The Lottery Club

ELLI LEWIS

For Mike

PROLOGUE

'If you're reading this then they're all dead. And I did it. Me.'
The writing was frantic, wild, frenzied. The multipack biro tore savagely at the cheap scrap notebook, almost ripping its crackling sheets apart.
'I did it because I was the only one who could. I did it because they wanted to die. They wanted it all to end. They just didn't know it'.
A final stab marked a decisive full stop and, having done its job, the shaking hand withdrew, trembling with the thrill of achievement. Then it froze.
No. No, it was all wrong. It was-
The pen clattered onto the desk, the paper ripped out before being crumpled and flung onto the growing pile of failure.
Four pensive fingers tapped rhythmically on the MDF surface. It was a shame there was no thunder or lightning. It really would have set the mood. This had to be right. This. Would. Be. Heard.
Well, read.
Noticed at least. Probably.
The tapping ceased, the biro raised once more.
'I knew of their pain. Like an angel of mercy, I knew. And I was there to end it.'
Another pause, this time more thoughtful. Considered. Not bad. The hand almost relinquished the pen, but thought better of it. It resumed its rabid scribbling.
'Please feed Dave'.

1

CHAPTER 1

Standing in the doorway of the cold church hall, Mark Jones was glad of the gloom that enveloped him. It allowed him to watch unseen. He had after all, just come there to look. To observe. He had no intention of actually taking part. No wish to join the six sunken souls in the centre of the cavernous room, all seated except one.
He wasn't like them.
He wanted to leave, but instead Mark found himself entranced by the single standing figure: The bald-headed beast who was currently holding court. As he gawped at the colossal mammal before him, a David Attenborough style monologue began in his mind.
'This. Is simply fascinating,' came the earnest hushed voice of Sir David. 'What we have here is one of the largest examples ever seen of the human species.' Here the veteran broadcaster would probably pause to allow the audience to gaze upon the wonder. 'Note, for example, its shape,' he'd continue. 'There is no hint of a neck or waist. This being is almost a perfect cuboid.'
Mark wasn't sure what Sir David would have made of the man's facial features, particularly his eyebrows. They looked so uniform they practically jumped off his face. Were they drawn on? His girlfriend, Jess would know. She was always nudging Mark and saying things like, 'too much Botox' or 'look at those lip fillers'.
'But wait,' Attenborough interjected now. 'He is about to speak.'
Mark held his breath.
'They warned me.' The words emerged slowly in a gravelly growl that would have made Bob Hoskins sound like Tinkerbell. 'They warned me it would be like this. But did I believe 'em? Oh no.' His voice cracked, revealing a hint of hysteria. It was like looking at a traumatised brick.

'The fights. The terror. The nights are the worst. I don't sleep anymore. I just sit awake. Waiting. Waiting for the worst to happen.' Mark was reminded uncomfortably of the horror stories they used to tell by scouts' campfire. 'They call it," the brick took a deep breath, "Abu El Banat.' Each word was drawn out, extended for maximum effect as his eyes focused on a point in the middle distance. There was a sombre silence.

'Oh yes,' somebody chirped, breaking the spell. 'It means "father of girls", right? I've seen that one. Isn't that from *Grey's Anatomy*?'

'No, it's *The West Wing*,' somebody else grumbled. Mark strained his neck, trying to get a glimpse of the speakers.

'You're always arguing when you have no idea what you're saying.' There followed a short if heated debate about the televisual provenance of the phrase, voices mingling and getting louder. Somebody was yelling something about Katherine Heigl when a sharp yelp interjected.

'Why can't we ever get through a meeting without a row?' This final statement was followed by an angry stillness. It was like walking in on a particularly dysfunctional family Christmas; all long-standing grievances and well defined roles.

'Don't you think you're slightly overreacting?' someone now ventured reasonably, ending the stalemate.

'You don't *know*.' The bare head was now shaking with insistent dogma. 'Wherever it comes from, it's bloody true. Three girls. Three. And each one of them's worse than the last,' he lamented. 'Mandy came home with a new boyfriend last week. Brian,' he spat out. 'Apparently he's a slash metal drummer by night and a shelf stacker by day. I told her I'm pretty sure he's just a wanker whatever time of day it is. She told me I don't understand his pain. Meanwhile Molly has given up her hairdressing course and came home to tell me and her mother that she wants to be a glamour model. I told her if she takes off so much as a shoe in public she'll be in a seminary faster than she can say Jordan.'

He paused before continuing in a ranting tone which spoke of 'and another thing'.

'And Dina's no better. She came home with a new nose yesterday. Apparently she wants to look like one of those Kardashians.' Mark didn't have time to wonder why a woman would try to look like one of *Star Trek*'s least appealing creatures before the man continued. 'You know, them chunky girls off the telly? It's like an obsession. I asked her if she was getting loyalty points at the surgery.' He laughed uproariously at his own wit, but the smile quickly faded into fearful remorse, as if he had been chastised, muttering to himself, 'She didn't like that.'

Then, as though a puppet master had taken control of his face, he forcibly brightened. 'Anyway, I said to her what you told me to say. I said, 'Dina, you're my wife, I love you, but I feel like I don't know you anymore.'' He looked around for approval. 'And I meant it. Really. I mean if she gets another bit of work done I don't think I'll be able to point her out of a line up.'

'What did she say?' The question was asked with the sharpness of a Fleet Street reporter, but Mark saw that its source was not a hard faced hack, but a smooth featured blond teen. Mark looked back at the man, who took this incongruity in his stride, answering the question without missing a beat.

'She said she thinks I could do with some more work myself,' he said glumly. 'Apparently they're doing wonders with chest hair removal.' He subconsciously fingered his chest area as if comforting a precious pet. 'And she has me planning Miley's sweet sixteen. It's ridiculous. She wants three hundred people. That's bigger than our wedding. I said that if we're going to throw a party that size someone is either dying or getting married at the end of it.' He stopped now and looked around. 'Right, well. That's it from me. Thanks for listening.'

As he sat down, there was a muted muttering of, 'thanks Paul' and 'well done', while the person to his left looked as though they were preparing to stand up in his place.

And that's when it happened.

The wall against which Mark was leaning somehow started moving. Why was it moving? Before Mark could think to himself, 'oh shit that's not a wall', the fire door which had been taking his weight started giving way. He began listing, then tipping, then definitely falling until, with an accompanying crash and a yelp, he found himself prostrate, face down. He allowed himself a moment to remain in his horizontal pose, but then he sensed them.

Like zombies alerted to the presence of living flesh, the people from the group had all shifted their attention to him. Mark closed his eyes firmly shut. He wondered, as he had as a child, whether if he didn't see them, they might not spot him. No such luck. He turned groggily onto his back, eyes squeezed tightly with pain before giving in to the inevitable. He would have to look. As he opened one eye and then the next, his gaze met the concerned but confused eyes of the bald man, staring down at him much as an ostrich might examine an iPad. 'You alright mate?'

Tell them you're lost. Ask for directions to the nearest pub. Or tube station. Or Sex Addicts Anonymous meeting. Think of something, anything, that will allow you to leave immediately.

Why was nothing coming out of his mouth?

Idiot.

It took several moments before Mark had the wherewithal to coordinate his fight or flight instincts and recover sufficiently to answer. There was an insistent pounding in his head and he was sure he'd dislocated an elbow. Still, there was no need to make a fuss.

'Quite alright. Thank you.' He was pleased with this. Well done, he thought. Play it down. Go to A&E on the way home.

'He's fine,' Paul said and in a swift motion Mark felt himself being winched upwards, a salmon helplessly plucked from its river, before coming face to chest with the man's bulk. 'That door latch needs seeing to,' Paul said with the expertise of a seasoned professional, looking up to examine it. He sucked his teeth disapprovingly. 'It shouldn't have gone like that. Plain dangerous. I tell you some of these cowboys.' He shook his head contemplatively before seeming to remember who he was talking to. 'Not a great start, is it? Hi, I'm Paul. You're here for the meeting then?'

There were too many questions. Mark raised his hand to his head.

'Well, no. I mean, maybe. I'm not sure.' Mark wondered when he had turned into Hugh Grant, all nervous stuttering in an accent so cut glass he would put his grandmother's WI group to shame.

'Has he got concussion?' Mark heard a well-spoken man ask.

'Have a sit down, love,' a grandmotherly voice intoned, a brew of pity and solicitude. Smiling with the weakness of someone who has overcome great adversity, Mark acquiesced. He was here now. May as well make the best of it. Also he could see what appeared to be a cup of tea over there. He wondered if there were any biscuits.

5

He shifted as he tried to adopt a natural sitting pose, legs astride, but not too wide, leaning back, but not in complete repose. Now in their midst, he took a moment to assess his neighbours. It was a bit too much to take in, but they certainly were a mismatched bunch. To his left were an elderly couple of whom the grandmotherly one was half, the man looking at him with a mixture of curiosity and mistrust, the women's face etched equally with wrinkles and concern. Beyond them, the sullen blond girl with a future in print press was staring at him, her look of boredom and disgust marring what was an otherwise pretty face, while three men and another woman of varying sizes and shapes watched from across the circle.

They all seemed so disconcertingly normal. So forgettable. Do I look that normal? he thought in alarm.

'Sorry, didn't get your name by the way,' Paul said jovially.

Oh Christ. His name. Should he tell them his name? It was like that moment of doubt when a website requested your personal details. Mark wasn't sure if he wanted these people to know his name. Would there be consequences? Would they share it with third parties? He considered giving a fake name - Prince Naseem, Tarzan, Jeremy Clarkson - but simply couldn't think of a plausible one that wasn't Mark or Paul. Not a single one. Mildred? George?

'Mark,' he said finally, abruptly. It came out more as an accusation than an introduction. Its utterance was followed by an expectant silence.

'Great,' Paul said. 'Well, Mark, welcome to the group. Probably best you just sit and watch for a bit then pitch in if you feel like it?'

Mark just nodded at this and Paul looked pleased.

'Right, who's next?' he asked, looking around.

At that point, a skinny yet somehow also flabby man with no discernible chin stood up eagerly. Mark hadn't really noticed him until now. He was wearing black tracksuit bottoms and a t-shirt that read *The light at the end of the tunnel is a train. National Train Day 2012.* Usefully, there was also a picture of a train, just in case an illustration was required.

Mark observed a few of the members exchanging glances and the blond girl rolled her eyes, but the train man didn't seem to notice. Taking a deep breath and with the nasal lilt of someone who had never known the touch of a woman, he began.

'Hi, I'm Derek and I'm a lottery winner.'

Like students chanting their times tables in a Dickensian nightmare, everyone else replied.

'Hi, Derek.'

CHAPTER 2

Graham Gill peered over the Part K compliant standard issue metal handrail down at the asphalt below. A handful of cars meandered in search of a parking space. He wondered if he would hit one on his way down. Unlikely. He was never one to inconvenience others.

He had to do it. Simply had to. The time had come. He straightened his posture, squared his shoulders and looked out into the distance, eyes squinting in torment. He was like Peter Parker in *Spiderman* or Bruce Wayne in *Batman*. Or maybe Edward in *Twilight*. He had issues. He had problems. Of course, unlike these plagued protagonists, he was never gifted with the powers required to transform him from zero to hero.

He turned his attention back to the scene below. He moved a foot forward, letting it peek over the edge. This was it. His heart jackhammered with the thrill of it. He could do this. All it would take was one more step. One. More. Tiny. Step.

It took several tries before he finally sighed and retreated. He checked his watch. It wouldn't be today. Nonetheless, he congratulated himself on the fact that it was the furthest he'd ever come. He almost laughed at the memory of the first time he'd come up here. He hadn't even looked over. This was progress. And there was always next time. Next week in fact. Wednesday at 1:30pm, just like every week over the past two years, weather permitting.

It had become part of his routine. Like brushing his teeth at 6:55 or entering the third train carriage on platform 2 at 7:30. At 1:25 he would take his lunch out of his drawer and walk up the fire escape up onto the roof of his office building. There he would sit or stand on the edge considering his options and willing himself to act. How was it that something could be so perfectly, magnificently straightforward and yet at the same time be so out of his reach? Graham, who considered himself a master of simplicity, had spent hours agonising over his inability to complete what should have been such an uncomplicated undertaking.

It wasn't fear that stopped him. He had determined that fact very early on. Yes, there was something unsettling about not knowing how the whole matter would conclude, but being frightened seemed something of an overreaction. It didn't fit.

Was there a religious element? A leftover of all those RE lessons? Perhaps early memories of the whisperings about the neighbour two down? He could still remember his mother shaking her head in disgust muttering about 'Those poor children.' Unlikely. For one thing, Graham didn't have any children. Only Dave.

He often liked to think about this, revelling in the possibilities, turning them over in his mind like a problem to be solved. A puzzle with intricate pieces. He couldn't deny that he found the process soothing. No irritants. No worries. Just the prospect that everything would soon be resolved to his satisfaction. Maybe, he thought, this was what other people experienced when meditating.

But then, at the same time it was also unutterably frustrating. And, on those occasions when annoyance or exasperation took hold of him, he had hoped the wind would blow him off in an inconsequential gust. Perhaps he would trip and fall. If only.

At around 1:43pm, he usually gave up and ate his chicken sandwich before returning to his desk in time for the afternoon appointments.

Nobody ever saw. Nobody ever noticed.

No-one had ever so much as looked up and seen him teetering on the edge. He had expected that to happen at least. For someone to notice his skinny bespectacled form with its sensible shoes peeking out over the sixth floor of the building. But no.

The world around him had simply gotten on with its day. The paperwork kept coming, as did the people.

This was nothing new to Graham Gill. Nobody had ever really noticed anything he had done. Not that he could blame them. Graham had always erred on the side of being totally, completely and utterly forgettable.

His entire existence had been an exercise in mediocrity. Born on Thursday, 7th of February in 1974, he'd weighed 7lb 6oz, incidentally the exact average weight for babies born that year. His Christian name was the 42nd most popular listed for boys that year. The doctor who had delivered him had been more interested in the announcement of a general election than in the emergence of the grey bundle he was bringing into the world.

From then on, everything he had done had been determinedly ordinary. He learned to walk at an unimpressive, but decidedly normal 14 months. The third out of five children, his own mother usually forgot his birthday while his father looked at him with a distant gaze that suggested he was an imposter. Even now, at work, it frequently seemed like he wasn't even there, but for the constant flow of his appointments. He wasn't even part of a team. He was able to operate on his own.

Graham sighed. He had a 2:30 meeting to get back to and a phone call before then. He'd better get on. He sat by the door to the roof on a discarded office chair eating his homemade chicken and sweetcorn on white bread before retreating back inside.

The open plan office was abuzz with phones ringing and people milling around holding folders and typing self-importantly at their desks. Graham's cubicle was the nearest to the coffee station, always a hub for people to gather and talk. Although his back faced the action, it was a useful spot from which to hear the latest goings on in the office: who was seeing whom and what plans were being made. What was more, nobody ever seemed troubled enough by Graham's presence to censor themselves.

People chattered there at the moment, laughter emanating as someone told a joke. It had been Smith. It was always Smith, Graham thought irritably. He sat back at his desk and removed the note he had stuck to it reading, *'Please feed my cat Dave twice daily, Whiskers Chicken for Adult Felines.'* It wasn't much by way of a suicide note, he knew, but everything else he'd ever tried had seemed overly dramatic. He had once gone as far as writing *'goodbye cruel world'* before realising that he simply couldn't carry it off. It would be like a gerbil performing Hamlet.

Why had he got a cat in the first place? All that feeding and petting and for what? He pictured the tabby's disappointed face as it had clocked hooded eyes on him that morning before slinking out of the cat flap so as to avoid having to sit with him. Whenever he did bother to grace Graham with his presence, Dave strode around the flat like he owned the place. There was even something condescending, superior about how he held his tail aloft, with its nonchalant flicks here and there.

Graham tried to block it all out. It was time to get back to work. Switching on his computer, he looked up the details of his latest call. Jennifer Beesley from Milton Keynes. He dialled the number.

'Hello?' There was a definite note of suspicion there. Of course there was. She wouldn't have recognised the number. Graham had to speak quickly if she wasn't going to hang up on him.

'Jennifer Beesley? Graham Gill here from Avalon calling to congratulate you on your win.'

He waited. There were three stock reactions to this line. Most people just started chattering excitedly. Even hardened construction workers and London cabbies turned into the equivalent of a four year old girl on her birthday, giggling and laughing and saying how excited they were.

The second type was dramatically stoic. Whether it was suspicion or disbelief, Graham didn't know, but this person barely uttered a word. This was his favourite type; the kind who let him do his job with minimal fuss. Graham considered them the most sensible. After all, it wasn't like he was informing them of their win. Most of them knew they had won and how much already from an email or just by watching the TV show. Others had checked their numbers online. His call was just to confirm it all and set the date for their meeting.

Jennifer however, appeared to be the third type.

'Oh, we've got a screamer,' Smith announced to the room as Graham's phone erupted with a prolonged and high-pitched shriek of epic proportions. Graham held the receiver away from his ear and rested his chin on his hand. It was always best just to let them finish. It took a good minute or so for the sound to die down.

'You are the lucky winner of £2.5 million,' Graham said, his well-rehearsed speech flowing easily. 'You must be delighted. I am your lottery liaison, Graham Gill and we at Avalon will be with you every step of the way,' he intoned while checking his emails.

'What happens next? When do I get the money?' Jennifer babbled. Luckily, this was the next line of Graham's monologue so he didn't have to deviate.

'Come on down to our offices and we'll transfer the funds straight to your account,' he said.

'Oh, fab! Is it central London? The big city? Ooh, I'll have to go shopping,' she giggled.

'We are conveniently located in Watford.'

This elicited sudden silence.

'Watford?' There was a definite note of disappointment on the other end, an air of uncertainty. This happened a lot. It was never being told they won the lottery that brought suspicion as much as being informed that the end of this particular rainbow was located in Watford.

The conversation was a bit more subdued from then on, something for which Graham was grateful.

He had just replaced the receiver when he saw Grace Perkins and Harry Hammond from management approach the coffee machine. They clearly hadn't seen him.

'We're going to have to do something about it,' Perkins was saying sotto voce. 'I actually had our local MP breathing down my neck this morning; it's not good for publicity. I mean somebody has *died* and they're laying the blame at our door.'

Hammond harrumphed in response as Graham heard the unmistakeable sound of the biscuit tin being excavated from behind him.

'How can they possibly say it was our fault? This is ridiculous.'

Graham knew exactly what they were talking about. It had been all over the *Metro* that morning and all over the office even before that.

'Lotto Winner Drowns in Pool of Pounds' the headline had read. It turned out that Raymond Deaks, who had won £3.4 million one Wednesday evening in November last year had filled his new swimming pool with £5 notes and had gone 'skinny dipping' whilst blind drunk. Unfortunately, it transpired that paper currency was an unsuitable medium for casual, let alone inebriated, swimming and Mr Deaks had expired at the bottom of the money pile. The coroner had deemed it death by misadventure. The press had deemed it a field day.

'Well, they *are* blaming us,' Perkins persisted. 'Apparently we didn't provide him with enough pastoral care.'

Graham could practically hear Hammond's eyes roll.

'What do they want? A nanny?' the large man demanded.

'Look I know, but I have to tell them something or else the top brass is going to be furious. The media is all over it. We have to be seen to be coming out ahead of this.'

There was a pensive pause. Hammond's mind was chewing the cud while his mouth was chomping something, presumably a Hobnob.

'I dunno, set up a counsellor or a, erm, support group,' he said, mouth clearly full. 'Yeah, people love that kind of thing. Caring Avalon.' He was seemingly warming to his subject. 'Tell the press people to put out a release. We'll trial it in one place then roll it out nationwide. Every lottery winner has access to support from a trained counsellor.'

For the next few days, the coffee station was boiling over with members of staff chatting about the new initiative.

'I tell you, it's the bloody nanny state gone mad,' Gemma from accounts had said to her friend Emma.

'I know. I mean what do they need support for? Oh no! I won the lottery! Poor me!' The two women tittered. Several similar conversations took place between different people.

But apparently the heads at the top liked the idea because the next thing he heard, Smith was put in charge of spearheading the trial of the support group for Avalon Cares.

'Ok, so we should probably trial it in the place from which most lottery winners originate,' Smith had suggested at the computer on the other side of the dividing panel from Graham. It was Liz's computer and Graham just knew Smith would be leaning and leering over her shoulder as he always did.

'That would be...' There was a tap tapping as Liz spoke. 'Romford,' she finished, probably having found the details on the system.

There was a long pause.

'Romford.' This time it was Smith again. 'What's the second luckiest place?'

Evidently Romford wasn't considered an ideal location for the trial group. Graham wondered why. Maybe it just wouldn't sound good in the papers. Typical. Always about the razzmatazz, he thought in annoyance.

Just then Liz spoke up again.

'I wonder if the winners stayed in Romford though. Why don't we look up where most of them live now?'

'Good idea,' Graham heard Smith say. 'You're not just a pretty face, are you?'

Graham seethed as Liz giggled at this. What did she find attractive or funny in this cretin?

A few more taps could be heard on the other side of the partition before Liz said, 'Ok, that would be...' The tapping stopped and Graham could almost hear their anticipation. 'Hampstead, North London.'

'Much better,' Smith said, elongating the first word.

The next thing he knew, flyers had been made up and all the lottery liaisons, Graham included, were instructed to hand them out in their initial meetings with winners.

'Make them understand that they have somewhere to turn. Remember, Avalon Cares,' Perkins had said slowly to the assembled liaisons in the weekly meeting. Nobody so much as flinched at this.

"Avalon Cares!" The flyer had yelled, like one of those 'activists' one found on Speakers Corner in Hyde Park trying to convince passers-by that the end was nigh. Graham read on. *"Worried by your win? Mulling your millions? Got nowhere to turn? Come and spend time with other lottery winners in a safe environment. Get your worries off your chest and feel a million times better."* Then it listed the time and place of the meeting.

After the meeting had ended, Graham had filed out along with his colleagues and went back to his desk. Logging into his computer, he checked his list for the day. His first appointment was with Paul and Dina Baker. Lucky them.

CHAPTER 3

With a cup of tea in one hand and a bourbon in another, Mark was now feeling quite recovered as he sat in his plastic chair.

'What's the best thing about winning?' This question came from the bald man, who he now knew as Paul. It was directed at a petite woman standing before them all, weight shifted onto one leg as she toyed with what appeared to be a wedding ring. She had introduced herself as Holly. Her demeanour was partly nervous, partly excited, but she also seemed to be in her own world, as if she was talking to herself.

'Would it be completely weird for me to say that I love the storage?' she asked as she scrunched up her nose. She must have been in her late thirties, but with her long red hair and almost translucent skin, she appeared fragile, like a porcelain doll.

'Um, yes, but continue,' someone replied and Holly laughed.

'Jamie calls it Pinterest perving,' she glimmered. 'That's my husband by the way,' she clarified in Mark's direction. 'Anyway, it's probably more interior design than just storage. Before the win, I used to drool over these gorgeous pictures of well organised larders and these cloakrooms with perfectly organised wellies and stunning kitchens with every possible gadget and neat rows of Tupperware and now,' she paused and shook her head as if in amazement. 'I have a shelf *just* for pasta,' she said, stretching out each word. 'I literally can't tell you how happy that makes me.' She laughed self-deprecatingly and a few of them joined in, but then she fell silent again as her smile dimmed.

'But I also feel quite guilty. I look at other people. The kids are still at their old school, you know. We've never been into private schools. Anyway, I-I watch the single mums struggling and the working parents making ends meet and I think, why us? You know?' She looked around for something, for approval or recognition. A couple of people, large Paul included, nodded. 'I feel so bad. It's not like we were rich or anything, but we had our semi in Finchley.' She paused. 'Mortgaged to the hilt of course.' She rolled her eyes and laughed as she said this, a small titter rippling through the group.

'But then again, if anybody heard me, they'd probably say, "so if you feel so bad about it, just give it away". And they'd be right, wouldn't they? I mean, we do give to charity. We always have and we still do. But is it enough?'

'You can't beat yourself up like that,' Paul said. 'That's life. Some people win, some don't.'

'And you've got your lovely children to look after.' It was the elderly woman this time, chipping in to the conversation and smiling up at Holly, who smiled back at her gratefully.

'Anyway, thanks. Thanks for listening. It's just good to get it out there.' As Holly sat down, Mark didn't feel able to look up so his eyes fell to his lap. There, his gaze fell upon the photos which Derek – the man in the train t-shirt - had passed around and which he was still clutching, quite hard as it happened. Noticing that he was causing them to crease, he loosened his grip.

They really were incredible – even unbelievable - images. Derek, it transpired, had more than a passing interest in trains.

'As some of you know,' Derek had said, after introducing himself. 'I like trains.'

And he did.

He really did.

In fact, to say that Derek liked trains was like saying that human beings enjoyed the odd breath of air. It was so true that it was beside the point. Mark had found it hard to follow much of what Derek had gone on to say, full as it had been of abbreviations such as the North London MRC – that apparently meant Model Railway Club – and lots of talk of different sizes of gauges, which he'd explained at length was the distance between tracks. The world of model trains was, it transpired, one whose deeply imbedded conflicts made the United Nations seem, well, united. There was great disparity between countries and even counties on various issues ranging from the scales of model trains to how the scales were calculated.

And yet, as this instance proved at least, a picture could paint a thousand acronyms.

'I am pleased to announce that Trainton Abbey is finally complete,' Derek had said in his adenoidal monotone, making his subject matter seem all the more surreal. 'As you know,' he continued with the chanting drone of a true obsessive, 'it has taken six months to adapt this 18th century manor house to integrate a propane fired 1:8 scale live steam train with 184-millimetre gauge-,'

'It's a house with a train running through it,' Paul had interjected, his voice in no way hiding his appalled horror.

And that's exactly what it was.

Like a terrifying amalgamation of Ridley Scott's *Alien* and *The Very Hungry Caterpillar*, an almost life size locomotive appeared to be eating its way through what might once have been a picturesque country estate. Gaping holes had been made through wood panelled walls, the kitchen had a ticket stand inside it and the garden was like Spaghetti Junction.

'What's that in the downstairs loo?' Holly had asked, turning the picture to try and understand what she was seeing.

'Oh, that's just some of the electricals,' Derek had replied earnestly, leaving Holly to look dubious.

'And the council let you do this?' Paul's tone as he asked this question implied that he was a man who knew of the difficulties of getting things past councils.

'Oh, well, um, no, that is to say,' Derek started defensively, cocking his head and flitting his eyes downwards as he spoke. 'We're still working on the details-,'

'Why would you do this?' The interruption came courtesy of the sullen blond girl, her voice conveying a considered mix of condescension and dismay. Mark thought he'd heard her referred to as Annie.

'Well,' Derek said, looking directly at her for just a second before needing to look away again. 'It's for the competition.' He looked around now, albeit fleetingly, to check for signs of recognition. 'The Annual Model Railways Exhibition?' Nothing. 'At the National Exhibition Centre? I mentioned it last week.' When this still elicited unilluminated silence, Derek explained with a weary sigh.

'The Annual Model Railways Exhibition,' he said slowly, pausing here as though determined to imprint the words forever in their minds. 'Is next month and Trainton Abbey is up for best layout. It's sort of a big deal,' he said apologetically.

Derek began to warm to his theme. Apparently the annual show was the talk of southern English model railways enthusiasts, attracting attention from around the country and even worldwide.

It became apparent that Derek was the black sheep of his own model railway club, The Railway Rangers, after an argument surrounding the official club scale had gotten out of control. It had reportedly descended into anarchy and something of a bloodless coup with someone called Albert taking over the leadership from Derek and summarily ejecting him from the group. He was now restricted to communicating with them over the internet on what Mark assumed was an official chat group reserved for the one-track minded.

'He always had his eye on the conductor's cap,' Derek lamented. 'I shouldn't complain really. It was always going to be him. He's got the pizzazz and the iron grip you need to really make it in the world of model trains.'

The stillness in the room was absolute as everyone tried to digest the indigestible. It was Holly who finally broke the silence.

'Were you a history teacher?' she asked with the air of someone who recognised him from somewhere, but couldn't place their finger on the source.

'Geography,' Derek had replied, somewhat defensively, eliciting a quiet 'ah' from the group as if that explained everything.

Annie had been next.

To Mark, Annie looked like the kind of eighteen-year-old every parent dreads. The sort who made you feel stupid just for breathing. With her blond locks, large green eyes and slight frame, she should have been pretty, perhaps even beautiful. And yet the world-weary expression on her face, the constant checking of her nails and her phone and the fact that she didn't seem to want to be there made her intimidating in the extreme.

Her long, coltish legs were imprisoned in tight, sparkly jeans and she wore a cropped jumper. Mark knew he was getting old because he didn't admire the hint of taut tummy peeking out beneath it. Instead he fought the urge to warn her she'd catch cold. But the most immediately striking thing about this girl was that every inch of her seemed to scream out the name of a label. Her top bore the initials 'D&G', her sunglasses (in October?) shouted 'Dior' on the side, while her bag had 'Louis Vuitton' written on it so many times it looked like a schoolboy had done it in detention.

'Hi, I'm Annie and I'm a lottery winner,' she had begun, reciting the words like a child forced to apologise to their sibling for setting their hair alight. Then, without any preamble, she made her next announcement. 'Matt's gone.'

Mark looked around in surprise as these three and a half words evoked a unanimous groan from the seated gathering. He heard someone grumble, 'Again?'

Annie seemed unperturbed by the reaction, apparently too busy being furious with the erstwhile Matt.

'He's gone off with Christa. Christa for fu-' she was clearly about to swear when she looked at Paul and changed her mind. 'Sorry. But I mean. I like basically, like, bought him his bike and his phone. And I was like checking it, you know, just to see, when I see a message and it's from Christa and it's all like "xxx" and he's replied and he hasn't even deleted it and now he's like gone off with her and I'm like, what has she got that I haven't?'

The words didn't so much emerge from her lips as pour out of them in a torrent of torment, the end of each sentence rising in tone as if posing a question even when there was none. This made comprehension a challenge and not one assisted in any way by her accent. Mark would probably have described it as cockney-ish. Mockney? There was something about it which rendered it inauthentic. It was as if she was borrowing it. Trying it on, like a toddler wearing their mummy's shoes and constantly falling out of them.

'Maybe you shouldn't be buying his affection,' a man's voice ventured. If Annie's accent was Hounslow, this one was more Hansard, displaying as it did the marbles in mouth pronunciation so characteristic of most politicians. Mark craned beyond Paul to see who was brave enough to challenge the terrifying teen.

He was greeted by a vision of Boris Johnson-esque scruffiness, complete with sandy blond hair that looked like it had been raked rather than brushed so haphazard was its distribution. His corduroys and shirt with top button undone were the very epitome of Westminster Hall chic, while the glint in his eyes screamed, 'vote for me'.

'Oh you can talk, Rickaaay,' Annie snapped, pronouncing the man's name with exaggerated distortion of the last syllable so that it came out sounding like the letter 'A' as opposed to an 'ee'. Mark recognised the pronunciation as imitating the way characters in *EastEnders* used to say that name in reference to Ricky Butcher. Annie continued in an acerbic tone. 'How is your new lady love? Out of the womb yet?' Her tone was part interrogation, part sarcastic sweetness.

'My name,' he began with emphasis, 'Is Rick not Ricky. And Brioche is twenty-three I'll have you know and very mature.'

'I'll bet,' Annie grunted, rolling her eyes. 'Just tell me this, how many of your wives are suing you at this precise moment?'

If anyone had ever wondered what it would be like to watch TOWIE go head to head with Prime Minister's Questions, Mark thought, here was their answer.

'That's enough you two,' Paul had interjected sternly. 'Annie, keep going.'

By the end of Annie's tale, Mark felt fully equipped to return to the playground for a good old game of he said, she said. Apparently, Matt had been juggling Christa and Annie for a considerable period of time. Upon discovery of his nefarious dalliances, it seemed that the court of teen infidelity deemed that priority was to be given on a last-in first-out basis. Thus, whoever had been going out with Matt the longest, got to keep him.

'Jenna says I've been going out with Matt for like miles longer than Christa but Jezebel swears on her life that he's been with Christa since like last Christmas.'

The group agreed that Annie had been going out with Matt for 'ages', while the single presiding thought in Mark's mind had been that Matt was either stupidly brave or intrepidly brainless. Either way the moron was doomed.

Rick was next to vent his latest saga. In answer to Annie's question, two ex-wives were currently suing him as well as a past business partner. With utter moroseness, he informed them that the courts had decreed that they could have their settlements reconsidered in light of his lottery win.

'My lawyer says they've got an excellent chance of taking at least half of the money,' Rick said glumly of his exes. 'Apparently they felt they hadn't had a proper bite of the cherry the first time because of my 'complicated financial arrangements'.' He put air quotes around the last three words. 'I did explain it was all perfectly legitimate. I happened to have a number of different noms de plume for professional purposes.' He looked down at Mark. 'I was a motivational master and author of several self-published self-enhancement books,' he explained in a stage whisper before carrying on. 'Bree is furious. But it's not exactly like I can do anything about it.' He looked annoyed, but the expression was fleeting. Within seconds his smile had achieved the kind of wattage no environmental activist would approve of. 'Still, it's great stuff for the new book, 'Love in the Age of the Lottery'.'

Finally, just before Holly had been the joint contribution of Margaret and Gerald Hughes. In their sensible shoes and M&S jumpers, the elderly pair looked to all the world like they had just come to the local bingo for an afternoon. They definitely didn't look like they had won several million pounds.

'We've just come back from Norfolk,' Margaret had been chattering indulgently, passing around some photos of their trip. It was hard to tell what was going on in half of them, what with the poor focus and odd angles. However, the more traditional shots showed either Margaret or Gerald looking happy and serene with one background after another behind them. Mark imagined that they must have hundreds of such photos at home, same smiles, same clothes, just different backgrounds.

'Just lovely there,' Gerald said. 'We got a great deal on a cottage and it was just by the local Tesco, which was great.' Margaret nodded at this emphatically before taking over.

'All the grandchildren are doing well,' she said, completely yet seamlessly changing the subject. 'Mason is walking and Parker is out of the detention centre.'

It was like being the recipient of their annual Christmas newsletter, Mark mused, somehow both entranced and bored by it all.

'Right, I think that's everyone,' Paul eventually said with a note of finality, looking around the group.

'What about the new guy?' Annie barked. 'If we have to talk then he does too.' Six millionaires fixed their eyes on Mark.

'Oh yes,' Paul looked like the thought had never occurred to him. 'Do you want to say anything? You don't have to.'

Caught off guard, Mark tried to think on his feet.

'I, um, I'm not sure how any of this works.'

'Just say what's on your mind,' Margaret had said kindly.

'Ok, well. Should I start like all of you did then? This is an anonymous thing, right?'

'What do you mean?' Paul asked, the very picture of confusion.

'Well, you know, the whole "hi I'm Mark and I'm a lottery winner", that's all like Alcoholics Anonymous, right?' A sea of blank faces greeted this, along with a confused silence.

'We're not alcoholics,' Margaret whispered, clearly scandalised.

'Ah, well. It's just the only way we could think of to do it,' Paul explained, somewhat sheepishly. 'Nobody was here to run the meeting so we sort of had to cobble it together ourselves and we'd all seen it done that way on telly.'

'So it's not anonymous?' Mark clarified.

'We've had a barbeque at Paul's house,' Gerald said. 'I think that means the cat is pretty much out of the bag there.'

22

'Plus most of us have been in the papers,' Annie said, in a 'duh' tone which unambiguously indicated she thought Mark was a grade A moron.

'Right,' Mark said, feeling very much put in his place. Then he thought of another question which had been irking him.

'So who does run these meetings?' He thought again of the leaflet he'd been handed by the man at Avalon.

Paul shrugged. 'Dunno. Bloke at Avalon said there would be a counsellor or something, but they never turned up, so...' he let the sentence trail off as if that explained everything.

'We just come every week. Well, most of us do,' Rick said.

'We've got refreshments,' Margaret added proudly, gesturing to the trestle table with its packet of biscuits and hot water dispenser. Clearly refreshments signalled that it was a professional setup.

'So go on then,' Annie challenged. 'Why are you here?'

'What Annie means is,' Paul said, 'Do you want to tell us a bit about yourself?' He now sounded like an alarming blend of Jeremy Kyle and the unlikely leader of a Nevada crystal worshipping cult. 'When did it all begin?'

That.

That was a very good question. Mark could actually trace that back precisely. Exactly.

It had all begun with Sanjeev at Jackson's Confectionary off licence in Hampstead High Street. He had been buying a sneaky packet of cigarettes after a night out when the usually reliable corner shop attendant must have misheard him.

'Ten Marlborough Lights please,' Mark had mumbled, keen not to be overhead. It wasn't like this was a regular occurrence. In fact, he'd quit. Really. It had just been such a long week at the firm, what with the Collerton case, he'd had a bit to drink and he needed something, anything to take the edge off. 'And a packet of Wrigley's Extra.' He wondered whether there was anything else he could buy to mask the inevitable after-stench of the smoke.

'What numbers?' The response from across the counter was robotic.

'What?' Mark looked up to find that Sanjeev had his hand on the lottery machine. 'Oh sorry, you must have misheard. Ten Marlborough Lights please,' he corrected, looking around quickly to ensure nobody had heard before diving into his wallet to retrieve his bank card.

'You need six numbers. What numbers please?'

Mark glanced up again, finally taking a proper look at his fellow conversant. Staring straight ahead, Sanjeev's glazed eyes had the deep red hue of someone who had long passed the point of tired.

Just then, a bell had sounded indicating the shop's door opening and a woman had walked in. Mark had panicked as she had stood behind him patiently waiting to be served, noting her sensibly cropped hair and wide legged cotton trousers, just like his mum wore. Mark had only two options. He could either try in almost certain vain to make himself heard, all whilst battling the guilt of buying ciggies in front of a woman who was basically his mother or he could just go along with it.

'6, 10, 35, 42, 43 and 48.' Mark rattled off the first numbers he could think of.

'Two pounds please.'

And that was that. His fate was sealed. Like an unassuming log dislodged from the riverbank and swept unknowingly towards a giant, gaping waterfall, he had found himself the owner of a brand new future.

Yes. It had definitely been Sanjeev's fault.

Mark had slipped the ticket into his pocket and thought nothing of it, except that it was lucky that he hadn't bought any cigarettes because Jess was already in a foul mood when he arrived home. Something about her sister. He knew that had she sniffed even a hint of tobacco on him that night it would have been the Branning stag do debacle all over again and nobody wanted that. That argument, which had stemmed from the questionable, but entirely unavoidable festivities of his best friend's pre-wedding jaunt to Magaluf, had lasted for days. A week in fact.

Mark had been eternally grateful to have been saved from a repeat performance of that indignity. Instead he had been free to provide the obligatory, unthinking responses required of every partner/boyfriend/husband/punching bag at such rantings and they had ended the evening with Jess angry at her sister instead of at him.

What with all the relief and drama of that night, he had forgotten about his unintentional purchase. He had actually left it in his jeans. The ticket may well have ended up in a 40 degree wash. It was only when Jess, having been doing the laundry, proffered the crumpled piece of paper to him a few days later that he'd remembered. The look on her face was much the same as the one he imagined Jack's mother would have borne when confronting him about those stupid magic beans and asking what the hell he thought he was doing.

'You were supposed to sell that bloody cow for money!' Jack's exasperated mother surely yelled at her pointless son. 'Not magic beans! What kind of moron have I raised?' And that's effectively - or at least generally - what Jess was thinking, give or take a bovine.

Fortunately, Mark had been on the phone at the time Jess had found the ticket so could avoid the excruciating 'stop buying pointless things' conversation that always accompanied a purchase such as this. He had been talking to his best mate, Jason Branning.

'What is it?' Branning's voice had intoned doggedly on the other end of the line, the very epitome of lacklustre despondency.

Having recently and simultaneously become a father for the first, second and third time thanks to a newly discovered but previously unknown family history of triplets, Branning had lost his usual sparkle. Not a surprising fact given that he was now a slave to some very small, very demanding masters. He was also chronically sleep deprived and feeling thoroughly sorry for himself. This was despite the fact he seemed to spend most of his time either on the phone or at the office. It was his wife, Gemma, who usually had all three on her hands.

Nevertheless, his friend enjoyed nothing more than a good moan and so had been regaling Mark with his latest trials and tribulations of what sounded like the multiple nappy changing Olympics when Mark had found the ticket thrust under his nose.

'Check the numbers!' Branning had cried, instantly sounding much more like his once-exuberant self. Mark could just see him salivating over the nanny-hiring possibilities of it all.

'Why? I haven't won. Nobody actually wins these things.'

'The jackpot is a triple rollover! I'll check them for you. What are your numbers?' Clearly too much Baby Einstein had driven Branning to the edge.

'Shouldn't you be changing something or feeding something or, say, helping your overworked wife?' Branning's wife had turned into a terrifying amalgamation of Mother Theresa and Attila the Hun, part care giver, part rampaging lunatic, all bundled up into a tiny, disgruntled package with unwashed hair. Mark wasn't sure for whom he felt sorrier, but he did know who did the most work and it wasn't the guy on the phone to him who had just recently debated the pros and cons of Game Boy versus X Box.

'Hold on,' Branning had said, sounding spooked. After a short silence, he came back on the line. 'Fuck, somebody's woken up. It might be all of them.' And, like a doomed protagonist in an action film whose headcam falls to the ground before switching off in a haze of buzzing black and white static, he was gone.

Mark had looked at his ticket nonchalantly. He may as well check, he had thought, before idly wandering over to the computer. As always, he reviewed his Hotmail first, finding nothing except for marketing dross, banks asking for his log-in details and several forwarded emails from Branning with improbable titles such as 'Chimp eats his own foot'. There was an email from his mum asking if he wanted to come to dinner and naming a date three months ahead, to which he knew he would forget to reply.

He had browsed the *BBC Sports* website and quickly looked at the news headlines when one of them grabbed his attention.

'*£10 Million Lottery Ticket Remains Unclaimed.*' He'd read on. '*A mystery lottery winner has yet to claim their £10 million pound triple rollover jackpot. The ticket, which has been traced to an off licence in North London, was bought at 10pm on a Tuesday evening by an unidentified, but apparently shifty looking male. The shop's proprietor, Sanjeev Bhattacharya, is quoted as saying, "We sold a lot of lottery tickets that night. I can't keep track of them all."*'

It was with now trembling hands and an acutely gaping mouth that Mark had opened a new window and googled the National Lottery web address. Clicking through to the results page, he felt his mouth dry of any perceptible liquid. Of course he hadn't won. Of course not. Of-

Bloody hell.

He ran through the numbers. Once, twice.

6, 10, 35, 42, 43, 48.

6, 10, 35, 42, 43, 48.

Half turning his head towards the door, but without looking away from the screen, Mark called out, 'Darling, can I borrow you for a moment?' So nonchalant, so very casual was his tone that he may as well have been asking her to double check the weekly shop.

'What is it?' she had called back. He could hear that she was in the bedroom, probably putting away some clothes He could also tell she wasn't interested. When he suggested that it may be best for her to look at the matter herself, she had stridden in distractedly.

'What is it, Mark? Sorry, I've just got a million things to do.'

As always, Jess had been immaculate. By complete contrast to Mark's appearance – ripped jeans with a ketchup stain near the crotch matched with Banana Man t-shirt and over washed bobbled hoodie - her blond hair was brushed and neatly tied back, her jeans were in one piece and she was wearing a top that almost certainly hadn't been purchased at the closing down sale of the Hampstead branch of HMV. Not for the first time he wondered what she was doing with him.

'Will you take a look at this?' His voice had cracked under the pressure of trying to sound normal. She had taken the proffered ticket as she might a legal brief. In fact, it was how she did everything, all officious efficiency. Mark stood up to allow her to sit on the office chair and, once she did so, she looked from the ticket to the screen several times. He could see the gleaming cogs of her pristine mind turning. He watched entranced as the reality of the situation dawned on her. It was like watching a fire being lit from two twigs, slow, billowing smoke and then: Ignition. The expression on her face transformed from mildly irritated to confused then shocked and finally settled on what could only be described as amazed horror. Then she spoke.

'Is this?'

'Yes.'

'And you?'

'Yes.'

'So we.'

At this point he'd decided it was best either to form a complete sentence or allow the internet to do it for him. Unable to form a cogent thought, he clicked over to the BBC article about the mystery winner. It took her mere seconds to digest its content.

'Bloody hell,' she had whispered.

Back in the church hall, the entire group was now looking straight at him, and he realised he hadn't actually started talking. Paul's fat face bore the wary look of someone who thought himself the victim of a wind up, while Mark could tell from her sympathetic, horrified face that the elderly woman, Margaret, was certain that he was a bit slow. Some of them, particularly Annie, had lost interest and were browsing through their phones.

'How hard do you think he hit his head?' Paul asked.

'Maybe Mark's just a bit shy.' This from smooth talking Rick.

For a split second, Mark bridled at being described in terms usually reserved for a six year old girl, but then he realised he was in no position to deliver a repost. He couldn't remember the question he was supposed to answer, but he knew he had to say something. So, he said the first thing that came to mind.

'I'm Mark. I'm 33, and winning the lottery has been the worst thing that's ever happened to me.'

Paul's reply came after the shortest but archest of pauses.

'Welcome to the bloody club.'

CHAPTER 4

Jess had to resist the urge to drum her perfectly manicured nails on the table. The guy was lying. And she was bored.

She was in room three at the Holborn Family Courts watching two barristers conduct an incredibly civil exchange about the dubious £10 billion fortune of the (soon to be ex) Mr and Mrs Antonovich. The preposterously prosperous pair was in attendance as their financial divorce settlement was being discussed before Judge Steven Templeton. Svetlana, resplendent in her furs, tight jeans and perfectly coiffed blond mane, Boris, an almost perfect orb with arms and legs protruding in the awkward pose of a stick figure in his Armani suit.

'Your honour if I can direct you to page 35 of the bundle, you will notice in appendix four,' the older, more doddering barrister, Andrew Filbin, was presently warbling. He had quite a task on his hands, trying to explain how his client had 'misplaced' a sum of money roughly the size of some national GDPs. To his credit, he seemed to be taking it in his stride, his face the very picture of apathy.

Jess looked over at the barrister her firm had hired to speak on behalf of Mrs Antonovich. As a solicitor, she was spared the task of appearing in court. Today, that was the job of – she checked the name she had scribbled down earlier – Dean Klein, the surprisingly young and good looking barrister heralded as an up and coming divorce whizz kid. For his part, Dean was rifling through the paperwork in between bestowing the occasionally lascivious smile in the direction of the buxom court transcriber.

As she observed Messrs Filbin and Klein go about their duties, she imagined how the exchange would have been conducted if Mr and Mrs Antonovich had been left to their own devices. It didn't take much to conjure it up. She had only to recall the less than convivial conversation betwixt the two when they had bumped into each other in the hallway.

'Where's the money, you arsehole?' Svetlana had hissed in her rolling accent, squaring up to her rounded former beau.

'Why, so you can spend more of it on plastic surgery? Don't you think you've had enough? Or maybe you want to lavish more presents on Andrei,' Boris had retorted, part angrily, part smug. The smugness was understandable. He had, after all, managed to make almost £5 billion seemingly disappear into thin air. Poof. No sign of it. It didn't matter how many private investigators or forensic accountants they hired, they simply couldn't find it. Poor Svetlana had to make do with splitting the remaining £5 billion. The exchange had soon deteriorated into a barrage of rapid fire Ukrainian with both parties having to be restrained.

However, thanks to the incredibly courteous and safely sterile format of the British legal system, the scene was the very picture of amicability, with each barrister taking their turn as the judge listened, limp face resting on his hand as he slowly turned the pages of the bundles. The trainee who had prepared these folders, Sacha, sat beside Jess, frantically scribbling notes.

This was what was known as a 'final hearing'. They had already undergone a 'first appointment', essentially the court appearance where all the housekeeping was done, and what was called a Financial Dispute Resolution or 'FDR'. The English courts made FDR mandatory. It as an attempt at settling matters. You had to try to settle your disputes out of court first, but everyone had known that that would not happen in this instance. Boris and Svetlana were not ones to accept what they saw as a first offer.

Even this 'final' hearing was just a first shot over the bow. Jess knew that, in cases such as this one, matters were unlikely to conclude in the fairly anonymous surroundings of court number three. Oh no. This would reach the Court of Appeal. Perhaps, if they could find a good enough reason, it may end up in the Supreme Court. Wouldn't that be a coup? A case in the Supreme Court would definitely raise her profile.

She imagined herself on the front page of *The Telegraph*, looking professional yet stunning in a Max Mara suit, her hair up in a loose chic chignon.

'We believe the right decision was reached today,' she would purr into the bank of microphones jostling before her, lightbulbs flashing all around. It would be the right decision, because she would have won. She always won.

And today was no exception. After three gruelling days in court, Mrs Antonovich flounced away with a more than ample settlement of half of her husband's known capital, as well as some fairly hefty ongoing payments. Allowing for the fact that they had yet to find Mr Antonovich's stashed sums, it was certainly satisfactory.

'Great work, Jess,' Anthony Guild proclaimed as she strode confidently back into the offices of the family department of Drakers LLP, one of London's top law firms. She glided flawlessly on her six inch Jimmy Choos with the ease most women only achieved in slippers. She felt his eyes linger on her long legs as he followed her into her office. He was a decent man, the head of the family department and happily married for twenty years, but he couldn't help it. And who could blame him? They were great legs. She worked on them at the gym daily.

'Thanks,' she replied breezily as she entered the room she shared with Sacha, Anthony following her in. 'I think the client's pleased, but we'll just have to wait for the appeal.' As she spoke, she removed and hung her coat then placed her bag on her desk.

'Yes, it'll come. Marshall and Shaw are infamous for their comebacks,' Anthony replied with an indulgent smile. It was the kind of expression one might expect of a grandfather watching his grandson watering flowers. You would never guess he was talking about divorce proceedings. He was, of course, referring to their rival firm, with whom they had been judged as joint first for divorce cases that year by Chambers UK. It was notoriously difficult to appeal a divorce final judgement, but Marshall and Shaw had managed it on more occasions than any other firm except Drakers. It had become a sort of game between the two firms to see who could outdo each other.

'Anyway, carry on like this and there are big things in your future,' he said confidentially. 'I hear Felicity has plans to make up some more partners this year. How does youngest ever partner sound to you?'

Actually, it sounded like her fair dues, her right, but Jess opted for a more modest answer.

'I'll work for it, Anthony,' she said simply. This was clearly the response he was after, as evidenced by his approving nod.

'I'm sure.'

He swept one last glance around her office before leaving to return to his room at the end of the corridor. His departure was followed by the completely silent return of Sacha.

Jess knew that Sacha was petrified of her. And she liked it. These newbies needed to know their place. She looked at the twenty-something girl over the top of her computer screen. With her sleek blonde hair, porcelain skin and lithe limbs, she was not unlike Jess herself, nor all that different from the other female trainees carefully selected to join Drakers. Their male counterparts meanwhile, were mostly tall, athletic and usually found running around the city at lunchtime preparing for some triathlon or other. Sacha would do well, yes, but she needed to harden up. That's why Jess liked to keep her on her toes.

'Where's the Brightman report?' Jess threw the question into the air as one might an unpinned grenade. Sacha's response was satisfyingly swift. She began sifting through her papers, presumably piecing it together. Jess couldn't help but admire the girl. They both knew that she had told Sacha to have it ready two full days from now. A stupider girl would have said so.

Jess worked through lunch, picking absently at a salad her secretary placed in front of her at some point. She completed several financial forms and checked a legal argument Sacha had prepared. Now she was reviewing the details of a new client she had met only a few days ago. She was Jemima Dear, girl about town and wife of a hedge fund manager.

Jemima's husband, Mr Dear had registered on an exclusive infidelity website, Solent & Mire. According to their tag line, S&M specialised in 'affairs of the discerning heart'. Somehow, in between running a multi-million-pound fund and being an all-round family man, Mr Dear had managed two such affairs, one dalliance and a one-night stand, all without being discovered for three years. In fact, it was only when the website was spectacularly hacked that his private activities found their way into the news. Quite impressive really, although it had been unspeakably stupid of him to use his own credit card for the website fees. Some people had so little imagination.

Mrs Dear had learned of his deeds while browsing the *Daily Mail* for her usual dose of celebrity gossip. Instead of the latest goings on in TOWIE or Hollywood, she was presented with her husband's S&M profile picture and the headline, *'Doh. A Dear Who Likes a Good Spanking'*.

Jess examined the photograph of the Dear home, an immaculate five-bedroom stucco fronted house in Chelsea. In the past, she had salivated over these residential masterpieces, jealously studying the flawless décor and vast expanses of kitchens, living rooms and labyrinth of underground spaces. Now, although not quite as wealthy as the Dears, she was certainly closer to their neighbourhood, financially speaking.

£10.43 million. That's how much she – or more precisely Mark – had won. To most people, that was a large sum. Some would say it was an indisputably large sum. But Jess had bigger ideas. Just look at Mr and Mrs Dear. Their home alone cost almost £8 million. She calculated the stamp duty on buying such a house. £873,750. After paying that there would hardly be anything left to spend on life's little luxuries. And Jess liked her luxuries.

She thought of her own maisonette in Hampstead with its period black and white checked pathway, two-tone kitchen and sleek bathrooms. Before the win, it had been satisfactory, but plain, uninspiring. Now, with her uninhibited touch, it had become worthy of any interiors magazine, with every room decorated to perfection and each finishing touch considered and executed flawlessly.

Jess had always known how to spend money properly. People underestimated that, but it was a skill in its own right. She understood that it wasn't just about the big purchases; the cars, the houses. It was about detail.

Jess had had every inch of their house perfected, from the storage solutions to the sheen of the paint. When somebody walked into their home now, they were presented with sheer excellence. Invisible temperature control, silently opening and closing doors, remote controlled lighting, a Quooker tap that doubled up to provide hot, cold and boiling water so there was no unsightly kettle in her pristine kitchen. Jess shuddered at the thought of people who didn't know how to spend their money. They simply didn't deserve it.

She thought back to that day when Mark had shown her the ticket. When she had realised what he had done. Her first thought had been, this is so tacky. Winning the lottery? Who wins the lottery? Call centre staff and purple haired pensioners. Not city lawyers. Not successful people. Of course she had later reconciled herself to it. It was a good stop gap. A way to enjoy life while she amassed her own fortune.

Pft. It was so typical of Mark to do something like win the lottery. Before the win she had already been sick and tired of him. Of his lack of ambition. Of his happy go lucky view of the world. She had originally thought he was going places. After all, hadn't they met at the Young Solicitors Group Pro Bono Awards? Hadn't he won an award for his work? Evidently she had misjudged him.

She should have known better. After all, he had been rewarded for giving free legal advice to old age pensioners on drafting their wills, not for his ground-breaking approach to mergers and acquisitions. It was hardly the sign of a man on the up.

She shook her head in exasperation, both at him and at herself for her naivety. But there again, she had only been 23 back then. Had just qualified as a family lawyer. In a way, hadn't she needed him? Needed his down to earth gentleness, his jokey light-hearted manner. It had provided the perfect counterpoint to the hardness of her day to day.

'Sacha, pull your skirt down. This isn't Saturday night at the club.' Jess said this without looking away from the photos of the Dear's property. She had no idea of the length Sacha's skirt just then, but the girl had been out at the photocopier for a bit too long. The trainee did as she was told, her face flushed with embarrassment.

Jess remembered the first time she'd seen Mark. She had just endured the first week from hell. A week which saw her being allocated a boss who made Cruella De Ville seem like one of the adorable puppies she liked to turn into coats.

'Go on and attend this little event for me, be a dear,' Jackie Sweeting had said to her, in dismissive condescension. 'You look like a party girl. More than you do a proper lawyer, anyway.'

And with that she had sent her to the awards ceremony blinking away tears. So when Mark had sat down next to her with his warm smiling eyes, it had been like coming in from the cold.

'Hi there,' he had said, his voice smooth and friendly. 'Looks like they've put us together.' He'd been boyish and handsome in his suit, the cheap, bad cut of which seemed adorable and lent him a sort of cheeky innocence.

She had loved to hear him chatter in his carefree way. He kept whispering stupid jokes about the people on stage, making her giggle and forget what lay ahead for her in the office the next day.

Now he just seemed utterly, unbearably immature. Yes, she knew better now, three years on. She knew that she needed someone more motivated. Someone more ambitious. Someone who was simply more.

She had known it that day. The day of the win. Her mood had been black as she'd angrily picked up the laundry scattered around the house, silently ranting to herself about how she had let herself sleepwalk into a three-year relationship with someone who had days of the week pants. Meanwhile, he was on the phone to that pointless friend of his. She was going to tell him that night. It was over. She had almost blurted it out when she had found the ticket.

But then he had called her in and showed her the winning numbers. To him, it must have looked like she was taking it all in. Like she was shocked at the sheer scale, the amazing fortune of winning such a sum. In fact, it had only taken her moments to calculate it all.

She remembered looking at him out of the corner of her eye. What did this mean? They still didn't know exactly how much they had won. Yes it was a triple rollover, but there might have been multiple winners. The papers might have it wrong. She needed time to think about her next steps.

'Bloody hell,' she had breathed and they had both laughed. It had been him who had done so first, an uninhibited, indisputably happy explosion that rang out. He hadn't laughed like that in years. Maybe not since they had first met. Then she had joined in, slowly at first, tentatively. But then it had felt more natural and they had sat there for what must have been minutes on end, eventually finding themselves in a tight embrace.

When they had pulled apart, his eyes had shone with excitement. 'Who should we call first?'

That had jolted her into action.

Arranging her face into what she hoped was the right mix of delight and earnestness, she'd appealed to him.

'Mark, maybe we shouldn't tell anyone quite yet.'

'What? Why not?' His incredulous expression had almost made her snort aloud. He had always been an open book. She had simply to skim read him.

She rubbed his arm.

'Think about it. We need time to consider it all. Who are we going to tell? Will we tell everyone? Will we go public? What if that means loads of people start asking us for money? What if our friends start treating us differently?'

He had no answer to this. She almost felt bad for dampening his mood, but it was for the best. She pressed her advantage.

'All I'm saying is, let's spend some time and consider what to do next.' She had kept her voice soothing, reasonable. 'Just for a bit. Our little secret.'

Reluctantly, almost petulantly, like a child told he had to give his brother his last Rolo, he had acquiesced.

That day they spoke to Avalon and Mark had dazedly wandered around like a cartoon figment recently hit over the head by an anvil. She'd researched holiday options and worked for a few hours. By 8pm she had known what she wanted to do. It was just a case of convincing Mark.

'This is nice you know,' he had mused, sipping the champagne Mark had bought at Sainsbury's with his arm around her on the DFS sofa he had bought straight out of law school. 'It feels like nothing has changed. We shouldn't let it change anything.'

'Mmm,' she had murmured in agreement.

That had been her thought exactly.

She turned to him, a bright smile on her face.

'What if we don't let it change anything?' she had asked. He had closed his eyes by this point, the wine having started to wield its effect on him. 'What if,' she continued, 'we let everyone think we earned it?'

'Yes, that's realistic,' he'd laughed. 'I, Mark Jones somehow earned over £10 million practicing wills and trusts law at Porpoise, Fielding and Smudge. People will definitely believe that.'

You said it, she thought dryly, but she'd persevered.

'Not all of it. But we could tell people you got a raise. A promotion. They don't have to know how much we've got. Just that we're doing well.'

She felt his bulk shift from beneath her, his arm dislodging uncomfortably as he sat up.

'You're serious.' His voice was the very epitome of incredulity and, to her distaste, had a holier than thou tone to it. 'Why don't you want anyone to know? This is fun. It's great. We've won the bloody lottery, Jess. There *is* nothing better.'

He was so excited, and Jess knew she shouldn't roll her eyes at this. Seriously, she would be embarrassed to her very core to tell anyone that they had *bought* a lottery ticket let alone won it. In her book, real winners *earned* their money. They struggled and clawed and climbed until they reached the top. Or at least inherited it. She didn't want anything just handed to her like she was a charity case.

'Just think how cool it would be if people thought we had earned it. That *you* had earned it. Think how all our friends would think of it.' He'd still looked unconvinced. That's when she'd pulled out her ace.

'Think about Lance.'

At this, Mark had frozen.

Bingo. She had him now.

Mark's face had morphed from dubious to ponderous. It wasn't a straight shift. It went through several permutations including annoyed, confused and exasperated. It had been the mention of her brother-in-law's name that had done it. Mark was a fairly secure, usually easy-going guy, but even he wasn't immune to the chisel-jawed, blindingly bright grinning arrogance of her sister's husband. Tall, handsome and with the body of a nationally seeded tennis player – mostly because he was one – Lance Smyth-Brynn was also a spectacularly successful real estate mogul who regularly featured in the *Sunday Times* Rich List.

'He's a glorified estate agent,' Mark always grumbled. 'And he came from money. It's not like he started off with a fiver and a dream.'

It had been a sore point for Mark ever since the first time they had been introduced. After all, it wasn't like he wasn't impressive in his own right. He was a well thought of member of a medium sized City firm. In most families he would at least have been on a par with the other partners. It was just bad luck that Lance was a property genius of international proportions. That meant that he got the lion's share of respect at every family gathering while Mark was treated like a beloved but ultimately useless pet.

That her sister, Amelie, had bagged a man infinitely more impressive than her own was something that irked Jess too, but for today anyway, he had served his purpose. She pressed on.

'Everyone would see how successful you are. It would have happened eventually anyway,' she had reasoned, albeit untruthfully.

'But I would have to be a partner to be earning anything like that kind of money and even then it would take years. I'm not sure it would even be possible.'

Jess knew he was right. Being a wills and trusts lawyer wasn't generally the route to the high life, but if there was one thing Jess knew, it was that being British meant people didn't pry. They might speculate wildly behind your back, but nobody would ever dream of doing something as outrageously forward as asking a direct question.

'We don't have to be extravagant. Much better to be subtle. You said yourself that we shouldn't let it change anything.'

And that's what they did. Yes, Mark had whined about it, had complained that he had wanted to tell at least his parents or even just one friend, but she had insisted on a complete blackout. Not a word to anyone. It was just too big a secret for anyone to keep for long.

They told friends and family he had been awarded a pay raise for good work and that hopefully partnership was on the horizon. Most people had smiled and congratulated him with the mild disinterest such news always garnered. People were always getting pay increases. So what? But it was the perfect explanation for any extravagancies; little treats if they were so inclined.

And here Jess had been careful to strike just the right balance. For example, they didn't move house. They were already living in a pretty maisonette in one of London's best areas; they just owned it now instead of renting. It would do. Their car had undergone something of an upgrade. For one thing, it was now cars, plural: Hers was a neat little Mercedes roadster and his some kind of Audi.

She loved her new car, but what she had relished most of all was the freedom of being able to pile on all the extras without giving a thought to the budget. She'd just chucked in all the various packages. She had no clue what most of it was, but she was never going to risk someone who *did* know noticing she was lacking in any way.

Her wardrobe had also improved exponentially. She had always been resourceful in her clothes purchases, finding ways to achieve the latest looks and chicest brands within her means. She always looked good, at the very least because she spun, soul cycled, yogalatised and ran to within an inch of her waistline, all while maintaining the eating habits of a stick insect. But now her wardrobe would meet the scrupulous standards of the staunchest of fashionistas. There were no more compromises. Instead of scouring the net for deals, she strode directly into the boutiques on Bond Street and had every stitch altered to her exact measurements. And in honour of her transformed clothing collection, she had converted one of the rooms in their house into a walk-in wardrobe that most girls would gladly die for just to look good in the casket. She adored walking along the lines of matching hangers fingering the fabrics. When she did, she felt like she was at the most exclusive of events, one to which all the supremoes of sartorial society were invited; where Giorgio and Isse mingled with Donatella and Miucia.

Still, there was a lot of work to be done. She was, after all, clutching the Dears' property information, a tangible illustration of exactly how far she had yet to go to achieve her life goals. Jess swivelled her chair to face the bustle of the city street encapsulated in her office window, fingering the glossy photographs of the regal residence reverentially. There was an inner circle she had yet to penetrate; an ocean of riches and wealth in which Mark's little windfall barely registered as a drop. She would get there of course. This injection of cash just meant she could be more comfortable along the journey.

CHAPTER 5

Boiling water splattered messily into Mark's mug, coating then drowning the husks of freeze-dried granules within to create the diluted, murky waters masquerading as coffee. He tapped his foot, eager to retrieve his caffeine then retreat to his desk. His office's kitchen was, like so many of its counterparts, designed to minimise loitering through a mix of shabby sterility and inconvenience. It was almost universally effective. However, the two secretaries nattering by the biscuits were proving impervious to the gloom of the space, their chatter boring into his brain as a jackhammer might infiltrate a slab of butter.

'Forty-three million, I mean!' Hillary, the shorter, fatter of the two was saying breathlessly as she shook her head in amazement. She was, as usual, dressed in colours one would never encounter in nature, a sort of bright neon pink dress that matched the lipstick residing as much on her teeth as on her lips.

'I know,' agreed Kelly, the unnervingly tall, broad one in her thick northern accent. Leeds? Maybe Macclesfield, pondered Mark. 'I've bought two tickets. Phil's gonna kill me, thinks there's more chance of being hit by lighting, but I've gotta try.' She dunked a biscuit into her tea, prompting two droplets of the dark tan liquid to make their escape, only to plop onto her black court shoes.

'It could be you!' her friend squawked and they both cackled. 'What would you spend it on?'

'I love this game,' chimed in the plummy voice of George, one of the trainees. 'What would you spend the lottery money on, right? I heard it's up to 43 million.'

George always had to have his say on debates in the office and insisted on doing so like an actor performing his pre-stage warm up. It was as if he was doing one of those tongue twister exercises in which you had to repeat things like 'Do drop in at the Dewdrop Inn' over and over. It was all diction, articulation and volume.

'Ooh a lovely holiday. Lanzarote or Majorca,' Kelly said dreamily. 'Then new car, new house. One with a swimming pool.'

'You're forgetting no more work,' Hillary chided her. 'That's always the first thing I think of. A bloody good lie in first thing.'

'Chelsea season ticket, Chelsea tractor, Chelsea house, Maserati, villa in Mustique,' George opined, rattling off his shopping list while counting it off on his bony fingers. 'Oh and Chelsea. The one who went out with Prince Harry? I'd like her as well.'

'Oh you pig,' Hillary guffawed before they all burst out laughing.

Finally, his mug full, Mark turned to leave.

'What would you do, Mark?' He froze. Crap.

'Me?' He turned only his head, the rest of him ready to flee. It was no use though. Their eyes were pinning him in place.

George, who had asked the question, nodded at him challengingly. 'Yes, 43 million pounds. What are the first things you would buy? Go.'

Mark actually knew the answer to this. Sure, his windfall had been a relatively meagre quarter of the current one, but he was pretty certain the answer wouldn't have differed dramatically regardless of the amount.

Upon realising his good fortune, he had stepped out to purchase a bottle of supermarket champagne, a copy of *The Big Issue* (because the bloke selling it outside the Sainsbury's where he'd bought the wine was bloody terrifying) and, on a whim, a new frying pan. Those were the first three things he had bought with his winnings. No, they weren't particularly exciting, but there were some compelling reasons for that.

Firstly, people forgot that, unless you were one of those monsters who played the Wednesday lotto, you were told about your win on a Sunday. That didn't really leave much time for massive purchases what with Sunday trading laws. After all, the shops opened at 11 and closed at 4 and who wanted to dash round the shops on a Sunday? The only other option was to go online and you weren't going to buy a sports car without a test drive, were you? That was just bad business. But that's not what people wanted to hear. It was a bit like advising his clients on planning in their wills. People didn't want to hear that, no matter how carefully you planned, you'd have to pay *some* tax. They wanted magic. Miracle solutions.

'What the hell am I paying you for if I still have to pay the tax man as well?' one particularly irate client, Mr Gregoriou, had yelled at him just the other day. Mark's boss, Goodwyn had had to appease him. He had stridden into Mark's office like Lancelot on his high steed and whisked off Mr Gregoriou like his very own Guinevere, if Guinevere was a fat middle aged Greek man with commercial property interests around central London.

'Mark, mate' Goodwyn had said to him, arm around his shoulder like he was consoling the last boy picked for cricket, 'You're good with the facts and the numbers,' he had smarmed sickeningly, 'But why not leave the people to me?'

'But he wanted to pay no tax,' Mark had argued sensibly. Was he the only one who thought that that was mildly unrealistic for a man who would be bequeathing a fortune in the region of £1 billion? Mr Gregoriou had actually demanded 'one of those Starbucks solutions'.

'Look,' Goodwyn had cooed, condescension dripping from sneering lips, addressing him much as he would a particularly dim cockatoo. 'You have to say it in the right way. Make it clear they're getting a good deal. The best deal. Make him believe you're the best.' Then he had patted Mark briskly on the shoulder and left to deal with Mr Gregoriou himself.

Looking at his colleagues now Mark thought he'd try talking the talk. What did he have to lose?

'You're thinking too small,' he started, rotating to face them full on. 'You've won £43 million not four. You're not going on holiday. You can buy a whole island. Season ticket? No, no. Buy a football club. And then something fun. Maybe a jetpack.' As he finished, Mark took a triumphant sip of his drink.

42

Everyone around him looked impressed. George shook his head in amazement, eyes wide, and said, 'I underestimated you, Jonesy. You're a dark horse, aren't you?' before slapping him on the back just enough to jostle Marks coffee and returning to his desk.

As Mark walked back to his own office, he heard Hillary say to Kelly, 'He's really made me think, he has. I need to start planning.' And they had both giggled.

Mark was pleased with his answer. In truth, none of those things had been his idea. He'd had to google it. 'How to spend ten million pounds' he had typed into his computer the Monday after their big win. They had each told work that they were ill, but in fact they were going to collect their winnings. With a couple of hours to kill before they were due at Avalon head office and, having already checked Facebook and BBC News, he thought he might research his options.

He had tried to daydream about how he would spend the money. All the amazing things he could do. All those incredible, wonderful things. But for some reason, he couldn't think of a single thing he wanted to spend money on. He'd clicked on the first link he saw.

It read 'What to do if you win a million'. Not exactly what he'd been looking for, but it was a start. It turned out that this was an article about national lottery winners. Mark had devouring the facts and figures on the screen. They were fascinating.

Apparently the average lottery win was £2.08 million and the vast majority of winners invested their jackpots wisely, such as in the stock market. He would have to start devising a plan. The article went on to detail a variety of frequent lottery purchases. Amongst the most common buys were £2.7 billion spent on property and £1.2 billion on gifts for others. Caravans were quite a popular choice for lottery winner apparently, with 300 having been bought with winnings. He'd never look at caravan parks the same way again. According to the stats, they were choc full of lottery winners.

So how would *he* spend his money?

Travel? That was a safe bet. He could go to Columbia or Peru. Or France. Disneyland! He had thought with a jolt of joy. But he didn't want to overdo it. He hated flying. All those people crammed into a tin can tutting at twenty thousand feet. Of course he could go business class. Or first. Maybe he'd call a travel agent. Later. Another time.

Then there was giving to charity. That seemed like a great idea. If he couldn't share the news of his win with his family, the very least he could so was share his winning with the less fortunate.

He had spent the next hour preparing an Excel spreadsheet detailing all the things he wanted to do before Jess had summoned him.

'We have to go,' she had called from the hallway and he had shut down his computer, meeting her as she opened the front door.

'Where is this place anyway?' he'd asked once they were in the car, peering at the email printout they'd received with driving instruction.

'Watford,' Jess replied deadpan. She turned the ignition on their Golf GTS and they started their journey towards the M1. 'Seriously, can't think of anywhere I'd less like to be today. I was supposed to be meeting a new client you know.'

He couldn't blame Jess for her reaction. He had grown up there. He knew it wasn't the most exciting or inspirational place, but he was a little hurt every time she talked about his hometown as she might of the favelas of Rio. It wasn't that bad, he had thought defensively.

'It's only a few minutes from my parents. We could drop in on the way back,' he'd said.

There was a short, but distinct pause, just long enough to communicate Jess's thoughts on this.

'Fine.'

Thirty minutes later, their car ambled into an anonymous business park.

'Is this it?'

'Yep.' Jess pointed at a sign with the National Lottery logo on it.

'Bit disappointing, isn't it?'

'What do you mean?'

'Well,' he gestured towards the windscreen. 'It's not exactly, you know, Avalon.'

'Were you expecting a castle?' Jess teased.

'No.' Mark could hear the petulance in his voice, but really, could anyone blame him? The name of the company was bound to elicit wildly high expectations, especially when coupled with its function. Surely they could have done something to inspire some excitement. Would a turret have killed them?

The greeting at the reception desk did nothing to elevate the experience.

'Can I help you?'

Mark almost recoiled from the face that greeted them. The girl behind the glass counter was a diminutive twenty-something, but her features had the jagged brutality of having been scrawled on with a blade.

'We have a 10am appointment,' Jess replied.

'Have a seat.'

'Somebody overdid the permanent makeup,' Jess muttered quietly once they were safely in the waiting area. 'Her beautician should be shot.'

Mark's eyes darted involuntarily towards the reception desk then away again. Bloody hell.

A few minutes of mindless phone swiping later yet another expectation was squashed like an ant underfoot when they came face to face with their lottery liaison.

If there was an opposite to what one might reasonably expect a 'lottery liaison' to look like, their one was it. To Mark, this job title conjured an image somewhere between the *Cillit Bang* bloke and Willy Wonka. Someone altruistic yet over excitable, definitely slightly unhinged. The truth could not have been further removed.

Grey.

That was the overwhelming impression one had upon meeting their lottery liaison. His hair was grey. His suit was grey. His shoes were black, but Mark could tell they felt out of place. Even his skin had a blue-greyish tinge, the kind one usually found in the elderly or the undead.

His voice also somehow managed to exude a grey quality.

'Congratulations.' It was clear that the grey man was aiming for enthusiastic in his delivery of that single word, but bless him he was only just about convincing them he was alive. Mark and Jess stared at him expectantly from across his MDF desk in his magnolia-walled office. 'You have won an incredible £10.43 million pounds. What a thrilling experience this must be for you both.' He paused here as though awaiting a reaction. It was like his script had said 'leave pause for applause'. Mark was about to say something, but clearly he had missed his moment as the man barrelled on.

'This must be a very exciting time for you both. But there are some things you need to think about,' he continued, his monotone chant taking on a muffled underwater quality as Mark zoned in and out. It was entirely devoid of all intonation. Obviously he had said these words at least once too often. It certainly sounded well-rehearsed.

Mark thought about something he had read earlier in the article. 'On average Avalon makes six millionaires a week.' Six a week. It must seem so dull to him. Oh here comes another one. No wonder the grey man looked so unimpressed. It run of the mill.

Run of the million.

Mark snorted, eliciting a fiery glare from Jess. He tried to turn it into a cough. But the grey man was unperturbed.

Mark would later be unable to recall much of what was said that morning, except that it very closely resembled a mortgage application meeting. They were quiet, attentive, well-behaved. They'd provided the requisite two forms of ID and then, with a few clicks of his computer, grey man had explained that they would receive all the money in one go; that they would be offered advice on private banks that might be able to assist them and some basic tax advice. Mark had considered explaining that that was unnecessary given his legal expertise, but he never got the chance. In any event, it felt like it was a bad idea to interrupt the standard monologue. Doing so, he feared, might cause the grey man to malfunction.

In the end, they had been ejected from the building with a handful of paperwork and a suggestion that they check their account as soon as possible. It felt like being spat out of a washing machine mid-cycle. They had simply sat in their parked car dazedly for a few moments.

'What do we do now?' Mark had asked.

'I guess we go,' was Jess's numb response. 'Still, at least that's done. That was one of the most depressing places I've ever been.' Mark had had to agree with her there. And with that, they had departed.

As they approached his parents' new build bungalow in leafy Bushey, bought two years prior in a downsizing move, he readied himself for the task ahead. He squared his shoulders and stretched his fingers, turning his neck as though about to take part in a World Federation wrestling match. He was arming himself. Preparing for battle.

It wasn't that he didn't love and adore his mum and dad. What was there not to love? Mary Jones was a diminutive stay at home mum who threw herself into charities and community events almost as much as she did the world of crime fiction. Meanwhile, David Jones was an ex antiques dealer and general businessman around town who enjoyed nothing more than a good natter.

Reactions to his parents were varied. They ranged from, 'They're so lovely!' and 'Your dad is a character,' to 'Are they ok?' and 'They're really quite loud aren't they.' This last observation had come from Jess the first time she had met them.

His parents had always been a handful. That was doubtlessly true. Mark only had to think about his childhood for a second to remember the time his dad had taken over the school Christmas dinner, mid cracker snapping, to lead the entire room in a medley of carols. Then there had been the time his mum had volunteered to chaperone a field trip, only to spend the entire coach journey loudly recounting Mark's last trip to the doctor, ending with the declaration, 'the smell was terrible, but luckily they were able to get it out.'

Today, his mum and dad were, as usual, in top form. At that moment, his mum was regaling them with a tale from the golf course.

'So I said to her,' Mary Jones was recounting confidingly, leaning forward, one eyebrow raised, 'If you think that's a hole in one, you've been doing it wrong for a while now, love!'

As Jess choked on her mineral water and Mark considered pulling off his own ears, his mum and dad laughed heartily.

'But honestly,' his mum continued, spearing a piece of roast beef onto her fork before shovelling it mouthwards and chewing vigorously, 'Who does she think she is? She only joined the club last year and all of the sudden she thinks she's Tiger bloody Woods!' She stopped for just a split second before saying, 'So any baby plans?'

Mark wasn't sure Jess was breathing at this point, but his mother just blinked expectantly.

'Because Sharon down the road is expecting her second and she was saying that when you hit 35 your eggs start disappearing.'

'Poof!' Mark's dad said, making a sort of explosive gesture with his hands, like a magician who had lost his magic marbles.

'Have you had your eggs tested, Jess? You can't have that many left. You're not a spring chicken anymore,' Mark's mum warned with stern eyes and a wave of her fork as his dad chewed energetically.

'Jesus ma, Jess's eggs are fine,' Mark said, even though he had no idea if this was true. Fact was, his girlfriend's eggs were not a topic to be discussed over a Monday roast.

'So how's work?' asked his dad, tucking into the mound of potatoes on his plate. His parents had been surprised to see them on a weekday, but they had explained that they had decided to take a day off together as they had holidays left which they couldn't carry over. 'I've been sending people your way, you know.'

'Yeah, about that dad, I wish you wouldn't,' Mark said. 'The last guy you sent was a complete weirdo. Kept asking me when he was likely to die.'

'You scared the hell out of George Hill the other day, David,' Mark's mum said, prompting his dad to laugh loudly and, mouth still full, gesture wildly as if to say, 'you've got to listen to this'. Mark's mum obliged. 'Started telling him that if he didn't write a will all his money would go to that awful daughter-in-law of his. The one with the squint and the angry chin.'

His parents started laughing uncontrollably, swaying back and forth and banging the table with their hands.

'I think he was on the phone to your office about ten minutes later,' his dad now said, almost in tears.

Mark snuck a look over at Jess who was busy fussing with her plate. He knew she hated roasts. Far too oily.

It took several moments for Mark's parents to get hold of themselves, his mother having to dab her eyes with a napkin.

'So what else is going on?' she asked, eyes dried, but still slightly out of breath.

This was such a non-question. It was the question you asked when you'd covered everything that really mattered. In most circumstances, important, life changing information would have been revealed far in advance of this particular question being asked. And yet, if Mark had decided to be truthful that lunch, this was his chance.

'Oh, yes, well,' he could say lightly. 'Did I mention we've just been down the road to get our lottery winnings? Twenty quid? Nah, more like £10 mil, give or take a few hundred thow.' But he could feel Jess's whole body tensing, as if she sensed his hesitation.

'I got a pay rise,' Mark said suddenly, abruptly. It was as if the tension had squeezed him like a blood pressure cuff until some words just popped out. His mum and dad responded in their respective typical ways.

'That's great!'

'How much?'

Later, on the way home, Mark had felt compelled to say something. He stewed and fretted as Jess held forth about how his mother considered potatoes to be a salad.

'Have your parents ever fed us anything green? I swear, your mum is trying to fatten me up.'

'Didn't that feel strange to you?' Despite the complete non-sequitur, he knew Jess would understand.

'What do you mean?' Jess's voice bore the sharp tone of someone who knew exactly what he meant. Her eyes remained firmly on the road.

'I *mean* not telling them about winning the bloody money. I didn't like it. It felt like lying.' He allowed his misery to penetrate his words.

'You're not lying,' Jess had said in mild exasperation. 'You're certainly not hurting anyone.'

'The pay rise isn't a lie?'

'Will you stop being so melodramatic.' There was a tense silence and, probably realising she had been a bit too harsh, Jess glanced over at him. Seeing that he was hurt she sighed and relented. 'That's a tiny little lie. A white lie. People can't exactly go round telling the truth all day, can they?' Jess said, her eyes now once again fixed on the road. 'Look, it's not like we can't go back. We can always decide to tell people later. But for now it's best if we just stick to the plan.'

A few nights later he and Jess were at dinner with Sophie and Jonty Macintosh. Mark hated going out with this particular pair. Sophie may well have been Jess's oldest friend, but she was also by far the most frightening. Mark wasn't even sure they were friends. They seemed to spend most of the time trying to outdo one another.

Jonty on the other hand was like the physical embodiment of the darker side of nature versus nurture. Weak jawed and frail of bone, it was obvious that as a schoolboy he would have spent much of his time at the mercy of the bigger, stronger boys, possibly with his head shoved down the toilets of his high-end boarding school. Yet, with the benefit of years of what was obviously some pretty hefty pep talks from his alpha male father and having made a fortune on the stock market, Jonty was now determined to demonstrate his superiority. Mark imagined that a psychologist would have a field day interpreting Jonty's actions. He probably suffered from the kind of reverse inferiority complex usually only experienced by the sons of military dictators. Watch out Kim Jong Un, he thought sardonically, looking on now as Jonty checked his teeth in the reflection of a spoon.

'So I said to the doctor,' Sophie was drawling, 'I can't help it if I am naturally slim. I eat like a horse. You know I do,' she said to Jess, flashing her a confidential smile. In fact she had barely eaten more than an edamame bean that night. 'But apparently my BMI is equivalent to that of a seven-year-old boy.' She said this with a mix of pride and horror.

'How awful for you,' Jess had replied, her own BMI probably exactly the same. Mark knew enough about Jess and Sophie's relationship to know that there was a whole subtext to this conversation. Indeed, competitive undereating was like a blood sport for women like these. Take that evening for example.

They were at one of London's most highly rated sushi restaurants, Roka in Mayfair. The food was, even to a sushi novice such as himself, delicious. What's more, Jonty had ensured that they had ordered everything on the menu. Twice. Looking at the prices, Mark couldn't help but think he might need a second lottery win by the end of the night just to pay the tip.

Nevertheless, despite the excellent food and plentiful supply, both women had indulged in the kind of food détente that made the Cold War appear like minor bickering by comparison. Neither was prepared to be the first to place a chopstick's worth of food near her mouth until the other did so, meaning their blood sugar was dangerously low.

At one point it had looked like Sophie might be about to accidentally inhale a grain of rice, but Jonty had made some apparently hilarious comment about skiing in January instead of February – something along the lines of it being so gauche – and Sophie's explosion of laughter had luckily prevented that potential fiasco.

Mark felt powerless as the tennis match of one-up-womanship continued. He knew from Jess's frequent past rants that she was sick of Sophie always making her feel like she was the downstairs to Sophie's up.

'How many bloody holidays can two people go on in winter? It's a wonder Jonty gets any work done at all,' she had seethed after their last night out.

So, when Sophie started talking about the 'simply terrible' decision she had to make between holidaying in Mauritius or the Maldives that year, Mark knew a strike by Jess wasn't too long in the offing.

'Oh, I know what you mean.' From Jess's pained tone as she said this, one would have thought they were commiserating about losing a family pet. 'So hard to find somewhere decent. We were thinking about the Caribbean.' She smiled sweetly across the table. Mark could almost hear the 'dun dun dun' drama of a piano signalling that a gauntlet had been thrown down.

To anyone else, this would have been an innocuous comment, but in this particular context it was a first strike. A poker move. A sign that Jess was going to see Sophie's holiday and raise the stakes. Jess may as well have told Sophie she was directing a missile at Harrods.

Judging by the flared nostrils, Sophie was pissed. She smiled slightly maniacally. 'How lovely. I didn't realise you were going on holiday. Don't you usually stick to just one a year?' The tension was palpable. The music would definitely have switched by now to the *Jaws* soundtrack.

'Oh yes, well, you know how it is,' Jess said, voice full of sympathy. 'Mark just desperately needs a break. I mean, yes he's earned a big pay rise, but it's just been so stressful.'

Game on.

Mark and Jonty had been silently watching their other halves. Now both of them looked to Sophie, waiting with bated breath for her response. You could never really tell how these things would end. True, both women had mellowed since hitting their thirties, but in the past arguments had started over things as simple as one copying the other's nail polish and ended with the slashing of one another's Stella McCartney dresses.

'How lovely,' Sophie beamed patronisingly, prompting Mark and Jonty to both exhale sighs of relief. 'So you're getting yourself a little treat. That must be fun.'

'Oh these women,' Jonty said conspiratorially to Mark, like someone out of a nineteenth century play, 'Let's talk of more serious things.' Jonty spent the next hour telling Mark about how he understood the markets better than anyone else and how nobody else knew how to invest. He then 'picked Mark's brain' about tax avoidance versus tax evasion and asked him which territory he felt was best for safekeeping funds.

Mark was thankful when the night finally ended with air kisses all round and promises to meet again like this soon. He was looking forward to going to bed and getting out of the line of friendly fire.

'Oh my g-d she can be nightmare,' Jess said of her friend as soon as they were in their cab and out of Sophie's elephantine earshot. She continued like this for the entire trip home. But Mark just relaxed into his drunken stupor and comforted himself with one fact. Jonty would be getting it worse.

CHAPTER 6

Mark knew he should be revelling in the beauty of the parkland before him. He should enjoy the visage of the rolling hills, rambling paths and ducks and swans paddling nearby. He should marvel at the wholesomeness of ruddy dog walkers and tiny mums with tank-like buggies strolling, running and chatting all around as he and Jess walked arm in arm, taking in the atmosphere. He should at least appreciate the fact that it was all within reach of a pub. Hampstead Heath on a brisk, sunny Saturday afternoon in November. What was there not to love?

And yet, the overwhelming sense he had at that particular moment was not happy serenity. No, no. It was sheer, unrelenting, thank-Christ-it's-over, relief. Indeed the last time he had experienced a sensation of liberation of this magnitude was when Branning had finally stopped telling him the grim birth story of his triplets complete with graphic snaps and agreed to talk of less bloody escapades. For, as he looked down at his attire of designer workout gear, gold Fitbit and flashy trainers, he knew that his torment had ceased, if only for the time being. He also knew he looked like a prick.

Onlookers probably assumed he had been dragged through the hedges. That was basically because that was what had just happened to him. For the past hour they had been hurtling through the Heath as though they were fleeing the state, Mark trying to keep up as Jess jumped over logs and ducked under trees like she was Jason Bourne.

According to Jess, it was all part of her plan to get into shape. Mark gritted his teeth at this. He knew that wasn't the real reason. Considering the fact that she did enough exercise to put Olympic Decathletes to shame, he had surmised that the real purpose of this little jaunt had Sophie written all over it.

He was sure that somewhere in between Jonty's ramblings the other night about how brilliant his latest investment strategy was and how he was a brilliant mind of the twentieth century (yes apparently Jonty wasn't aware of the millennium), he had heard Sophie harping on about 'running through nature' or 'getting fit outside' or some other such nonsense. This definitely had something to do with it. A morning which had not started with the lie-in he had hoped for, but instead with Jess shaking him awake like they had to evacuate the building, throwing his clothes at him and demanding that he be at the door within ten minutes.

This was nothing new. In fact, many of the random activities Mark found himself undertaking in his spare time could be traced back to Sophie's whims.

He thought back to other examples. There had been the time they had ended up on holiday in what could charitably be described as a shack – complete with bathroom dwelling goat - in a northern Italian shanty town on the basis of Sophie's recommendation that it was 'so incredibly rustic and unspoilt'. Then there had been the month that Mark had been forced to wear pink shirts and ties every single day in order to prove that he was every bit the enlightened modern male that Jonty claimed to be. Goodwyn still called him princess. Now it was enforced running. Where would it end?

He looked over at Jess. She looked fine. Good even. She seemed to be glowing rather than perspiring. Wearing a pair of black leggings, Flashdance style leg warmers and a vest under her jacket that showed off her cleavage to great advantage, she was the very picture of urban exercising perfection.

Mark was just trying to foresee the next craze in an attempt to forestall it when something huge and hairy came barrelling in their direction and straight at him.

'What the-,' he started, just about managing to throw his hands out in self-defence when the creature crashed into him. He heard a loud roar emanate from behind the beast as he stumbled backwards, only just manging to keep upright.

'Snuffles! Down!'

It was a bloody dog. A large, slobbering, panting, grinning black Labrador which was now standing up, his face intimately close to Mark's, his paws resting affectionately on his arms, like they were about to make a bid for the Strictly Come Dancing golden trophy.

'Mark? Mark!' The deep disembodied voice came from beyond the salivating canine.

The dog was eventually dragged backwards, offering Mark the chance to get his bearing. The first thing he saw was a furious Jess. Arms folded, she looked at him much as a mum did at the toddler who jumped in the giant puddle in their Sunday best. He shrugged at her as if to say, 'how is this my fault?'

It was only when he managed to recover from her silent censure that he caught sight of Paul. It was such an unexpected sight that Mark couldn't quite get his head around it. Paul from the church hall. Paul of the lottery group was smiling broadly at him while trying to restrain a dog whose attentions had shifted to a small, unsuspecting poodle by the lake. Taking a closer look at the enormous man, Mark wasn't sure how he had missed him before now. With his bulky frame covered head to toe in hi-vis active wear, he looked like a tennis ball.

'How are you, mate? Good to see you.' Paul managed to maintain his enthusiasm while still keeping hold of the improbably named Snuffles, a battle which was becoming more difficult by the minute as the dog's excitement grew.

Realising that a response was required, Mark tried to recover. He plastered on what he hoped was a smile on his face.

'Paul, hi. Funny seeing you here,' he managed. 'Great dog,' he added.

'Yeah, he belongs to my girls,' Paul said fondly. 'Somehow I ended up being his walker. Always the way!' He chuckled. 'So, I take it this is your good wife?' He looked over at Jess, whose suspicious gaze was firmly fixed on Snuffles, clearly wary of her own immaculate outfit being in peril.

It was only now that Mark realised the serious trouble he was in. Because, as much as Mark never saw himself as the kind of person who would join a support group, Jess would have considered such a move as the first step towards irrefutable insanity. Or at least towards a life on a trailer park in one of America's vowel states. He knew exactly what she would say. What kind of loser goes to a support group? No. Telling Jess had never been an option. So how would he explain Paul?

'Jess this is Paul, Paul, Jess, my girlfriend,' he said, trying to buy time. 'Paul and I know each other through,' he paused for just a second before alighting on the only possible answer. 'Work'.

Jess's eyes immediately brightened from the dull, polite glaze she had when talking to the dishwasher repair man to the dull, polite smile she bestowed on people she deemed to be one rung further up the ladder. Jess liked to preserve her social energy, only unleashing her most glittering smile on those she deemed worthy.

'Hi,' she smiled. 'Are new you to the firm?'

Seeing Paul's confused gaze, Mark piped in. 'Paul's in the IT department at the *law firm*. Really good with computers.'

A light of recognition glimmered in Paul's eyes as he cottoned on. In fact, as the light grew brighter, Mark had time to consider that he may have ignited something he would be powerless to control.

'Yeah, yeah, I'm part of the furniture, me. Me and this one go back,' Paul was now chuntering, slinging one potato-sack arm around Mark's shoulder. 'The number of times I have to say to him, 'have you tried turning it off and on'?' He shook his head in mock exasperation, eyes to the sky.

'Oh, right,' Jess said, now visibly dimming the wattage of her smile. 'How lovely.'

'And you should see him at the canteen,' Paul said, now clearly warming to his new role. 'Always takes the last yoghurt. I always say to him, 'oi, Mark, leave some for the ladies'.' He winked at Mark.

Jess looked as though she had just swallowed a bee, while Mark felt all the blood leave his face at the thought of the possibilities ahead. They had to leave. Now.

'We're just off for a drink at the Spaniard's Inn,' Mark said, referring to the closest pub and hoping his tone indicated a near end to the encounter.

'Oh! Why don't you come round to ours?' Paul said excitedly. 'I know Dina would love to meet you and one thing you can count on at ours is that the bar is stocked,' he chortled.

'Oh no,' Mark and Jess began at once before Mark finished with 'We can't impose.'

'Nah! I insist. It's the least I can do after my mutt ruined your gear,' he said.

Mark couldn't think of how to get out of this. He looked over at Jess who was similarly lost for words. She was just mutely shaking her head, mouth open as if about to say something that wouldn't come out. Mark knew that being 'stuck' with a man like Paul was not Jess's idea of a profitable way to spend her spare time. Just as at work where Jess had to justify her time in six-minute increments, she ensured that every moment of her weekends and evenings served a purpose. And this would not pass muster.

Mark, on the other hand, wouldn't have minded if it hadn't been for the fact that he and Paul shared their terrible secret. He liked Paul. He seemed like a genuine guy. Looking at him now as he led them out of the park, a tail-wagging Snuffles leading the way, Mark considered that Paul himself was not unlike a puppy. Boundlessly friendly and completely unstoppable.

The journey to Paul's house, as it turned out, wasn't too long. In fact it was a matter of moments before they were standing in front of a pair of gargantuan gates on one of London's most famous roads. The Bishop's Avenue was a wide street in between the affluent areas of Hampstead and Highgate which boasted some of the Capital's most ostentatious houses. Whilst not the billionaires' haven it once had been, it certainly should have been out of the reaches of 'Paul from the IT department'. If he had existed.

Shit. How would he explain this one? Jess was clearly flummoxed by this turn of events.

'So, this is where you live?' Jess asked as Paul keyed in a code and the gates began to open, more than a hint of surprise and doubt in her voice.

'Paul's wife inherited some money,' Mark explained quickly. Possibly a bit too quickly.

'Oh yes,' Paul said in agreement, nodding erratically as he realised his mistake. 'Old aunt. Just died. Very sad.' He was about as convincing as a nun at Oktoberfest.

Mark could almost detect a reluctance, a sort of embarrassed torpor in the gates' movement as they opened with a slow, low whine. He couldn't blame them. As Mark, Jess and Paul stood surveying the scene before them, it was hard to put into words the vision that greeted them.

'Welcome to Casa Baker!' Paul spread his arms as he said this in a grand gesture.

'Is that?' Jess started, a quiver in her usually solid voice.

'Buckingham Palace?' Mark finished slowly.

'Yep,' Paul said. 'It took some convincing and quite a bit of planning, but we managed it. It's a perfectly proportioned mini Buckingham Palace.' He had his mitts on his hips in the image of a man who had cobbled this together with his two bare hands.

'Well, it's just,' Jess began.

'Majestic' Mark croaked in conclusion, after a short pause.

'Look at you two lovebirds finishing off each other's sentences,' Paul laughed. 'Come on in then, meet the missus,' he added, ushering them towards the oversized doors, on either side of which stood gnomes wearing Queen's Guard uniforms. Mark could practically feel Jess shudder.

As the ridiculous doors opened, a gust emitted from inside and they walked in to find a foyer the size of an average ice-skating rink. It bore other resemblances to this as well, with its bright white marble floor and high ceilings. A huge dark wood staircase coiled its way upwards to a second floor, while there were doors leading off in various directions. Red, black and gold marble seemed to be vying for attention on every surface, battling for supremacy with gold leaf and leather. Mark felt like he had fallen down the rabbit hole. Or perhaps into a sixteenth century French brothel.

'Hold on a sec,' Paul said as they went in. 'Let me just find her.' And with that, he scurried away across the expanse of the white marble, but not before shooting Mark a meaningful glance.

Mark and Jess didn't speak over the period of minutes while Paul was away. Jess just mouthed emphatically at him and kept pointing at the front door in a way which signalled unambiguously that she expected him to get them out of this mess. Mark could hear loudly hushed conversation somewhere in the near distance before Paul re-emerged. As he did so, Mark and Jess mirrored his all too bright smile.

Paul strode over the marble with the flamboyance of a bullfighter. It took Mark a moment to register the sound of determined clattering which approached as Paul did. Quiet at first, it drew closer and closer.

A pair of heels.

Yes, definitely. And they were propelling themselves in their direction. A small red figure was now visible in the distance, one that was jiggling with the exertion of its rapid pace. As the sound and the legs attached got nearer, Mark imagined that this was like what one must feel like on the business end of an approaching nuclear missile; utterly defenceless.

'Hello!' cried a voice attached to the heels, waving a short arm as it neared them. 'Welcome!'

Mark had never seen anyone, or anything, like it. Except perhaps on reality television. Indeed, the wildly gesticulating woman before them would probably be deemed slightly tacky by the cast of *The Only Way Is Essex*. Her scarlet dress was so tight, Mark was sure he could see her appendix. The terrifying spectre of her body and her ballooning breasts bundled into the tiny garment was in direct contrast with the vast construction of determinedly crimson follicles that added five inches to her height. Her lips, cheeks and somehow even her eyes meanwhile had the appearance of having been inflated, so exaggerated was their appearance. It was almost as if the constrictive dress had forced them to pop out. A hand shot up to her swelled chest.

'I,' she pronounced, somehow managing to imbue even this single word with her heavy Essex accent before pausing for effect, 'Am Dina. And I am so pleased to meet you.' And with that she clasped first Jess and then Mark in chokingly fragranced hugs.

Upon her release, Jess smiled tightly, looking about as pleased as if she was about to undergo a root canal under the auspices of the local butcher. Mark meanwhile was still getting accustomed to the fact that he had just involved his new acquaintance in what must be the strangest set of lies on earth. What had he been thinking?

'Come on then,' Dina squawked. 'Let's retire to the lounge.' As she led them through the aircraft hangar of a house, Mark thought that if the outside was a replica of royal proportions, the interior was straight out of the most lurid, outlandish and vivid photoshoots of *OK! Magazine*. In fact, massive posters of *OK!* and other magazine front covers graced every wall, Dina and Paul's faces staring out from them with headlines such as *'My Lottery Hero'* and *'We Haven't Let Our Win Change Us'*.

He surveyed the passing photographs of their hosts. Through them, one could track the transformation of Dina's face and body from fairly normal and plain to increasingly more rounded and inflated. It was like watching some bizarre version of evolution in action.

'Hold on, I'll just ask Mirka to fetch the drinks,' Dina said. Mark and Jess nodded politely before Dina turned her head and without further warning screamed, 'Mirka!' so loudly that one of the photos on the enormous faux fireplace threatened to topple.

A skinny, dour faced woman in a badly fitting French maid's uniform clumped into the room.

'Ah, Mirka,' Dina said, pursing her lips. 'Coffees all round please and some biscuits por favor.' She waited for Mirka to go before saying sotto voce, 'Lovely girl, but doesn't always get things right.'

Mark wondered if this was because Dina was speaking Spanish to someone with an eastern European name, but decided to keep silencio. Paul led them to a vast corner sofa and, as they sat down, the suite swallowed them up. It was like sinking into quicksand. Dina sidled up to Mark and Jess, albeit with some difficulty, her breasts bobbing up and down with her exertions.

'So, you both know Paul from work,' Dina ventured, her face too much a picture of innocence. Her eyes were open so wide, there was a serious chance they would escape. Oh God, thought Mark. She knows. We have to get off this topic.

'Just me,' Mark blurted. 'Jess is a family lawyer at a different firm. Lovely home you have here. Is that a real tiger over there?'

Dina grabbed Jess's hand. 'You're such a pretty little thing and a lawyer as well! Hold onto this one, Mark.' And she let out a cackle.

'So that's divorce then,' Paul looked from Jess to Mark. 'Family law?'

Jess's face was a picture of patronising distaste.

'That's part of it,' she said. 'We deal with all aspects of family life in a legal context. Marriage dissolution, children, assets, that kind of thing.'

Jess hated this kind of questioning. She was undoubtedly plotting her escape. Nevertheless, her manners would never permit her to leave before imbibing at least one hot beverage. Jess was nothing if not obsessively polite.

'So is it just you two here?' Mark asked. As soon as the words came out he remembered that Paul had three daughters.

'Oh no,' Dina enthused. 'Our girls, Miley, Mandy and Molly are at finishing school,' she said as proudly as if her children had self-driven to the moon.

It was then that Mark noticed the army of photos of three teen girls scattered strategically around the room. They were aggressively blond, large of arm, bright of red lip and each more orange than the last.

'You know, if they're going to get the,' she leaned in and lowered her voice, 'right connections,' she whispered so loudly she may as well have been using a megaphone. 'They have to be in the best place. So, when we was choosing I did what I always do,' she continued, now pausing for effect. 'I asked myself, what would Carol Middleton do?'

Jess coughed, probably to avoid spitting out her own tongue.

'So of course, I sent them to Marlborough. Not that it lasted. So instead they've gone to learn their P's and Q's. You alright love?'

'Fine, thanks,' Jess croaked.

'Course they've started talking with so many marbles in their mouths half the time I don't understand what they're on about,' lamented Paul. 'But they're good girls.'

'Do you still work at the firm, Paul?' Jess asked.

Mark's eyes darted to Paul.

'Oh, well, just part-time. Keep my hand in, that sort of thing.' Paul fumbled.

'Very admirable,' she said. 'A lot of people would have just quit.'

Paul had clearly just risen in her estimations.

'Oh, well I love my work,' Paul replied nervously. Was he sweating? Mark thought he saw a glistening on his head.

This was unbearable. The conversation felt like they were playing chess using fire ants as the pieces. Every time someone thought they had made a move, the board changed inexplicably. This had to end.

Just then the faux French maid entered with the drinks and plate of ginger nut biscuits, practically slamming them down on the glass coffee table.

'Thank you, Mirka,' Dina said icily.

After coffees and teas were distributed, they sat in silence.

'So, you two keeping fit then?' Paul asked jovially, nodding at their outfits. 'I could do with a bit of that,' he laughed and patted his rotund belly.

'We were running in nature. It's the latest thing in urban exercise,' Jess informed him, unable to resist the opportunity to lecture. Mark couldn't help but think that running outside wasn't the latest thing in anything. Wasn't it pretty much what man had been doing since the dawn of time?

'Ah, well, cheaper than a gym I suppose,' Paul guffawed.

'We have our own gym now,' Dina informed them with a smug grin. 'Running machine and rowing and all that. Top of the line. You can come over and use them whenever you like.'

'Mmmm,' Mark and Jess nodded simultaneously.

Mark tried feverishly to think of topics that were unrelated to Paul's wealth or 'work'. He was still clueless as to Paul's actual pre-lottery-win job. He'd have to ask, but for now, he couldn't think of a single sodding thing to say.

'I like playing golf,' Paul cried. He too must had been searching for a safe subject. 'Do you play, Mark?'

'No,' Jess answered moodily, pre-empting him. This was a sore point between Mark and Jess. She had always insisted he should play, insisting that it was the ultimate way to network and schmooze with clients and partners. As though that was a *selling point*. He barely wanted to speak to those people when he had to. The idea of choosing to do so while traipsing around a glorified field with long sticks was anathema to him.

'Oh you should come and play with me,' Paul said excitedly. 'It's great. Spoiling a good walk and all that. I joined this club. You should come.' He looked genuinely thrilled at this idea.

'Sounds great,' Mark replied. In fact it sounded like pulling teeth, but as long as they weren't talking about law or computers, that was the main thing.

'We'd best be off,' Jess said, managing to maintain her poise as she lowered her cup. 'I'm so sorry, but we have people coming over this afternoon and we have to prepare.'

'Of course,' Dina said with an emphatic edge that implied that she understood completely. She jumped up as though forcibly ejected from her seat. 'It was lovely to meet you both. Always nice to meet Paul's colleagues.' And to Mark's horror she winked at him. Luckily Jess appeared not to notice.

'Thanks again,' Mark rasped as the rest of them stood up. There was then much bustling and air kissing before Jess and Mark were released into the bright serenity of the outside.

It was only once the door had closed behind them that he realised he had been holding his breath. He discharged the air with a swoosh of relief.

'Oh my god what the hell was that?' Jess hissed at him once they had emerged from the gates. 'That house. Those people.' She was shaking her head in disbelief.

'They were nice,' Mark defended.

Jess ignored this. 'Seriously, some people shouldn't be allowed a credit card. That was the crassest thing I have *ever* seen.' Jess's face crumpled into a puzzled frown, something she never did for fear of wrinkles. 'And what the hell was wrong with his eyebrows? Were they drawn on by a child?' She paused for only a second before ruining the rest of Mark's morning with the words, 'Right, do a quick stretch and we'll run back.'

CHAPTER 7

Mark surprised even himself when he arrived at the hall on time for the next meeting. He had found the perfect excuse for leaving work early. His back.

If there was one thing that was sacrosanct in the world of office health and safety it was the spine. You could drink like a fish, smoke like a chimney and eat like it was your last meal every day, but if you so much as turned your waist incorrectly, the big bosses paid attention. You only had to look at his office furniture to see this. Offices around the country were at pains to ensure that workers sat correctly, that they were furnished with the sturdiest of lumbar supports and that they swivelled at only the most advantageous of angles. His own swivel chair had a future career as the first office apparatus in space, so advanced was its technology.

So, when the firm's health and safety worker came round for their bi-annual check of everyone's seating positions, Mark simply let out a well-timed groan upon turning in his seat. He had imagined that this could lead to quite the dramatic scene, something akin to an episode of *Casualty* or *Grey's Anatomy*, one where the young medic has to think fast in a storm with a bus load of injured nuns and the four horsemen of the apocalypse on their way.

'This man needs a chiropractor,' the young and beautiful health and safety officer would say to her colleague. 'Stat.'

Mark would then be airlifted to a hospital where he would have the best care, perhaps interrupted by a quickly resolved hostage situation.

Instead, Mark was faced with the disdainfully dour visage of Bob from the firm's 'elf 'n' safety team, who tutted, wrote something on his clip board while shaking his head wearily and handed him a referral to a back specialist. Sure, it wasn't the heroic scene he'd envisaged, but it did achieve his ultimate goal. From that moment on, Mark had an early finishing time every Wednesday afternoon for his fictitious back appointment. Perfect.

As Mark walked into the church hall, he noticed a table with some digestives and two flasks along with some Styrofoam cups. At the end of the last meeting he had learned that this was done on a rota basis, with each member expected to contribute. He wondered when it would be his turn.

A couple of the members were already there. Mark wracked his brain trying to remember their names. There was Holly, the mum of two from Totteridge via Finchley and Derek, the train lover. Today, his rumpled T-shirt simply read 'Choo Choo Choose Trains'.

'Hi there,' said Holly, turning to look as he entered. She was dressed simply in a pair of skinny jeans and camel coloured knee-high boots with a grey oversized wool jumper, a pair of diamond studs in her ears. It was a simple look, but one which Jess would describe as 'preened'. She looked so friendly and open, Mark immediately felt at ease. Derek meanwhile was staring fixedly at his phone, but looked up just to offer him a nod of acknowledgement.

'Hi,' he replied, sitting on a seat with empty ones on either side, applying his Londoner code of giving people as much personal space as possible, whenever possible.

'You've come back,' Holly said, looking pleased. 'Thought we'd scared you off.'

'Nah,' he laughed. 'I'm made of sterner stuff.'

They laughed. As he recalled the last meeting, he felt the need to explain himself.

'Sorry about last time. I guess I just wasn't sure what to say,' he said. In fact, after his initial sentence last week, he had been struck dumb. He had just stood there, like a stupid fish, mouth opening and closing silently. He had been unable to string together a single cogent line of coherent speech. 'I blame the head injury.'

'Oh, don't worry,' Holly assured with a giggle. 'You did well compared to most of us. I didn't speak until my third meeting.' As if in assent or just to punctuate the moment, Derek hoisted up his sagging trousers.

Feeling at ease, Mark wondered if this might be a chance to learn a bit more about the group.

'So, how long have you all been coming here?' he asked her, a touch tentatively.

'Oh, well, I'm fairly new,' Holly said. 'Only six months. I think the group's been up and running for about two years. Paul and Ricky are probably the longest standing members.'

'So you won about six months ago?' he asked. He wasn't sure what the protocol was for this kind of questioning. It seemed odd to ask about Holly's win. It was like discussing someone's salary in forensic detail. The only people he knew who did this were Americans – at least according to the films he watched – and Lance, Jess's brother-in-law. He had to resist the urge to shudder at the thought of him.

'No, it was actually about a year ago. I wasn't going to come to the group, but then,' she paused, her eyes getting that faraway look again, like she had had last week, 'It started to feel a bit lonely. Ben, my other half, he's my rock, but I hated burdening him with all my worries. So I thought I'd try this,' she finished brightly.

'And it's helped?' Mark asked.

'I don't know if 'helped' is the right word, but I've made some great friends.'

Mark's face must have betrayed some doubt or perhaps an inkling of horror because Holly laughed.

'I know,' she said, a wide smile on her face. 'We're a bit of an odd grouping, but everyone is actually really nice once you get to know them.'

As if on cue, Paul came in together with Rick, who Mark remembered as the well-spoken fellow with all the ex-wives. They were followed in quick succession by Margaret and Gerald, the older couple.

'Hello mate,' Paul said, looking genuinely pleased. 'Glad to see you back.'

Mark felt a distinct sense of embarrassment at what had happened in Hampstead Heath and a need to apologise, but Paul cut him off.

'Good to see you on the Heath the other day,' he winked at him and tapped his nose conspiratorially.

Soon, all seven of them were sitting in a circle, several of them holding piping hot cups of tea and coffee, the teenager, Annie rounding off the group.

'We're in *OK!* again next week,' Paul's opening volley was delivered with complete resignation. 'They say they're going to give Dina a column. Something like 'lottery lady around town'. Apparently we'll have to go to parties and premiers and things,' he mumbled, definitely on the way to moaning now. 'I just want to stay home. Quiet life and all that. What's wrong with that?'

'Have you told her how you feel?' Holly asked.

'Well, sort of,' Paul said. 'I mean I've tried. She says I'm just not 'embracing the experience'.' He put air quotes around the last three words. 'What does that even mean?' He looked around.

Nobody was able to answer him.

'She's threatened to make more cosmetic improvements to me. Seems like she's taking a break from her body and focusing on mine. Apparently there's some new procedure that can make me look ten years younger in ten minutes.' He shook his head. 'I mean, I already look like Noel bloody Gallagher thanks to the eyebrows,' he said, touching them subconsciously, 'I can't take another procedure.' He said the last word in a pained manner.

When Paul finally finished his tale of woe, he sat down and looked over at Mark. At first, Mark just smiled at him, assuming he was looking for reassurance, but Paul kept on looking. It was unnerving.

'Go on, mate,' Paul said.

'Oh, it's my turn,' Mark said, lifting his hand to his chest.

'You can do it,' Rick said beside him, slapping his back in a macho 'we are men' sort of way. 'We don't bite!'

'Um, yes, well, sure, of course,' Mark stuttered before getting to his feet. As he looked around, he caught Holly's eye. She winked and gave him a thumbs up.

'Hi, I'm Mark and I'm a lottery winner.'

'Hi Mark,' everyone chorused.

'I'm not sure where to begin,' he looked around again questioningly.

'How much did you win?' Annie yelled out like a heckler at the Comedy Store.

'Well, um, we won ten million or so.' He looked upwards as if trying to remember. '10.43 million give or take a few pounds and pennies.'

There were a few nods and Annie looked impressed.

'We?' Annie prompted.

'My girlfriend Jess and I,' he elaborated.

'That puts him, what, fourth?' Annie said. She looked around before her own eyes went to the ceiling, showing that she was deep in thought.

'It's not a competition Annie dear,' Margaret said soothingly, but the girl was unperturbed.

'I won 4.3 mil, you already know that Derek won 8.1 and Rick won 9,' she listed with the force of a freight train. 'So that puts you after Holly who won 13 mil, then there's Paul with his impressive 30 and finally,' she paused for effect, 'Margaret and Gerald with a staggering 53 million.' She cocked her head and raised an eyebrow.

Mark wasn't sure what to say. Margaret and Gerald were looking wide eyed and embarrassed.

'Um, well done,' he hazarded. 'That's great.'

'Oh, yes, well, it's very nice,' Gerald said in amidst bouts of clearing his throat, obviously deeply uncomfortable with the attention.

Sensing a need to help the older pair and take away the attention, Mark felt it incumbent upon himself to keep talking.

'Well, my girlfriend, Jess, and I won a few months ago,' he said. 'And we decided not to tell anyone.'

'Just family, that's sensible,' Holly said, nodding sagely.

'Yeah, wish we'd done that,' Paul said. 'You wouldn't believe all the people that come out of the woodworks when they sniff a bit of money.' He shook his head in disgust.

'So you didn't go public,' Annie confirmed.

'No,' Mark said. 'I mean we didn't tell *anyone*. You're the first people I've told.'

Six pairs of eyes visibly widened, but it was, of course, Annie who spoke first.

'Your friends and family don't know?' she enunciated. Her tone expressed a horror she might have used in questioning a fondness for sniffing strangers' underwear at the gym.

'Nobody does,' Mark said. He was suddenly feeling very nervous. Telling this group he had won over £10 million on the lottery had barely raised an eyebrow, but this revelation had floored them. He was finding it hard to reconcile this.

'Um, Why?' Annie asked. 'Do you hate your parents? Are they horrible or something?' There was some relish in these last two questions which Mark did his best to ignore. He thought of his bubbly, fun parents and almost laughed at the incongruity of it all.

'It was my girlfriend's idea,' he said. 'Jess. We. We wanted people to think we'd earned the money.' It was a relief to be saying these things out loud. To be able to see others' reactions when he did so. Witnessing the varied expressions on their faces, he felt like he could pick and choose to adopt one as his own.

'And you just went along with it?' Rick said, his confusion evidenced in the tight drawing in of his brows atop narrowed eyes.

'Well, I could see her point,' Mark said. 'It's nice to have people think we're doing well. Jess comes from a very high achieving family. So it just looks like we fit in.'

'So, what?' Paul interjected. 'You've just gone on living your normal life like nothing's happened?'

'Sort of,' Mark replied, feeling like he was a football manager fielding a press conference after a particularly controversial match. 'We've bought new cars and redecorated. It's been good.'

'But don't you just want to yell out, 'I've won the lottery!' at everyone you see?' Paul asked, eliciting a laugh from several of the group, Mark included.

Mark thought about Goodwyn and his smug face. He had definitely been tempted to shove his resignation in his face once or twice since the win.

'Sometimes I want to say that to my boss,' he admitted. It was only when an audible gasp rippled through his rapt audience that Mark realised he'd said anything strange.

'You still go to work?' Annie asked, with a face so aghast he may as well have told her he enjoyed dismembering small animals.

'Yes, well-'

'What do you do, Mark?' Rick asked. His manner was part macho confrontation, part apprehensive chat show host. He was leaning forward, face a picture of concentrated concern, elbows on knees. It was clear that Rick was used to discussing such things.

'I'm a wills and trusts lawyer,' Mark said. He heard the shame in his words. It was actually more like sheepish embarrassment. He wasn't sure why. Why on earth was he embarrassed at being a lawyer? Lots of people said it with such pride. Most likely it was the wills and trusts bit that tripped him up. It was hardly rock 'n' roll was it? Corporate litigators, divorce lawyers, barristers, they were the cool crowd of the legal world. They were seen as thrusting and interesting. When they told people what they did it evoked images of late night dramas on Channel 4 where attractive personnel exchanged witty arguments about fascinating subjects and had torrid affairs. He belonged with the pension analysts and the tax experts. The most exciting thing that happened in Mark's world was when one of his clients died. It was then that the office really came to life.

The reaction of the group was like a display of all the reactions he ever got. He thought of taking a photo of it, so accurate a depiction was it of how people saw him. Holly and Margaret had their mouths open in wide 'O' shapes, the polite, 'we don't know what to say to that' look. Rick and Gerald clearly knew of the importance of his role, but saw him as the bin man of the legal system: necessary, but not interesting. Annie looked appalled and Derek didn't look up at all, still fixedly monitoring his phone screen, occasionally typing frantically.

'I work in the City and that's sort of how I met Jess,' he hurried on. 'We were at an award show for young lawyers and Jess is a family lawyer in another firm.'

'What does she look like? Your girlfriend. Show us a photo,' Annie demanded. Mark just shook his head at this, mouth open in uncertainty.

'Annie will you stop bothering him?' Paul said.

'Are you good?' Rick asked, all boldness and bravado. He struck Mark as the kind of guy who always needed to be involved in a conversation, just to ensure his voice was the last anybody else heard.

In any event, he never knew how to field interrogations like this. Lance always asked him those questions: 'How much are you billing?', 'Do you get a percentage or a fixed bonus?', 'But you only save people money once they're dead, right?' He was always so flustered. So taken aback by the chutzpah of it all. Any answer he gave wouldn't be taken as it was supposed to. He usually tried to be empirical, basing his answers on the facts. It was just what came naturally to him. He'd say something like 'I am the fourth highest billing associate at my firm and am on track to save an average percentage per client serviced.' This never impressed Lance, who invariably sneered in response. This time, Mark thought he'd try a new tack.

'Well, yes. I am,' he said simply. And the look on Rick's face. Mark wanted to preserve it and wave it in Lance's face it was so approving. This was great. Why had he never before discovered the wonders of the concise answer?

'So you work and you don't tell anyone you've won. I can pretty much guess the answer I think, but tell us in your own words. Why are you here?' This came from Paul. Everyone leaned forward. Even Derek, face in iPhone, seemed to shift in anticipation. Mark considered his answer. He could sense that it was important not just to him, but that it would affect everyone else in some way; that his reason for being there might illuminate something for them.

'I guess,' he said. 'Well, I suppose I feel like I'm living a double life.'

And there it was. It felt so good just speaking those words. Hearing them fill the air. He had bottled it up for so long, had ignored it at first. He had told himself it was ridiculous to be upset at winning the lottery. How could he possibly be anything but elated? Then he had blamed it on his own neuroses. He'd just have to learn to deal with it. Jess had.

'Mate,' Paul said on an out breath, shaking his head. It was a neat summation of Mark's situation.

After that, Mark felt drained. It was like the effort of saying what was on his mind had robbed him of all his left-over energy and so he mutely sat down and surrendered the speaking platform.

As if having been coiled like a spring, Derek shot up like an irate Jack-in-the-box and started shaking his phone, spilling forth before he was even fully upright.

'Ok, so Albert has been trash talking all over the message boards, saying that I'm a sell out and that I should be banned from the NEC show because the only reason I'm even a contender is because of my money. He's turned them all against me.' He was almost yelling now. 'It's the gauge debate all over again.'

Margaret, who Mark was learning had a macabre knack for understatement, gently followed up this tirade with, 'It doesn't sound like this Albert is your friend. He actually doesn't sound very nice at all.'

Derek ignored this. 'I'll show him at the NEC. He'll never beat me at best layout. His idea of a good figurine is a Lego man. Pah!' He barrelled on. 'And then Margot said that we should have a proper chat forum instead of being on the Railway Magazine one and Albert said that she was welcome to try if she wanted, but who was going to moderate it? Who does he think he is?' He shook his head at them in disbelief.

Derek revelled in his ranting for another fifteen minutes, running them line by line through his online conversations like a twelve-year-old girl who hadn't been invited to the sleepover. Who knew the model train world was so unforgiving?

'Where are you off to?' Holly asked Mark conversationally as they pulled on their respective coats after the meeting. Mark noticed a group of impatient seventy-something women outside in exercise gear, yoga mats in hand, obviously waiting for the space.

'Oh, just home,' he said. 'Hopefully Jess will have finished work at a decent time. You?'

'Adam and I are taking the kids out for dinner,' she said. 'Saves me cooking. And saves them from my cooking,' she added self-deprecatingly. They both laughed as they passed the tutting grannies on their way out to the evening air, waving as they went their separate ways.

As Mark sat down in the driver's seat he checked his phone. The first thing he saw was a message from Branning. He opened it up only to wish he hadn't. There on the screen was a picture of three soiled nappies with the caption, 'THIS is my life.'

Mark almost threw the phone across the car, but instead he typed back a desperate message.

'Mate! Never show that to me again.'

There was also a message from Jess telling him she would be late and one from his dad talking about the football fixtures.

Mark was deep in thought as he typed a reply to his dad when a knock at his window made him jump. The situation only worsened when he jerked his head up only to find his window filled almost entirely with a giant head.

Paul. Heart still pounding, Mark wound down the window and tried to match Paul's smile with his own.

'Rick and I are going to look at the Porsche garage across the road. Wanna come?'

Mark looked at the garage and back at Paul. 'You thinking about buying one?'

Paul looked noncommittal. 'Meh, thinking about it. It's also fun watching Rick try to outdo the salesman in talking bullshit.'

Mark hesitated for a second, but then remembered Jess's message. It wasn't like he had anything better to do. So, he climbed out of his car and followed Paul.

The light of the showroom was a complete, blinding contrast to the outside darkness. Silently, as if by prior agreement, they all wandered off in different directions, reverently looking at the luxury cars in their midst. Rick had already cornered a nervous looking guy in a suit who looked like he was about to have a terrifying first day on the job. He could hear words such as 'horsepower' and 'alloys' being bandied about with testosterone filled competitiveness.

Mark stopped to admire a metallic grey Cayman with its sleek lines. He had always loved Porsches. Always liked the look of them, the idea of them. He remembered watching Tom Cruise drive on in Risky Business and wanting one of his own. The only reason he'd chosen his Audi was because Jess had sneeringly deemed the sports car a "mid-life-crisis-mobile".

'It would look ridiculous,' she had said dismissively. 'A TT is much classier.'

'But it's my car,' he had said, a touch whiney. He still couldn't remember why he had relented. Some argument or another that she had made had seemed to make sense at the time.

He walked on languidly, lost in his memories. And that's when he saw it.

It really was a thing of beauty.

'Nought to 62 in four point five seconds,' he heard from somewhere in his consciousness.

He took in the stylish convertible with a mix of lust and awe.

'375 horsepower and a top speed of 180 miles per hour.'

It was now that Mark realised that the voice he was hearing had a Birmingham accent. Moreover, it was not in his head, but rather being whispered seductively in his ear. He turned to find a small, but sturdy bloke in an oversized suit standing uncomfortably close to him. His short, but extremely muscly frame made him look like the Mr Man, Mr Strong.

'Harry Ford, nice to meet you,' the little man shook his hand and Mark responded.

'Mark.'

'Gorgeous vehicle isn't it, Mark,' Harry intoned lugubriously. 'It's the new Boxster Spyder, a return to the original glamour of the roadster.'

'Lovely,' Mark said tightly, wondering why the man felt he had to stand so close to him.

'Smart guy like you,' Harry rasped seductively. 'You'd look great in this. The ladies love it you know.'

'Yes, well-,'

'Can you see yourself in it?' Harry interrupted, placing a tiny hand on Mark's shoulder while his other painted a vista ahead. 'Wind in your hair, lovely lady next to you. Driving on the M6,' he intoned. The M6? Mark thought the choice of road was an unlikely one until he realised it led directly to Birmingham. 'It could be yours.'

I could buy this, he thought. I could buy this £60k car right now without so much as breaking a sweat. The very idea of it gave him a little thrill. Subconsciously he reached into his pocket where he knew his wallet was. Looking at the beautiful machine he felt like a helpless hobbit in the thrall of the One Ring. It was out of his control, like an invisible force was moving his hand.

'I'll take it.'

CHAPTER 8

'So we're getting your mother that cordless vacuum cleaner she wanted and your dad a day at Silverstone with a friend. What about,' Jess consulted her list. 'Branning?'

'Do you think we can buy him a full night's sleep?' Mark asked and they both laughed.

It was only the first week of December, but already he and Jess were sitting in their study, glasses of wine perched on the desk, with Jess in full organisational swing making her Christmas list. If Santa ever wanted to retire, Jess would be the perfect replacement. She had the spreadsheets, judgemental capabilities and the erratic driving tendencies necessary to determine who was naughty and nice, select the perfect gifts and get them to their recipients on time. Of course at least three reindeer would probably require counselling from the whole ordeal and she would never agree to put on that much weight, but the job would be done. Properly.

Indeed, true to her logistically minded-self, Jess had already bought all the presents for her friends and family. She was now, as usual, dragging Mark through the process of picking for his, something he'd have left to New Year's Day.

'I simply won't go through the humiliation of turning up empty handed again,' she had snapped when he'd protested the activity.

'I saw a stunning Vera Wang photo frame with space for three pictures,' Jess said. 'Perfect for photos of the triplets, no?'

Mark thought of the last time he'd spoken to Branning as he'd been lamenting his depleting finances.

'It comes in as money and goes out as baby poo,' his friend had moaned of his pay packet. 'We just seem to spend it all on food,' he had explained mournfully. 'And nappies and wipes,' he had added after some thought. Given this, gifting him a designer picture frame seemed like the modern equivalent of letting him eat cake.

'Can't we get him something practical?' Mark asked, wanting to be a help to his friend. 'What about some vouchers for dinner at his favourite restaurant along with a promise to babysit on the night in question?'

Jess had looked incredulous. 'You want to babysit new-born triplets?' Mark thought about this. In truth he had thought that Jess would take charge of that, but seeing her expression he realised that that had been folly of the highest degree. 'Picture frame it is,' he said quickly.

Oh and I've bought myself a Porsche, he intoned silently. He had to tell her. It had been two weeks. The car was on order. It was on its way. She would notice when it arrived. He needed her help anyway in dealing with the council. The new car would need a parking permit after all and she was so much better at those things.

Maybe later, he thought. She looked like she was having such a good time organising and sorting and typing up the lists; it seemed a shame to spoil it. Also, they had spent so little time together of late. She seemed to be working double the hours. He knew there was a good reason for this what with the promise of imminent partnership on the horizon so he didn't mind, but given the rarity of their time together, shouldn't it be spent happy rather than with her slaughtering him like a sated spider finished with her beau?

'I bought a car.'

Apparently not. Jess looked up at him. He could tell that she had understood him immediately. That was the advantage of dating someone fiercely intelligent. Very little explanation was required.

'What car?' Jess's question came out with such a flat lack of intonation, it was barely a question at all. Mark was regretting this already.

'Boxster Spyder,' he squeaked, wishing his head could retract into his neck.

Jess didn't yell. She didn't get angry. She didn't even look at him. She just said, 'Fine' tetchily and began typing on the keyboard with the rapid-fire cadence of an AK47.

'Oh come on Jess,' he started. 'It's not a big deal. We have all this money, let's enjoy it.'

The good news was, this made Jess stop typing. The bad news was, she had fixed him with a laser glare so potent it would leave scorch marks on the wall behind him .

'That's funny. I thought we were on the same page,' she said with terrifying coolness before resuming her typing. 'We agreed we would wait and buy things over time. We agreed that if we spend like crazy, people will start asking questions.'

'And so what if they do?' Mark asked pleadingly. 'Who cares? We can tell them. It would feel good to tell them.'

'Christ you can be so selfish sometimes,' Jess sniped witheringly. 'The partnership is around the corner. Do you think millionaires get made into partners? No. They'll think I don't need it. They'll give it to someone else.'

'That's insane. People get partnerships because of the work they do for the firm. You bill more than anyone else there. Why wouldn't they reward you?'

She rolled her eyes. Never a great sign.

'You are so naive,' she breathed exasperatedly. 'You think partnership is some sort of achievement prize? Christ, Mark. Maybe if you actually attempted to get ahead even a little bit, you'd understand. But no. You've never even tried to fight your corner; let alone in the way *I* have to.'

'I'm just not interested in their stupid little games,' he said. He was in dangerous territory now and he knew it. This was becoming a discussion about glass ceilings and his position at work. This was the kind of discussion that would very much turn into a blazing argument. He didn't want that. He didn't want hours of accusations, revelations and recriminations. The football was on telly in an hour. He was ready to dial things back. He was about to issue a placating remark; one which would calm things and allow them to get on with their day.

But then Jess guffawed. It was a patronising, sardonic, pitying breath that fuelled a rising anger and indignation in him; the kind that overtook common sense and made him say things like the thing he said next.

'What? You think you're the only one who struggles at work? Just because I don't have ambitions of world domination doesn't mean I don't work bloody hard. In fact, I have to work harder *because* I work for a moron.'

'Yeah, and instead of getting promoted so that he works for you, you let other people get ahead because you can't be bothered to play their little games.'

She used her fingers to put quote marks around the last four words. He hated that. Goodwyn did that. Goodwyn who didn't know the difference between a bare trust and a staff team building exercise. And who thought 'in statu pupillari' was an eye condition rather than in fact referring to someone being 'In the state of being a ward'. His boss. The moron. But that didn't mean Mark wanted to be the boss. He just wanted a better one.

Shit. He'd zoned out and Jess was still ranting.

'You don't even have a hobby,' she was saying when he tuned back in, which was so off topic that he worried about what he'd missed her saying beforehand. 'And, no, yelling at Watford FC in your underwear on the sofa doesn't count.'

'What does that have to do with anything?'

'It means,' she was shouting now. 'That if you can't actually *achieve* anything, the least you could do is play along when I make it up for you.'

And off she stormed, paper flying in all directions in her wake.

***

It was a few days later when Mark entered the now ubiquitous church hall on a drizzly afternoon to find most of the group were already there. He had been looking forward to today. After his row with Jess and the Porsche purchase he had a definite and urgent need to unburden himself.

Rick and Holly were chatting on one side of the circle as Margaret was handing out homemade cupcakes. Mark felt his stomach rumble at the thought of them. Gerald was reading an actual paper copy of *The Times* while Annie meanwhile, was reading something on her phone.

'He's still at it,' Annie said in a sing song voice, showing the screen to Rick and Holly.

'Oh, yeah, I saw that,' Rick replied, nonplussed.

'Is it Kai again?' Gerald asked and the other two nodded.

'Who's Kai?' Mark asked, feeling slightly left out at what was clearly their joint past.

'Kai Mangle,' Annie said to him as if he should know what that meant. 'The Lotto Layabout?'

When Mark still looked blank, Derek hitched up his trousers, ready to take pity on him.

'Kai joined the group when I did. Won five mil two years ago. He's been spending it all on motorbikes and drink and drugs,' Derek explained. 'Bought a massive house in Hertfordshire and drives the locals mad with massive raves and drag races.'

'He used to come to the meetings drunk as a skunk and just rant at us,' Holly added. 'Felt a bit sorry for him actually.'

'I didn't,' Rick said, arms folded defensively. 'That idiot had an advantage most people would kill for and he's wasting it. Worse than that, he's using it to make other people's lives a living hell.'

'But he doesn't come anymore?' Mark asked, half curious, half nervous at the thought. The guy sounded unpleasant.

'No, he's basically run out of money now. They're repossessing his house and all his things,' Holly replied.

'I heard they've written a musical about him,' Annie said excitedly.

Just then, the door creaked as Paul walked in. After a big round of hellos, Paul sat down, gratefully accepting a steaming cup of tea and a cupcake from Margaret.

They all settled into their circle and looked towards Paul. He was holding a pile of paper which looked like a print off of something.

'Right, well, before we start, I thought I'd bring this in,' he said, waving the paper bundle. 'I don't know if any of you have been approached yet,' he looked around. 'It's the thirtieth anniversary of the lottery so they're assembling all the biggest winners in Hyde Park for the biggest ever gathering of lottery winners. They're doing it for the Guinness World Book of Records.'

'So?' said Annie. 'I've got better things to do than stand around in a park.'

'So,' Paul said patiently, obviously on a mission, 'This article is about the last reunion. The one at the twentieth anniversary.' He started handing out the paper copies as he continued. 'They were asking all the old winners about what they'd done since their wins. You have to see some of these answers.'

As each person started skimming the words on the pages, their eyes seemed to widen and then dull, like they had been surprised and then disappointed in quick succession.

Mark was no different. He read about people who had given everything away to charity, who had travelled the world or set up businesses. Each and every one looked fulfilled and happy.

'That's disgusting!' Annie said before reading aloud one of the entries. 'Winning the lottery has allowed me to write my cupcake cookbook and raise my daughters as a stay at home mum.' Her tone was mockingly high pitched and she followed up her performance by sticking her finger down her throat in a being sick gesture. 'Give me a break'.

For once, it seemed Annie and Rick were on the same page. Or printout at least.

'That's all rubbish,' Rick said. 'It's like Facebook or Twitter. These people just *look* happy. I bet they're miserable.' There was a rumble of assent.

'But they've at least got something to say when they're asked what they've done, haven't they?' Paul asked, looking more animated than Mark had seen him. 'What have we got going for us?' He started looking round the room. 'Rick, you spend most of your money on battling your ex-wives, Derek plays with toy trains-,'

'Now wait a minute-,' Derek said, but Paul wasn't stopping.

'Annie, you bought that bloke you like lots of presents, Margaret and Gerald, you never spend a penny, most of *my* money has gone into transforming my wife into someone I don't recognise and Mark. Mate I don't know you very well, but it looks like you pretend it hasn't happened. You live almost exactly the same life as what you did before you won.'

Everyone was silent. It was never particularly pleasant to have your shortcomings pointed out to you, least of all when it was done so succinctly. Paul, for all his plain speaking, had a way of cutting to the chase.

'So what are you suggesting?' Rick asked.

'I don't know,' admitted Paul. 'All I do know is, I don't want to have nothing to say when they ask me what I've done with my money. What I've done since the win.'

Mark could see exactly what he meant. The prospect of being asked about his achievements had always been a daunting one, but now that he had all this good fortune, there would be something more to prove. Luckily, he was an anonymous winner. He had Jess to thank for that at the very least. Not even his own parents knew. That meant he wouldn't be on the radar of those asking the questions. He probably wouldn't even go.

'So let's achieve something.' This came from Holly. 'There's still time. This isn't until May and it's only December. Plenty of time.'

'What? Like find a cure for all diseases or something?' Annie sneered. 'Yeah, sure, I'll just get on that.'

'Seriously what has crawled up your bottom?' Rick asked her. 'Holly's right. We can do things. We can *achieve*. So, what are we going to do?'

'What if each of us picks one thing? One thing we want to achieve,' suggested Gerald. 'I think that's manageable.'

'I know what I want to do,' said Derek plainly, causing six heads to whirl in his direction. He stood up, putting his hands on his hips like Superman, his strange paunch heaved forward. 'I'm going to win the Annual Train Modelling Competition at the Birmingham NEC,' he said proudly. 'It's in a month and I just know I've got the best layout.'

Everyone smiled politely and Margaret and Gerald clapped half-heartedly.

'Ok, great!' Paul said, now taking charge again. 'Who's next?'

Margaret held her hand up as though she was in a classroom. 'Gerald and I have been talking about taking a holiday,' she said tentatively.

'You should travel the world!' Rick suggested excitedly.

'I think we'd need passports for that,' Margaret said, looking slightly concerned. Everybody stared at her before Annie spoke the collective mind with her inimitable tactlessness.

'You don't have passports? Who doesn't have passports?' Annie's voice reflected the horror of the rest of the group, if not magnifying it.

'Maybe start by getting that sorted,' Holly ventured carefully.

'This is stupid,' Annie said. 'So far, we've got one person who wants to win a poxy train competition – sorry Derek – and they've just landed a trip to the post office. We're really setting the world alight.'

'Go on then,' Mark said, 'What are you going to do?'

'Oh, ok, well if it's stuff like that then I'm getting Matt back,' Annie said sulkily, her arms folded.

'Brilliant,' Rick retorted. 'Aim high Annie. That's what it's all about. We're talking about changing our lives or those of others. And what are you doing? Trying to win the affections of what is by all accounts – and I'm being as generous as possible here – a complete and utter knobhole.'

'I *am* changing a life. Mine,' she scowled. 'And his. What are you going to do?' she challenged. 'Get an even younger girlfriend? You'll get arrested.'

'Actually, there is something I've been thinking about for a while,' Rick started, leaning forward as though about to make them co-conspirators to a plan of the highest confidentiality. 'Have any of you heard of the Three Peaks Challenge?'

A series of blank faces stared at him, all with the exception of Mark. He'd read about this.

'That's the one where you climb Britain's three highest mountains in 24 hours, right?' he asked.

'Yep. Snowdon in Wales, Scafell Pike in the Lake District and Ben Nevis,' Rick replied, checking them off on his fingers. 'I've always wanted to do it. Well, maybe now's the time. I'd love the challenge and it would be a great way to raise money for a good cause.'

'Sounds tough,' Paul said doubtfully.

'Count me in,' a voice piped up. It was only when everyone turned to look at him that Mark realised it had been his voice. He hadn't thought about it for more than a second. Had replied before his brain was properly in gear. But as soon as the words had registered he knew that this was what he wanted to do.

Jess's words still rang in his ears. Had been irking him for days now. No ambition. No hobby. Wasn't this the way to fix it? He could do something really worthwhile. And how hard could climbing a mountain really be? It wasn't a Himalaya. Or three. Britain wasn't known for its peaks. And he'd been hiking before. Hadn't he just run through the Heath? It couldn't be much harder. A good, brisk walk and he would have something to put to his name, even if he was anonymous.

'Yes! Brilliant,' Rick enthused. 'Who else?'

'I'll do it.' Now it was Paul's turn to be the centre of attention for uttering the last three words. 'I will,' he insisted. 'It's time I lost some of this weight and what better way than also raising money for charity?'

'Hold on.' Annie had her hand up in that talk-to-the-hand way Mark detested and feared in equal measure. 'Correct me if I'm wrong, but you three are bloody millionaires. Why are you asking other people to donate money? Just give the charity your own money you cheapskates.'

Shit. She had a point. All optimism was sucked out of the room leaving a void of melancholic futility. What was the point of raising money when they had it to give? And if they weren't doing it for charity, could they do the challenge anyway? Would there be any point? Mark darted a glance at Paul, hoping he'd have the answer, but the big man's jaw had plummeted roughly halfway to the floor, along with his shoulders.

Nobody met anyone else's eyes. Everyone, except a smug looking Annie, wore an expression of utter dejection.

'We'll match it.'

'Match what?'

'Every donation we get, we match with our own money.'

'That's a great idea, Rick,' Holly enthused. 'Plus you'll be raising awareness.'

'Well done mate.'

This seemed to galvanise the group. Shoulders and backs straightened with renewed hope and there were murmurs of "great idea" and "good thinking". If they'd been American, they might have jumped for joy or high fived, but instead they exchanged some reassured smiles and sipped at their drinks.

'No way,' Holly laughed, when Mark asked if she would join them. 'But I want to do something.' She paused. 'I might do a masters.'

Mark could tell the idea was forming as she spoke.

'That's great. Any ideas on subject?'

'Nope. But I've always wanted to study more. I've just been lazy,' she said. 'There's just one thing.' In a louder voice, she added. 'Annie, you need a better goal than the one you've picked.'

'What?' Annie looked affronted. 'You lot might be miserable, but I'm not. I'm fucking fine thanks.'

83

It was at that moment that Holly gave Annie a look of such force and fortitude that the teen capitulated almost instantly. It was a perfect mix between guilt, hostility, disappointment and hope. It was a mum glare.

'Ok, fine,' Annie sighed. 'I'll finish my A-Levels. Is that good enough?'

'Perfect,' Holly said, her smile now beatific.

The rest of the meeting was taken up with all of them making plans, excuses and coffee as they chattered about the reunion and their tasks. Mark decided to take a quick look at what was involved in climbing the Three Peaks. He googled the phrase 'Three Peaks Challenge' and first saw Wikipedia's explanation:

'The National Three Peaks Challenge is an event in which participants attempt to climb the highest mountains of Scotland, England and Wales within 24 hours.'

That seemed fine. It was only then that he decided to click on the image results. Paul must have been doing the same thing because, just as Mark thought it, he shook his head at his phone and muttered 'Oh, shit.'

CHAPTER 9

'So are they firing people?' Graham had heard from behind him.

'I'm not sure. Possibly. All I know is that there are definitely cuts on the way. Apparently the fat has to be trimmed. '

This conversation, conducted between Hammond and Perkins on a Tuesday morning in early December, was the first inkling Graham had that things were about to change. Perkins was clearly on a diet as she had chosen a milk free coffee that morning – something she did like clockwork every two calendar months for a period of exactly three days - while Graham was sure that the low snuffling sound he heard behind him was that of Hammond as he had stuffed a mince pie into his mouth without so much as a second thought. Did those two not have offices? They seemed to conduct all their important conversations at the coffee station.

And yet, now, just over a week later as he returned the office after lunch, Graham was pleased that he could guess at the reason for the presence of the two professional looking children that were rummaging through the office like they were ransacking the place. Surely these were the people assigned with the task of 'streamlining their costs' as Hammond had euphemised.

The sight was all the more depressing given the gaudy Christmas decorations some of the secretaries had put up around the place. Gold and silver tinsel was hanging off every available surface, while a medium sized fake fir tree weighed down by budget baubles stood in the centre of the room like the drunkest girl at the party.

'We'll need to see numbers. Budgets, expenses, salaries.' This dark uttering came from the younger of the two, a grim-faced twenty-something girl in a dark suit and grey stilettos as she opened her laptop at an empty desk. The indecently tall man – boy? – with her was struggling to walk through the room, constantly having to negotiate his way through a jungle of tinsel.

Graham would learn later that these two were cost cutting consultants sent by Formby Haste Consultancy, slogan, 'we're saving you… more'. The girl, Emily, was the more brutal of the two, while the boy – yes he was definitely a boy, Graham decided – had a gormless expression that could charitably be described as forgetfully aggressive.

While these two were running around like kids at play, the rest of the staff was at their desks, studiously typing at their computers while obviously listening in. As he passed Smith's desk, Graham saw that he was simply typing the letters 'f' and 'u' over and over onto a blank Word document.

Graham didn't care. He had more important matters on his mind. For one thing, it was Wednesday. It was his day. And he had just returned from the roof.

He had pushed the boundaries especially far that day, allowing his feet to teeter further than ever over the roof edge. The whole front of his shoe had peeked out, leaving only his heels for support. He'd even experimented with an arm, waving it about in the air above the drop. He had never felt so close to actually doing it.

And yet, in that glorious, powerful moment of being the master of his own destiny. Of nearly realising his ambition, he was struck by complete clarity.

That day, on the rooftop, he had reached a momentous realisation. A life changing epiphany. And one that had frozen him to the spot.

He wouldn't do it.

Or maybe he couldn't do it. He wasn't sure which it was.

Whether it was fear or squeamishness or knowledge of a higher purpose, he, Graham Gill, was not going to jump. He would live another day. He would survive. Whatever the purpose – and he was certain there must be one – he was not meant to jump off that seventh storey building on a Watford industrial estate. He was meant for more.

In every sense of the phrase, Graham stepped away from the edge.

As he had removed his sandwich from its foil envelope, the realisation of his reprieve had awakened a plethora of emotional responses. At one end was relief. He wasn't going to feel the pain or the fear of plummeting. That was a plus in his book, he thought, chomping contemplatively. But there again, what now?

He was still him. Still Graham Gill with his pointless job and annoying colleagues and rubbish flat. He thought of Dave, waiting for him at home, a sanctimonious expression on his feline features. The one that said, 'oh, still here are you?' He bristled.

There would have to be another plan.

CHAPTER 10

As an unlikely sun shone on a late December Saturday in Birmingham, Mark looked around at the huge swathes of people walking towards the vast NEC complex, bees making their way to the hive. The group had just disembarked from the coach they had hired to take them to the Annual Model Rail Exhibition for Derek's big day. It was him, Annie, Margaret, Gerald, Rick and Paul. Derek was already at the venue.

'I have to be there for my interview and to set up my presentation,' Derek had explained a week earlier when they had made their plans.

Now, as they surveyed the buzzing scene before them in awe, Holly was the first to speak.

'Wow,' she breathed as she surveyed the crowd. 'I had no idea model trains were so popular.'

'It's like a rock concert,' Margaret agreed, clutching her purse anxiously as she inspected the crowd.

The unlikely group shuffled along with the hordes around them.

'Which way do we go?' asked Mark, realising that people we splitting off into different directions.

'Excuse me sir, which way is the entrance?' asked Rick, addressing a man in an NEC t-shirt.

'You here for the graduate fair?' The man looked at them doubtfully. They indeed looked like the last people on earth to be attending a graduate fair. With the exception of Annie perhaps.

'No,' Rick said, 'The Model Rail Fair.'

'Oh,' the man said, his face adopting an expression of newly found understanding. 'You want entrance F,' he said disinterestedly, pointing them to his left and in a very different direction to that being chosen by the rest of the crowds. As their eyes followed his pointing finger, they saw what was no more than a glorified tent in the shadow of the NEC. Beside it was a rumpled printout blue-tacked to a makeshift easel reading 'Annual Model Train Fair, Birmingham NEC'.

A heavily bespectacled man in his sixties was standing by the entrance, the tide of his paunch held back by what looked like a tool belt with random objects shoved in the pockets. There appeared to be a walkie talkie, a pen and some loose change. He looked more than a bit surprised to see them approach, especially Annie, who he eyed with wary curiosity.

'We're here for the model rail show,' Mark said, a hint of nerves in his tone.

'Five pound each please,' the man said in a Black Country accent, obviously trying to maintain a sense of professionalism.

Each one of them meekly handed over their five pound notes, except Margaret and Gerald who gave him the amount in a collection of coins, painstakingly extracting each one from Margaret's purse. It was quite awkward to watch really, but the man appeared accustomed to this kind of display, nodding approvingly as the change was handed to him.

'We've got a carriage full en route,' the man said seriously into his walkie talkie as they walked in, not a hint of irony in his voice.

Once inside, they surveyed the scene before them.

'It's like the waiting room to hell.'

Nobody bothered to correct Annie's blunt observation, perhaps because of it had some merit. The large white expanse of the tent seemed to almost sag in disappointment at being drastically under filled. Mark estimated there were no more than one hundred guests inside it. The demographic of those present could generally be described as overwhelmingly male, invariably clad in train related garb and almost entirely of pensionable age. Derek, who they now spotted in a corner in deep conversation with a tall man wearing a vintage train cap, was by far the youngest. In fact, even accounting for Margaret and Gerald, their group had brought the average age of the room down by a decade, if not two.

'Gosh I hope they have medics on standby,' Rick said amazedly as Holly waved at Derek. 'One small shock and half these fellows will be clutching their chests.'

When he saw them, Derek practically bounded over, like a fat, middle aged puppy about to be taken out for a walk.

'Ah, good, you're in time,' he panted. 'They're about to start the first rounds of awards'. 'Rumour is,' he added, lowering his voice to a whisper, 'There's due an upset in the locomotive division. New entrant from the Far East.' He nodded his head upwards in the direction of a diminutive Chinese man standing in the corner stock still. He was eerily stoic and motionless.

'Albert's over there,' Derek said resentfully, tilting his head in the direction of a fish-eyed man by the stage. He was painfully thin and all angles and jagged edges. It was like encountering the human embodiment of a stick insect. 'He's already telling everyone he's going to win.'

'That's your old club with him?' Rick said, referring to the anxious yet simultaneously dejected looking group of five men and one woman surrounding Albert. They were looking around uneasily, but it seemed to Mark that they were studiously avoiding looking in Derek's direction.

Derek nodded. 'Yes, the Railway Rangers,' he said mournfully.

'Have you got anyone else here?' Paul asked.

'My parents,' Derek said, motioning to a pear-shaped pair huddling in a corner.

Just then, there was a screech of static as a microphone was tapped, prompting everyone to turn in its direction. A balding man in his sixties wearing a red chequered shirt and brown corduroys stood on a stage, his mismatched blue blazer emblazoned with several British Railways badges. He even had a tie with the British Rail logo on it. He reached into his pocket and pulled put a whistle which he proceeded to blow.

'ACME Model 658!' Somebody yelled from the crowd, eliciting a murmur of agreement.

'Very good, very good,' the man smiled. 'Yes, this is the traditional rail guard's friend,' he said amiably. 'Welcome everyone to this the fifteenth annual Model Railway Show at the NEC.' This announcement was met with a ripple of applause. 'My name is Gordon Wells and I'll be your conductor today.' He made this pronouncement like a ringmaster to his rapt audience. 'Let's start with model railway photographer of the year.'

And that was all Mark could remember of the next hour because he simple glazed over. All he knew was that there was round after round of awards and presentations for what seemed like endless categories of model train matters. Obscure categories were announced, from best locomotive to longest operating train and most realistic shrubbery. Luckily Rick nudged him when the best layout category came up.

'This is Derek's bit,' Rick whispered.

'And now to our flagship award of best layout,' Gordon bellowed. Mark felt the atmosphere in the room shift and thicken. 'Now I know there's been a lot of attention on this this year, a lot of chatter on the net. Model Rail Magazine is even planning on doing a feature I believe,' he said solemnly. 'So let's get to the three finalists. As you know, it is too onerous to have the layouts brought over and set up. In the past, photographs have sufficed, but this year we have plumped for films of the entrants. Let me tell you, you will not be disappointed.' Gordon's cheeks had turned a deep shade of tomato red.

The suspense, the gravity, the sheer excitement in the air, Mark imagined it could be mistaken for the Nobel Prize or perhaps the MTV Music Awards for its propensity for drama.

A large white screen was rolled into the centre of the stage, wheels squeaking as they turned reluctantly. It took several minutes and four attendants to get the computer working with terse utterances such as 'no it's this button' and 'if you'll just let me finish', at the end of which Gordon retook centre stage.

The lights dimmed and the screen lit up, pounding music swelling as the film began. What followed was like a music video nightmare of Dante-esque proportions. Visions of a locomotive and carriages were flashed up on screen together with random trees and buildings, all indispersed with phrases such as 'O gauge' and 'Lionel Pennsylvania Flyer LionChief locomotive'. At a certain point the camera precariously panned out to show a scene straight out of the American North East, complete with evergreen forests and impressive mountains.

Then the screen filled with the words 'Albert York presents...' soon joined by 'The Pennsylvania Flyer's Return'.

'Show off,' mumbled Derek, looking over at a smug Albert nearby.

The film lasted only three minutes, but Mark was sure that they had been the longest one hundred and eighty seconds of his life. How many times could one film extol the detail of plastic trees or miniature figurines?

A stunned silence followed, eventually engulfed by a decent round of applause.

The next film began with the unmistakeable opening bars of The Flight of the Conchords. Derek excitedly whispered, 'Here we go.'

To be fair to Derek, what unfolded on the screen was undeniably impressive. The vision of a good-sized model train tunnelling through an eighteenth-century English manor was enough to make even Annie pay attention. Added to that the realistic images of people and buildings and trees en route and it seemed to Mark that the result was a foregone conclusion.

Derek beamed with delight as the images faded to black, his chest so puffed out so far it made a Frigatebird look like a squashed pigeon.

'That was brilliant. Well done,' Holly yell-whispered in Derek's direction, a smile of genuine pride on her face.

'I feel a bit sorry for the poor sap that has to follow that,' Rick muttered to Mark, who nodded.

It was then that the next video began playing.

'Is that...the Chinese National Anthem?' Rick murmured.

'How the hell would I know?' Mark asked, wondering how Rick would have a clue either.

As if reading his thoughts, Rick replied, 'Pub quiz fodder. Need to know your stuff these days,' he explained, sotto voce.

Those were the last words either of them – or anyone else – uttered for at least three and a half minutes. It was, after all, fairly difficult to speak when one's mouth was hanging open as all of theirs did for that duration, the duration of the film and a decent amount of recovery time thereafter.

The final entry for that year's best layout was a fully functioning, fully automated exact replica of Beijing's vast railway system, complete with at least five high speed bullet trains, what seemed like a city's worth of moving figurines and trees that swayed as the trains swished past. In amidst the organised chaos was what appeared to be a small military parade, with tiny marching soldiers and the odd missile for effect. It was hard to keep up with the action, but the overall impression was undeniably astounding. Just as the action seemed to have come to an end, the camera focused on two soldiers holding a rolled up banner. On perfect cue, this rolled down to show the Chinese flag.

Nobody was quite sure how long the silence lasted as the lights came on, but Mark thought it was safe to say that it was definitely longer than any normal model rail competition entry could expect to elicit.

'Right,' said Gordon, coming to his senses with the slow confusion of a coma patient after ten years under.

Looking around, it was clear that the message boards of the national rail modelling community would be busy tonight. Derek wore an expression that could only be described as stunned, while Albert's face rested somewhere between indignance, anger and confusion.

The room started to buzz with conversation.

'People, people,' Gordon said, his hands up in a mollifying gesture. 'Let's have some decorum here. We're not plane spotters.' This evoked a titter.

Everyone watched as a plump woman ascended the stairs to the stage with little to no urgency, handing Gordon an envelope.

'Right, now. The results are in for this year's Best Layout Award.' Gordon paused, presumably for suspense, but possibly to genuinely catch his breath. 'In reverse order, the second runner up is.' Gordon cleared his throat. 'Albert York.'

Albert, who was clearly unaccustomed to losing, let alone losing well, stomped onto the stage and grudgingly took his certificate.

'First runner up is,' Gordon continued.

Mark knew he was holding his breath and sensed the tension amid his group. Could Derek win it?

'Derek Flat,' Gordon said, a clear note of disappointment tinging his voice. 'Well done Derek.'

But the look on Derek's face as he climbed up on stage was not upset or frustrated. In fact, if Mark had to describe it, he would have to have said smug with a hint of vindicated delight. Derek even shot Albert as self-satisfied smile as he waved before accepting a small trophy. Clearly beating Albert was almost as good as winning overall, if not better.

'And finally, the winner of best layout 2017 is,' George said, pausing for just the right amount of time. 'Wei Zhang.'

It was then that the unassuming Chinese man who Derek had pointed out earlier walked quietly onto the stage and meekly claimed his trophy from a stunned Gordon. He walked straight back down the stairs and departed the tent.

The coach ride back was a subdued affair, with everyone quietly thinking about Derek's loss.

'It just shows, doesn't it, that all this money doesn't really mean anything,' Holly said to Rick, Paul and Mark as they sat at the back of the coach like the cool kids on a school trip. Annie was listening to music and Margaret and Gerald were at the front reading.

Although they had offered Derek a lift back, he had declined. After the competition had ended, they had all had a drink at the small bar in the tent before Albert had approached Derek and shaken his hand with the gravity of a great statesman. By the time the rest of them had been on their way out, Derek and Albert were in deep discussion about the whys and wherefores of the competition and were scouring the rulebook to check if international entries were permitted.

'Well, yeah, but isn't that why we set ourselves these ridiculous tasks?' Rick said. 'Derek and his competition, you and your degree, us and the Three Peaks. Isn't all a way to make our lives mean something? I mean, what's the point of any of it if it ends up making us feel worse?' Rick really had a way of finding the darker side of the rainbow.

'Weren't you a motivational speaker or something?' Mark asked irritably.

'It's not all bad,' Paul said. 'The training's been fun. I even think I might even have lost a few of the old LB's,' he said, patting his noticeably smaller stomach.

Mark and Rick nodded in pensive agreement. This was true. Ever since they had decided to undertake the Three Peaks Challenge, they had taken to training twice a week, once on Wednesday evening after their meeting and once on a Saturday morning. At first, their efforts could charitably have been compared to a scene out of Dad's Army, the three of them breathing heavily as they climbed the tallest local peak they could find, Box Hill.

'How the hell... are we... going to climb... the Three... Peaks,' Mark had gasped intermittently. 'If we can't even manage the highest point in Surrey?' He had wondered this aloud in between pants as they sat at the top.

'I dunno mate,' Paul had said, embarking on a coughing fit so loud and ferocious Mark was waiting for a lung to pop out.

They had then collapsed on the grass, three varied lumps of human imperfection, as the clouds had passed above them, lying there for half an hour before any of them could face moving.

And yet they had persevered.

Twice a week, every week, they had negotiated Hampstead Heath. They had started by power walking, Paul in his bright yellow garb, Rick in his hi-tech gear and Mark in the clothes Jess had bought him. Rick brought a new gadget every time, from glow in the dark pedometer to a shirt that monitored his mood.

'It changes colour depending on how I'm feeling. Helps me to understand my body,' Rick had explained.

'What does mouldy green mean?' Mark had asked, looking at the shirt dubiously.

Rick had consulted his manual, but finding nothing to match that particular hue settled on his being 'ready to profit'. Or possibly significantly depressed. It was hard to know really.

They had started slowly, often being overtaken by other joggers and the odd elderly woman, but soon they had graduated to running. They now had a regular route which ended at The Wells pub for a stiff half pint.

Jess had been delighted when he told her he'd joined a running club and said he was definitely looking fitter. And he knew it too. No longer did he pant when the lifts weren't working in Holborn Tube Station, requiring him to climb the stairs. No longer did he use the lift at work, instead choosing the stairway.

All three of them had accumulated more and more elaborate gym wear and gadgets, including top of the range footwear and even high end water bottles. There was no doubt it was exhilarating.

'Less than two months to go!' Rick said and they all smiled. He was right. They had all been excited when they had booked their private Three Peaks Challenge online for the first week in March. There were public versions of the challenge and they had considered those, but they took place much later in the year. Most of them were too late to be in time for the reunion.

'Let's just get this done,' Rick had said. 'I say we book privately and just go for it.'

'Yeah,' Paul had agreed. 'I'm not too keen on sweating it out in a massive group anyway. It's good it'll just be us three.'

And so, they had booked at the earliest opportunity they could. Any earlier, they had been told, and they would have had to have been experienced climbers due to the snow and unpredictable weather generally.

'They want to know if we're doing it for charity and which one,' Paul had said. 'We can tell them any time before the big day, but obviously we need time to raise some money. Any ideas?'

This had been a difficult decision. They had immediately decided to opt for one of the lesser known charitable causes.

'It would be nice to give to a place that doesn't usually get picked,' Paul had said to pensive nods of agreement from the other two.

This had led them down a path which included everything from small local organisations which relied on government funding to survive to more unlikely causes such as one which was attempting to promote accordion playing in inner city schools. Looking at the despondent faces on the charity's website, Mark couldn't help but think that, if there was ever a lost cause, that was the very definition of it.

It was when he was on the phone to his mum one evening that Mark alighted on the answer.

'How's Branning?' she asked. 'Three babies! Oh it's just lovely, but what a handful. To be fair, the last time I saw him he looked like he'd been in the wars.'

Trust his mum to come up with that very concise summary of Branning's demeanor. Most of the time that Mark spoke to his mate, it seemed like he was either under fire or under cover, but always in battle.

His mum had paused thoughtfully. 'You weren't all that easy yourself, let me tell you,' she said, sounding like the memory was very much fresh in her mind. 'You never slept and you pood more than anyone else's baby. We thought there was something wrong with you.'

'Thanks mum.'

'Is he still having a hard time?' Mark's mother had persisted.

This had set Mark thinking. He remembered how Branning and his wife had struggled from the very first day with their triplets. It hadn't been a very auspicious start for one thing.

Gemma had gone into labour at 33 weeks. This wasn't unusual for triplets and Branning had been warned. Repeatedly. Yet, despite the constant reminders that 'they could come at any time', Branning had been playing the Question Time Drinking Game at Mark's house on the night in question while Gemma was at home.

The rules were clear. Players were to take a shot upon the following occurrences:

1. Each time Jonathan Dimbleby mentioned @bbcquestiontime;

2. 'No, the lady behind you. The one with the red top,' or other inane sartorial reference points;

3. Every time somebody blamed the last government for the woes of today's;

4. Any time a grey suited politician compared themselves to 'those men in suits in Westminster';

5. Each time somebody suggested we 'have a sensible discussion about immigration'; and

6. Whenever a member of the audience heckled.

There had been a mooted seventh drinking cue – at the mention of Brexit – but it was abandoned for fear of alcohol poisoning. Even without this however, sobriety was out of the window about ten minutes in.

Mark had no idea how Branning knew the Welsh national anthem, but he was singing it enthusiastically by the time Gemma's mum had called Mark's phone asking where Branning was.

'Mate, Gem's in labour.' When this elicited only a glassy look, Mark had added. 'The babies are coming!' This was at great personal cost. His own befuddled brain was struggling to function. It was fortunate that Jess had come home at that point. She'd driven them to University College Hospital where Gemma was ready for him with a list of expletives so impressive, Mark had noted some down.

As it happened, the birth – births? - went relatively well. The children – for there were indeed three of them – were healthy considering they were so premature. Branning had told him that, in hindsight, the premature birth was a good thing. It meant that the babies were kept at the hospital's neonatal department for a few weeks; a few weeks that had meant space for him and Gem to recover and get used to their new status as multiple parents. It gave them time to take stock. This, they had thought, would mean that they would be prepared for the babies' homecoming. They would be calm. They would be ready.

This, unfortunately, was about as accurate as saying that the run down the hill prepared the Light Brigade for the task ahead. When the children were finally healthy enough to come home, the Brannings found themselves on the wrong end of a full-frontal assault.

'There are always three of them, man,' Branning had said two nights in. 'Three. Always. If I'm not feeding one, I'm changing another. I haven't slept in 48 hours and the shit is pretty much perpetually in the fan.'

It had been Gemma's mother who had found the details of 'Multiple Parent Rescue', a charity that specialised in helping the parents and carers of multiples.

'They call us 'multents' instead of parents,' Branning had explained with the air of a new convert. 'They've offered us counselling, a night nurse and spare clothes.' The relief in his voice had been palpable. From then on, they had had at least one night's sleep between them per week and looked more likely to survive the experience.

Mark thought it would be so rewarding to help the charity that had helped such a close mate of his. After he'd mentioned his thoughts of the charity to Paul and Rick they had looked over his shoulder as he googled them.

'They're named by Mumsnet as the most hated charity in Britain,' Paul had read.

'And the Daily Mail has called them the Robin Hood of parent scroungers,' Rick added. 'Comments here are quite brutal. 'If you can't afford triplets why have them?', 'Nobody paid for my night nurse', 'Some people shouldn't be allowed to breed'.

'Are you sure about this?' Paul had asked.

'It's perfect,' Mark had said.

'I guess there are parallels between us and them,' Rick had said. 'We've all sort of won the lottery and can't cope.'

That had sealed the deal, but when Mark had tried to enter their details on the charity info section, it wouldn't accept them. He thought he might be entering them incorrectly, so he phoned the charity. The voice on the other end had been thoroughly confused.

'Are you from the government?' it had said when Mark had talked about giving them a donation.

'No,' he explained. 'I'm raising money for you in the Three Peaks, but I can't find your details on the Just Giving website.'

'Oh,' the voice said furtively. 'Hold on.' There had been a minute or so of mumbling and paper shuffling before a different voice had answered.

'Hello,' it had said in the wary tone of someone expecting to be pranked. When Mark had repeated his question about how to enter their details in in order to donate to them, the voice admitted, 'This doesn't really come up. Most of our donations are either from former beneficiaries or from the government.' It paused. 'And even they have us down as waste management in case there's a public outcry.'

In the end, a solution had been found and Mark felt more than ever that they had made the right choice. Now there was just the small matter of actually completing the challenge.

CHAPTER 11

'What you need to do is get in there fast. Does he have a study? An office? Yes? So get in there and grab what you can. Now Francesca, before it's too late.' After she finished speaking, Jess listened intently to the frenzied rummaging on the other end of the line.

This was her favourite part of the job. Dealing with the big numbers, managing newsworthy cases, getting the better of colleagues, that was all fun, but there was nothing like the thrill of a surprise attack. This must be what SAS men feel like when they storm an enemy compound, she thought gleefully.

Francesca DeFornicus had just caught her husband cheating on her with the nanny. Yes, the nanny. Who else? Jess never understood these women. Did they purposefully hire young girls to look after their children? It was like *importing* a mistress. Why go out of the house for your extra-marital needs when there's a perfectly good twenty-two-year-old in residence?

But there again, maybe that was exactly the intention.

 Jess thought of the photo she had seen of Mr DeFornicus. Fat, balding and on the wrong side of fifty, he might be one of the City's top analysts, but he was also one of its least attractive – and that was a tough competition to win. Perhaps Francesca was simply ready to move on. If so, there was no quicker route to a quickie divorce and a sympathetic judge on the financial front than a cheating husband. It was what Jess might have done in the same situation: Manipulated matters so as to create a faultless divorce on her part. Not that she would have been stupid enough to have children with a man who looked like that. That really was commitment.

'No I don't need the family albums,' she replied in exasperation. 'Just the paperwork. Anything with numbers.'

It was lucky really that Francesca had happened to see her husband and Chanel – for that was the nanny's name – in mid-'fornicus', but that they hadn't spotted her. This gave her the ultimate advantage – the element of surprise.

'Got it all? Good. We need to copy it and return before he gets back. And remember, not a word about divorce before we're sure we have it all.'

As she rested the phone back in its cradle, Jess felt a sense of true fulfilment. She looked out at the view of the city she had from her window. Sacha, her trainee, was typing feverishly at her desk across the room, her face flushed at the telling off she had endured just half an hour earlier for looking one of the partners directly in the eye. But really, she had to learn.

Just then there was a knock at the door and Zane Stevenson popped his head round. Zane was the latest hotshot in the department. Headhunted from their rival firm, Marshall Flynn, he was known for his innovative approach to legal loopholes.

It was he who had spearheaded the case which was hailed as a game changer in the divorce stakes when he had successfully argued that the ex-wife of a pro-footballer should pay *him* maintenance rather than the other way round despite the fact that she had the children. The winning argument had been that, given she had persuaded him into fatherhood, it was her fault that his scoring average had plummeted, leading to him being benched. Zane had presented scientific evidence, backed by several expert witnesses, that having children reduced men's abilities to play competitive sports. It was something to do with passing on their best men, so to speak.

As a member of Marshall Flynn, Zane was more accustomed to representing husbands than wives, the usual remit of Drakers, but that was precisely the reason the partners had pulled out all the stops to get him. They were diversifying. Zane brought with him a long client list of husbands who switched wives like other people switched cars. What's more, having presided over some of the biggest wins for husbands in the past few years, he provided an invaluable alternative perspective. He also offered undeniable eye candy for the multitude of newly single, on the rebound, soon to be ex-wives that frequented their offices every day. Jess studied him now.

With olive skin, laughing eyes and the kind of dark spikes you couldn't help but want to run your hands through, he was definitely handsome, a fact helped by his tall, athletic frame. Jess had no doubt that there would be bets around the office as to when she and Zane would get together. It would only be natural. The rabid City world loved nothing more than a good wager and a torrid affair and she, being his equal in both job and in the looks stakes was the obvious choice. Not that the secretaries didn't give it their best shot.

'Hi there,' he said lightly. 'Can I borrow you?'

Jess gave him a withering look. 'Sorry, I'm busy, can it wait?' This wasn't strictly true. She was in fact at a convenient break point between one case and another, but it wouldn't do to look like one had spare time. That's how rumours started.

'Not really,' he said, his almond eyes flashing and his tone now brisk, 'I have a client meeting and need an extra pair of hands. Anthony wants a show of force.'

Now he had Jess's attention. Saying a partner's name was always a winning move, the ultimate check mate, open sesame, but none more so in the family department than Anthony's name.

Without needing any further nudging, Jess stood up and picked up her Donna Karan blazer, seamlessly slipping into it as she closed the gap between them in long strides.

'Come on Sacha,' she said as she followed Zane out. If Anthony wanted a show of force, it was always good to throw a trainee or two into the mix, just for the numbers and the sight of at least two people frantically writing down what was being said.

As they walked to the lift, Sacha scurrying behind them, Jess dug for details.

'Who is it?'

'Actress. Fenella Feign. Comes from aristo roots, about to divorce-'

'Dan Feign,' Jess finished, her voice not disguising her astonishment as much as she'd have liked. To say that this pair was well known was an understatement. They were the current golden couple of the film world, she a lissom, blue blooded blond bombshell who had starred in every major Netflix drama in the past year and he the East End boy done good, a rapper turned film director who had released several critically acclaimed gritty tear jerkers about life on the tough streets. Of course, the toughest street he saw nowadays was Kensington High Street at rush hour.

Jess couldn't help but wonder what had torn the pair apart. The last time she had seen them they had been cuddled up in the party pictures section of *Tatler* attending a book launch or an art gallery opening or maybe the launch of a sandwich shop. Whatever it had been, they had looked ecstatic. There again, she of all people should know that one should never judge a person by their magazine cover.

After descending in the lifts, they entered the impressive lobby with its triple height ceiling and enormous vases of lilies and plush velvet sofas. There, they found two people waiting. One had a face she would know anywhere. Those pouty lips, the exaggerated brows, the acute curve of cheekbones, Fenella Feign was like a 1950's siren come to life. With her was a broad, silver haired man probably in his sixties, although something in his eyes made him look a lot younger.

'Mrs Feign? I'm Zane Stevenson and this is one of our top associates, Jess Jones and trainee solicitor, Sacha Flood,' Zane said flawlessly as he approached her, hand outstretched. 'Anthony Guild will be down shortly,' he added.

'Nice to meet you,' Fenella said, surprisingly self-possessed for one so young. 'And this is my father, Sir William Force.'

Jess had never known Fenella's background except that she was from one of London's oldest families. She had no idea that her surname was Force. Fenella Force. She had been destined for the stage and screen.

'Good to meet you,' Sir William said in a deep, powerful voice. Jess noticed he had a definite glint in his eye. 'And Fen's being silly, just call me Will.'

It transpired that Fenella and Daniel's marriage had been one of convenience rather than real love. She had needed something to rough up her elite image and he had wanted the publicity of marrying one of Hollywood's rising stars. It had been perfect. That was until Daniel had been caught canoodling with his personal trainer, Benjii – yes with two 'i's'. The pictures were currently on sale to the highest bidder so it was a mere matter of time before they appeared in the papers.

'We need this done quickly and quietly,' William was saying to what was now a room so filled with legal minds, it was hard to find comfortable seating space. Jess was also pretty sure that some of the people in the room weren't so much lawyers as cafeteria staff dressed up in suits to make up numbers. Anthony really had pushed the boat out. Most of the department was there and was that Fliss from the IT team?

'Not a problem,' Anthony assured him.

'And the pictures?' Fenella asked sharply.

'Well, there are things we can do,' Anthony said, 'But there are no guarantees. We can make it very unpalatable for them to publish them and get some very decent injunctions, but it may still end up on the net.'

'Well, do what you can,' William said with a touch of finality.

Jess stayed quiet throughout the exchange. She was definitely surplus to requirements from a professional perspective. Having said that, she was certain that there had been an alternative motive for her presence if the lascivious looks from William were anything to go by. Obviously Zane had thought that a great pair of legs would be a great asset. She didn't care. This kind of thing was always being done and it wasn't just because she was a woman. The great thing about the City these days was that everyone was equally objectified.

For the rest of the day, Jess was busy with the Feign case, liaising with their press department, ordering Sacha to draft the right forms and documents for the divorce proceedings and managing the financial aspects. Luckily, Fenella and Daniel had entered into a prenuptial agreement drawn up by the old family solicitor, now passed away. They also had no children, for now obvious reasons, so that made things easier. They would each walk away clear and dry.

It was gone nine before she crossed the threshold of her and Mark's Hampstead home and let the darkness envelope her.

'Mark?' she called out. Nothing.

This had become a more and more frequent occurrence, Mark being out. And it was something of which she wasn't sure she approved.

In the past, he'd usually been home at least an hour before her, his job not requiring the kind of commitment that hers demanded. Even if he stopped in at the pub on the way home, he'd still manage to get there before her. Yet now things were different.

Putting down her bag on the coffee coloured matt hardwood floor of their hallway, she walked straight into their enormous back room, complete with bi-fold doors looking onto their small but perfectly formed garden. She was unaccustomed to having to switch all the lights on as Mark had usually lit up the house like a Christmas tree by now.

She thought about texting him to see where he was, but instead decided to find that bottle of Malbec she'd seen the other day in their larder. Much more civilised. He was probably out with that running group again, she thought sullenly.

As she poured the rich red liquid into an oversized wine glass, she briefly considered the possibility that he was having an affair and almost laughed out loud. Yes, with most men that would have been the correct conclusion. Weight loss, more time away, increased enthusiasm for life generally, all the characteristics Mark was newly displaying. And yet she knew certainly, incontrovertibly, that that wasn't the explanation here.

There were two reasons for this. The first was simple. Because she said so. She knew enough about cheating spouses and the signs and the feelings to know that that wasn't what was going on here.

Secondly, Mark was just too good. He was a *good guy*; the kind of guy that opened doors for women not because he should, but because he wanted to. He was a stickler for the rules and appalled by everything from tax fraud to bad parking. This was not a man who would cheat.

She thought back to a time when she had told him that her friend Natasha was two-timing her boyfriend. Natasha had been boring her to tears on the phone that same evening with her pros and cons list of which man to keep. Mark had been incandescent in arguing that she should just break up with her boyfriend if she didn't want to be with him anymore.

'But she doesn't know if she wants to be with him or not,' Jess had retorted indignantly. 'That's the point.'

'Just do me a favour,' Mark had said finally. 'If you ever don't want to be with me anymore, just leave. Don't start having affairs or making lists about whether I snore too loudly or don't make enough money. Just break up with me.' His tone had had the flip quality of someone who knew that there was no risk of that happening. It had been near the start of their relationship when everything had seemed so easy and clear cut. Sure, they rowed, but the arguments were petty, almost fun. They just added some fire to their interactions. Or at least that's how she had seen it.

She remembered how she had yelled back, 'Erm yeah! Obviously!' in the same 'duh' tone her teenage-self had used with her little sister before she had decided to gain the higher ground by stalking out and slamming the door. Always leave first. That was a definite rule.

And she had been telling the truth at the time. If she didn't want him anymore, she would have left. It was obvious. She didn't need a man and would always put an end to a relationship when it had stopped working. She had been planning on leaving in fact. She couldn't believe how long she had let the relationship just drift. Three years. But there were good reasons for that. For one thing, she had been busy. It took a lot of time and effort to succeed as she had at work. She hardly had the spare time to reconsider her relationship. What's more she was a practical girl. She knew that breaking up with Mark would bring with it the hassle of moving out. That would mean more time wasted.

And what about work functions? Mark was presentable at office parties so there had been no harm in letting it go on. Plus it was good to show the partners that she was able to commit to someone. It sent good messages about her as a loyal employee.

Nevertheless, she had finally gotten round to it. She had been going to tell him. To break it off. Three years was long enough.

And then he had won. He had won the money and changed everything.

Because here was the thing. It was Mark who had won that money. The money was his. Not hers. They weren't married; she hadn't so much as lent him a couple of quid for the ticket. They weren't even engaged. Morons who listened to fishwife tales thought that there was such a thing as common law marriage in England: one where you earned the rights over time. But that simply wasn't true. Without a ring on her finger she may as well have been the guy who sold him the bloody ticket for all the good it did her being his girlfriend.

She had balked at the win at first, but now she was accustomed to the lifestyle it had brought with it. She wasn't ready to leave it behind, especially not until something better came along. Which it definitely would.

Jess sipped her wine as she perched at the breakfast bar, checking her emails on her phone. Anthony was delighted by the outcome that day and had sent round a slew of instructions. There was an email from Zane with an update on the paperwork regarding the Feign prenup and several excitable missives from Fran DeFornicus about the findings of her private detective. And then there was something else. An email from S W Force.

Jess looked at the subject line. It read simply 'Further to Our Meeting'. She couldn't help a smile creep over her lips.

>*'Dear Ms Holder*
>
>*It was a pleasure meeting you today, even given the less than agreeable circumstances. I was wondering whether you might like to meet for a slightly better reason?*
>
>*Yours, hopefully*
>
>*Sir Will'*

CHAPTER 12

'Would you like some sherry, Mark?' Jess's mum, Caroline asked in her best approximation of Violet Crawley from Downton Abbey. Not that the Dowager Countess of Grantham would ever serve her own drinks, but there again she could learn a thing or two from his girlfriend's alarmingly scrupulous mother. Mark took one of the small glasses proffered with a smile and muted thanks.

They were, as usual, having Christmas lunch at Jess's parents' palatial Hertfordshire mansion. They never even discussed it. It was just given as read. His parents were relegated to Boxing Day. He had once suggested that they try to see both on the same day, but the response had been less than positive.

'They're only fifteen minutes apart by car,' he had reasoned.

This had been met with the kind of horrified astonishment he would have expected had he announced a new career in bank robbery.

'And what part of my mother's lunch would you like to miss? The starter? Maybe the dessert? Would you like to just take our presents and run out of the door? We can topple over the carollers while we're at it. Honestly Mark, if it ain't broke.'

And that had been the end of that. So, for the past three years this had been his Christmas. And, to be fair, it wasn't too bad. He had to admit, Mr and Mrs Holder certainly knew how to throw a Christmas do.

There was the decoration to begin with. From the handcrafted tree baubles expertly swirling their way around the giant 100% real evergreen nestled in the crook of their regal staircase to the shimmering sea of fairy lights outside and the magical yet understated Vera Wang table settings, the Holder house was the very pinnacle of elegant festive cheer. It was the kind of thing that put most Hollywood films to shame.

Then there was the food. Mark had no idea what kind of genetic modifications it had presumably undergone nor what kind of furnace from hell could possibly cook such a thing, but the Holder family turkey was the size of a pregnant wildebeest. Had he seen it stand up from the table and go on to take down the family beagle, he would not have been surprised. It was simply massive. And it had to be. For the Holder Christmas wasn't an intimate family affair. Oh no. Mr and Mrs Holder were the ultimate hosts, inviting a slew of well-heeled friends and esteemed colleagues.

He thought of his parents. They had gone to his uncle's house with his mounds of cousins and their children all making a mess of wrapping paper and turkey in the shadow of a synthetic tree. It was true that it was hardly the height of glamour, but at least it was laid back. Not like this.

It was always so nerve-wracking at Jess's parents' house. You never knew who you were going to be sitting next to. Mr Holder was in publishing while his wife was the author of a series of terrifying books with unlikely titles such as 'Grabbing Life by the Cohunes' and 'Friends are Great, Enemies are Better'. They were so preposterously forceful he always wondered who could possibly be her target audience. Maybe aspiring warlords? It didn't bear thinking about, but what it did mean was that the guests were, to say the least, eclectic.

Now, as Christmas carols sung by the choir of St Paul's played softly over the wireless speakers, Mark was cornered.

'So, we thought that the ants were transporting the food faster when they heard Vivaldi than when they heard Wagner,' the man with the basset hound features beside him was saying. 'But we were wrong.' Mark couldn't quite remember his name. Was it Earnest Lewis or Lewis Earnest? What did it matter? All he knew was that dog face had been holding forth about his experiments on the effects of music on the common garden ant – or lasius niger - for the past twenty minutes.

'So what was the effect of the music?' Mark asked. He may as well know, he thought despondently.

'It turns out that there isn't one,' the man said desolately, disappointment mixing with a realisation of the cruelty of life etched on his loose features.

'Oh, right.' What was Mark supposed to say to this?

'It's a bit of a blow actually,' the man chuntered on. 'Five years of experiments and not one verifiable result. Bit of an anomaly in the science world. You'd usually at least get a coincidental effect.'

'Dinner's ready everyone,' Mrs Holder said with a tinkle of her sherry glass. Mark breathed a sigh of relief. They all made their way to the table and to find their place names. Nothing was ever left to chance here.

Luckily, it wasn't one of those years when the Holders decided to play seating roulette, separating husband from wife and boyfriend from girlfriend so he would have Jess beside him. Unfortunately though, the seat on his other side was occupied by Amelie, Jess's obnoxious younger sister. At a mere twenty five years old, Amelie was certain she knew the answers to life, the universe and everything. Or at least anything worth a bit of money. She was forever asking him about his job and whether he was in line for a promotion and even what he was paid, all with the disdainful gaze of a girl who clearly didn't understand what her sister saw in him.

But there was worse to come. Worse in the shape of Amelie's husband, Lance. Lance was the very epitome, the very picture and sound and feel of that hellish creature known as an estate agent. Yes, he styled himself as a property magnate, but he was an estate agent. With his slicked back black hair, absurdly square jaw and teeth so bright they could be used to direct ships, he perpetually bore the expression of one making a finger gun, just without any discernible irony.

When he spoke, Lance did so to promote Lance. Lance was always busy. Lance had a full and exciting life which could be followed closely on Facebook and Twitter. Lance spoke in the third person and was usually busy extolling his latest ventures. And these ventures were always the very best and most impressive. Because Lance wasn't just a run of the mill estate agent. He was like their king. Not for him driving around is some crappy green mini with a logo on the side. Oh no. Lance had an Aston Martin complete with the number plate L13SSS.

'I don't get it,' Mark always said to Jess. 'Surely people wouldn't buy from him if his number plate actually says 'LIES'?'

'But he's an estate agent,' Jess retorted. 'They expect him to lie. At least he's honest about it.'

There had been no sensible response to this.

Moreover, Lance didn't sell country cottages or suburban semis. Lance restricted his nefarious selling techniques to shifting only the biggest, most expensive piles the Capital had to offer.

Today, Lance and Amelie bore their usual self-satisfied grins as they all air kissed and shook hands in greeting.

'Mark,' Amelie said, her face bobbing in the air on either side of his face. 'How are things?'

'Hi Amelie,' he said. 'Yeah not bad.'

'Still not a partner?' Lance asked in his typical macho tone.

'Nope.' he responded, mirroring Lance's tone. 'Have you finished cramming London full of Kazak billionaires by persuading them to buy third homes they don't need?'

'I'm working on it, but I'm only one man,' Lance replied with a wink at Jess.

'Excellent.'

The lunch went by as it always did, with lively conversation and laughter. To anyone in the world it would look like the ideal Christmas lunch. A picture of peace on earth. Only if one listened carefully would one hear that Mrs Holder was telling her neighbour about her upcoming tome, 'Enemies: They just got closer'.

'My publisher was just crying out for it,' she was explaining languidly.

Amelie meanwhile was grilling Mark on his progress at the firm.

'I just don't understand how you're not a partner yet. You're forty, right?' Her face was a picture of innocence and concern as she waved her fork about like she was conducting the Philharmonic.

'Thirty five,' he said evenly.

'And you do go to the office every day, right?' she asked, her eyes wide. 'Surely *anyone* would be a partner after ten years at the same firm.'

'Have you tried negotiating?' Lance asked, mid enthusiastic chew. 'It's like Lance tells his team. Don't take no for an answer, don't answer until you know.' He seemed pleased with this. Mark wondered what on earth it meant.

It was taking every ounce of Mark's self-control not to poke either of their eyes out with his salad fork.

'I've won £10.43 million.' He should say it. Say it. Go on. That would definitely shut them up. But he could see that Jess had read his mind and was shaking her head in an emphatic 'no'.

'Mark's had a massive pay rise, sis,' Jess said. 'He's just too modest to say so.'

'Really?' Amelie asked. She looked doubtful. 'Oh, ok.' Mark was relieved. Maybe she would let it go.

'Keep going Markio,' Lance said, slapping his back with a giant paw from behind Amelie while employing one of the many irritating nicknames he had devised over the years. 'You can do it. Or you never know. You might win the lottery.' He and Amelie had laughed uproariously at his wit, thereby allowing Mark to get his coughing fit under control without being noticed.

And then Lance began talking about how 'Lance and Amelie' had been on a 'simply fantabulous' trip to Bali and how nobody ever relaxed like they did or knew how to snorkel properly or which seat in first class was best.

Luckily this gave Mark time to sit quietly without the need to so much as utter an agreement or dissent.

'Lunch' ended at 4pm, allowing for hours more fun. Other than a present giving scenario which saw Lance and Amelie give everyone a mind-bending calendar with each month being a different professionally done photo of themselves in various cringe-worthy poses and the section of the late afternoon which had involved an excruciating round of monopoly where Lance had won – 'Bad luck El-Markus, just one more thing I smash you at, eh?' - the day was uneventful and aided by copious amounts of alcohol.

Mark and Jess finally collapsed into a taxi at 7pm and silently travelled home. Once they got there, Mark took his phone off silent to check for messages. Paul had written something on the group WhatsApp for their challenge which included the two of them plus Rick.

'So who's overeaten besides me?? Need a run and now.' Mark smiled.

'Drunk as a skunk mate! Tomoz?' This popped up on the screen from Rick.

'I'm up for that,' Mark tapped into his phone. 'Evening?'

'I'm thinking of leaving my wife.'

This was the staggering revelation made by Paul twenty minutes into their Boxing Day evening run, just at the point where the uphill started evening out. This was supposed to be the easy bit, but not today. Rick stopped entirely and Mark turned towards Paul mid-jog, almost resulting in him hurtling shoulder first into a tree.

'Mate,' Rick said, running to catch up to where Paul and Mark were now standing.

'What happened?' Mark asked.

They were all slightly out of breath and visibly sweaty.

'I dunno,' Paul started. 'I just don't feel like I know her anymore and-'

'Don't say it,' Mark said, knowing exactly what was coming.

'Mirka understands me.'

Mark sighed and rubbed his hand over his face.

'Who?' Rick asked.

'Mark's met her, haven't you?'

'Have I?' Mark wracked his brain. The only person I've met besides your wife is-,' and that's when it hit him. 'Your cleaner?'

'Housekeeper.'

'For fuck's sake.'

'You don't understand,' Paul said, now pleading. 'Dina has changed so much. The magazine shoots, the column, the plastic surgery, it's like she's a completely different person. Do you know she's even got them doing a piece about me doing this charity event?' He was sounding nearly hysterical now.

'Right, I think this conversation would be most profitably continued in a pub, don't you?' And with that, Mark stalked off in the direction of The Wells.

Seated by a roaring fire a few minutes later with three pints and a bowl of Kalamatas, the three men delved deeper into Paul's dilemma. Paul hadn't needed any prompting. He started chattering the moment they were all seated.

'It's been four months. She asked me whether I wanted my collars starched and the next thing I know I'm telling her about my childhood nickname. We talk whenever Dina's out.'

'Have you *done* anything?' Mark was glad that Rick had asked this question. He couldn't even bear to think of his oversized mate engaging in any kind of bodily activities with the straight-lipped, dead-eyed Mirka. The thought of asking him about it was stomach turning. He took a swig of his beer as he waited for Paul's response.

'No, just talked.' Paul's gloomy tone matched his expression.

'Good, don't,' Mark said. 'Take time to think about this. You've been happily married for, what, ten years?'

'Twelve,' Paul admitted.

'It's natural that the lottery win has affected her. And you,' Mark said pointedly. 'Don't go doing anything rash.'

'Maybe,' Paul said.

'Look. Just try. Talk to Dina. Don't throw it all away over something that might get better.' Mark could see the battle waging on Paul's face as he listened.

'Hate to say it mate, but I think Mark might be right. Divorce is not a simple thing. Take it from the guy who's done it twice,' Rick said into his drink.

They sat contemplatively for a moment as an unspoken agreement formed between them. No further. They had probed all they could into Paul's private life for today. Any further would become uncomfortable.

'How is all that going by the way?' Mark asked tentatively. 'With your exes?' He actually wanted to know how Rick had come to be divorced twice, but wasn't sure how to ask that question.

'Oh, just great. I've got two ex-wives that hate me, two kids who don't want to know me and a legal bill so big I think their law firms are going to offer me loyalty points,' he moaned. 'The good news is, they're getting on famously. I saw a photo of them together on Facebook. Bree's angry as well. Thinks I'm letting them take advantage.'

'That cannot be good,' Paul said.

'No. Just you then Mark in a happy relationship,' Rick said. 'How is your Jess?'

'Oh, yes, well. You know. Just the usual,' Mark said non-committedly. He didn't tend to devote much thought as to whether he and Jess were happy. They just were. They existed. He found her attractive and she, presumably, felt the same way about him. Their sex life was pretty decent and they were used to each other now. There was no need to rock the boat.

His two friends seemed to get the hint.

'Did you know that cows have best friends?' Rick said by way of conversation changer.

'Is there any end to the useless information you keep inside that giant head of yours?'

'They get stressed when they're separated.'

'Shut up.'

CHAPTER 13

Graham sat in his corner of the office as the merriment overtook his colleagues.

9pm. The karaoke attempts had long since passed the point of tonal control and the night had already witnessed its first casualty – Janet from accounts falling off an office chair in a swivelling competition. Graham surveyed the sorry scene. This, he thought mournfully, was so festive. It was always like this. They were like pent up puppies. The moment they were set loose they ran amok.

He would have gone home by now, but he had been deep in thought. The Christmas season always made him a bit more pensive. He sighed. Ever since he had decided to give up on killing himself, life had lost all meaning. What was he supposed to do now? There seemed no end point. Nothing to look forward to.

And the past month had seen many changes in the office. He hated change. The biggest of the changes related to those two young consultants who had so suddenly appeared in their lives that late November lunchtime and had since become regular fixtures in the office.

Emily and Peter. The moronic moles as he had silently nicknamed them. They had used almost every trick in the book to cut down the costs of the lottery arm of Avalon Group Plc. The stationery cupboard was now under lock and key. Graham imagined it would be easier to find the Coca Cola recipe than obtain a ballpoint pen at that point. Sick days were now monitored with the careful suspicion of red clothing under McCarthy and most of the smokers were now covered in nicotine patches because they were only permitted one break a day. It was all being done in the name of economising.

At one point the coffee station had been replaced with a water cooler, but that had caused such outrage, such consternation that that particular decision had been reversed quite swiftly. And this was a good thing for Graham. For, while he never imbibed the evil bean, he did rely on its power to draw everyone in the office to the kitchen. That's how he learned what was really going on. Indeed it was in the last week of November that one particular conversation between Emily the consultant and Hammond had caught his attention.

'Hello,' Hammond had said cheerily, approaching the biscuit tin. Emily had been at the coffee machine, pouring herself an espresso. That girl really could handle her caffeine.

'Ah, Mr Hammond, I'm glad you're here,' Emily said pleasantly. Despite the fact that he was staring at his screen, Graham could hear the smile spread on her face. This was what she always did. Cushioned her blows with sweetness. She was like one of those Venus fly traps and Hammond was like an overweight fly that was always in the wrong place at the right time.

'Oh?' said Hammond, crumbs probably spurting from his lips by now.

Fly away while you can you moron, Graham thought at him furiously. Can't you see she's about to swallow you whole?

'I was going to pop into your office in a minute, but it's just a quick thing. Would you indulge me?'

Graham rolled his eyes at her honeyed use of the word 'indulge'. Did the woman have no shame?

'The thing is, I've found this expense that comes out regularly from the client care account. It's £200 paid to the Hampstead Diocese of St Mary's?'

There was a rustle as Hammond presumably looked at the paperwork.

'I'm not sure what this is,' He paused. 'If that's a charitable beneficiary it shouldn't be coming out of there and we don't usually give these things in instalments anyway.' When he next spoke, Hammond was directly over Graham's shoulder looking into Liz's cubicle. 'Do you know what this is?' The paperwork went over Graham's head.

As usual, Smith was chatting to Liz and so was there to provide an answer. It took Smith just moments to examine the document. 'Oh yes, that's that support group trial we did for lottery winners. Giving them pastoral care after they win. Avalon Cares.'

'Trial?' Emily said in disbelief. 'From what I've seen this has been going on for over two years.'

There was a silence as both men struggled to form any words.

'Does it work at least?' Emily continued. 'Does anyone even go?'

'Um…'

'Er…'

Smith and Hammond were clearly both lost for words.

'I mean, it seems a bit mad really. We're paying £200 a week to support a group of people who have won millions.' When this still met with no reply she said, 'Ok, well this seems like a no-brainer to me. It's gone.'

And that, apparently, was that. Graham had looked at the pile of support group leaflets on his desk. Did they have to go as well? Probably. Over the past two years, he had handed them out to every winner he had met. He wondered how many of them had taken it up. And who were these people who needed help to come to terms with their good fortune? He remembered thinking that it was people like him who needed the support group. The invisible people. It was unfortunate nobody knew where any of them were.

And yet, he was struck with a pang of fury. It was such a fresh, raw feeling he was actually thrilled by it. It was real. Not like the dullness of his day to day. It was a sensation so authentic, so true and fresh, it was almost tangible. All that work. All those leaflets. He had incorporated the support group into his appointments, made it part of his routine. They couldn't just take it away.

These thoughts had stayed with him, festering and growing. He had been consumed by questions. What would he do now? Would he just accept it and change his routine? He could fill it with some more platitudes. Or he could suggest counselling in general without the flyer. That could work. But it might lead to questions. Questions were distracting so that was no good.

He watched as Smith and Perkins stood on a desk, warbling loudly along to the music, the screen which they were facing reading 'With a Little Help from My Friends' by The Beatles.

'What would you do if I ask out of tune? Would you stand up and walk out on me?' They yelled, ironically with little reference to the tune. They had their arms around each other and were swaying with the lack of control of a ship in a storm.

Graham's own thoughts were also vacillating perilously. It had been like this ever since that day he had decided not to jump. He had spent weeks trying to give his life some meaning. A focus. He needed that. He required an objective. But if not the ultimate objective, then what? He looked again at his wayward colleagues.

'I get by with a little help from my friends!'

He couldn't help himself, no. He had proved that. The whole jumping thing had been folly of the highest degree. A pipe dream. He didn't have it in him.

'Oh I get high with a little help from my friends!'

So, given that he was incapable of self-help, was there a more altruistic solution?

He wondered how many people were like him. How many were just staggering through life waiting for someone to help them out of it. There must be hundreds. Thousands? After all, it couldn't just be him.

'Gonna try with a little help from my friends!'

Could he help others? Could he do for them what he couldn't do for himself. After all, those who can't, teach. He chortled at the thought.

By the time the song had ended, everyone in the room who was still passably conscious and didn't have their face glued to that of another member of staff was singing along. There was a sense of camaraderie in the air and of exuberance. For once, Graham felt connected to it.

He could free those who couldn't free themselves, he thought in awe. Yes.

But who, he thought, ignoring the fact that Smith and Perkins were now being joined on stage by Hammond for a rowdy rendition of Human League's 'Don't You Want Me?' It wasn't like he was going to pick someone at random. He needed to identify the truly worthy. Someone who was crying out for help.

Was there anyone here who needed him?

'Don't you want me bebe,' the tuneless chorus rang out.

No.

He would have to give that some thought. Maybe create a spreadsheet.

Then there was the matter of how.

'Don't you want me, oh-oh-oh-oh!'

There were options of course, but not all of them open to him. He wasn't strong, he didn't know anything about poison and firearms were almost certainly out of the question. So what? Maybe run someone over? More food for thought , he considered, just as Perkins fell off the makeshift stage.

CHAPTER 14

'Are you serious?'

'That's disgusting!'

'No, no, I think it's a serious point.'

'Wait! Mark, what do you think?'

Mark looked up unsteadily through eyes glazed with gin. Paul, Annie, Holly and Rick were all looking at him with baited breath, like football fans waiting for the final goal to be scored. Since when had he become the tie breaker? What was the debate now anyway?

The idea of a night out had been mooted by Annie at the last meeting. They were going out to celebrate several achievements. Firstly that Annie had got a B in a piece of English coursework, the first she had submitted since being accepted for a late start of her A-levels at a local sixth form college and secondly that Holly had been accepted to a photography course for next year. Rick claimed to be celebrating the fact that Brioche hadn't left him yet, although the deathly look she had thrown him before she was ejected from the flat was enough to put that in doubt.

Margaret and Gerald had declined the invitation while Derek had simply left early pleading tiredness, although Mark was pretty sure it had something to do with the Amazon package he had waiting for him at home.

'It's the latest Hornby British Rail Class 71 Electric Locomotive,' he had said excitedly to Mark over his vodka and lemonade in the first venue they'd entered. 'I've had it on pre-order for months.'

Mark had listened as much as he could as Derek had enthused about the Double Flywheel Dual Bogie Drive and something called a 5 Pole Skew Wound motor, but in truth he had been looking around nervously at the all too trendy crowd around them. At 33, he still very much considered himself in the 'young and carefree' category. So why was he looking at the girl with the nose ring and repressing a tut at her visible cleavage. Why was he lamenting the lack of 'excuse me's' as people shoved past him? And why was his head pounding at the sound of this ridiculous music? It was as if one part of his mind was holding a silencing palm over the other part that wanted to yell out 'in my day!'

Luckily, Holly and Paul had similarly concluded that a trendy bar in Hoxton was no place for anyone who could remember dial up modems and so they had all agreed on a sensibly hasty retreat. Annie, on the other hand, had wanted to stay and had had to be dragged away from a bloke who looked so scruffy and dazed, he would make Pete Doherty look on the ball. Rick didn't care either way. But finally they had left the madness behind and withdrawn to the safety of Rick's 'gaff'.

When they had first arrived they had still been on the relatively sober side, so the subjects of conversation had been sensible and controlled: the underinvestment in primary schools in London, confusion about road traffic signs and Strictly versus X Factor, that sort of thing.

Yet as the night went on and the drink flowed, the topics meandered into every territory considered to be taboo, from religion: 'I have seen Essex and let me tell you that God has had nothing to do with vajazzles!' (Paul to Holly), to politics: 'if the Government is overthrown don't you think lottery winners will be the first to be shot?' (Rick to Annie).

Voices had gradually risen and gestures had become increasingly pronounced. Annie, for one, looked like she might be directing traffic, so wide were her arm gestures as she laid forth about why she thought Niall Horran was the backbone of One Direction. Indeed, it was the portion of the night that saw Annie pronounce that 'One Direction is miles better than Take That' was the one that had true combustion potential, with Annie and Holly at lethal loggerheads.

'Come on Mark,' Annie prodded him, almost falling over as she did so, 'Prenups. Yes or no?'

'Mark would never get Jeb to sign a prenubsual agreement,' Rick held forth, his mispronunciations and slurring words underlining the ridiculousness of the situation. '*That*,' he continued, finger pointing in the vague direction of up, 'Is true love.'

Rick hadn't had a simple three months. For one thing, his ex-wives had formed something of a union, clubbing together to hire a lawyer who seemed to be part Emmeline Pankhurst, part bloodhound in her demeanour. He had spent every one of his turns at the weekly meetings filling them in on their latest arguments against him, ranging from his rampant adultery to refusing to take the bins out.

'Mark?' It was Annie.

As if awoken from a dream, Mark looked around to see that he was still under scrutiny. He tried to focus and seriously consider the question that had been posed. Was he for or against prenuptial agreements? It was one issue he had never given any thought, primarily because he had never needed to before. After all, before he had won the lottery, all he'd had to lose was a rental agreement and a six year old Volkswagen Polo. But did it make any difference now that he had more stuff?

He was pretty sure that sober Mark would be appalled by the idea of a prenup. What kind of person got married while preparing for divorce? There again, was it arrogant and irresponsible to ignore the statistics? In a life that was so long and unpredictable, could anyone say with absolute certainty that marriage was 'til death did you part?

Jess for one relied on divorce for her livelihood. As such it would almost be rude to ignore it. Impractical. Just the other night she had been reading out some numbers from the Office of National Statistics – she kept abreast of these much in the way that bankers kept an eye on the markets. She had shaken her head sadly as she told him that approximately 42% of marriages in England and Wales end in divorce. Meanwhile 34% of marriages are expected to end in divorce by the 20th wedding anniversary. It was sobering stuff. Or at least it would be if he had drunk anything less than the six shots, three pints and a glass of the random concoction Annie had made upon arrival at the flat.

Of course Jess had shaken her head and lamented, 'we really had hoped it would be higher by now.'

'Is he ok?' Holly asked.

'Hold on,' Paul said, staring at him intently. 'I'm pretty sure he's about to say something.'

Finally, Mark spoke. 'I dunno,' he said, to groans from the crowd before they started shouting at the tops of their voices again.

Flopped back on the sofa, Mark looked at them in a fond haze. It was funny to think about it, but since he had first fallen into their lives all those months ago, he had come to think of this disparate, unlikely group as his friends. It was unsurprising really given their weekly meetings and all the things they'd shared in that time.

He looked at Rick. For all his persona of well dressed, well-spoken and well versed, he was actually utterly clueless when it came to the practical things in life. For example, he had been floored to discover that you shouldn't necessarily believe everything a cold caller told you and, in fact, Annie had had to school in him the whys and wherefores of caller blocking. On the other hand, he was unstoppable in a pub quiz, being the only one to know the answers to 'who wrote the original tale of Goldilocks and the Three Bears?' (Robert Southey) and 'how many cantons make up Switzerland?' (26).

Holly on the other hand was as practical as they come, something which they had discovered on one motorway journey when she had changed a flat tire without so much as smudging her mascara.

'Trust me,' she had said. 'Get stuck just once on the hard shoulder with two hungry toddlers and you too will learn the basics of car mechanics.'

They had met Holly's children, Jake, 3 and Sam, 5 as well as her husband, Mike, at a barbecue one Sunday afternoon at their Totteridge home. Mike had been every bit as friendly and laid back as Mark had expected, while Holly's children had been little bundles of energy, running around and chattering away.

'My daddy has an Audi! Not a Nissan!' Jake had informed Mark on several occasions, while Sam had tied Rick up as a hostage in a game of pirates.

They had stayed there all afternoon, eating and laughing, enjoying the day. Mark had felt guilty on that idyllic day for not bringing Jess, especially as Paul had come with Dina and Rick with Bree, but there again even putting aside the fact that she would never approve of him joining this group, Jess was busy anyway. She was certain now that partnership was on the horizon and was working evenings as well as weekends in her mission to succeed. Was it his imagination or had she become visibly more terrifying as a result? There was a manic glint in her eyes nowadays that Mark couldn't help but compare to the bottomless, staring tunnel vision of Gollum in search of his bounty.

He had begun to wonder where his relationship with Jess was going, something he had never questioned before. Would he ever have to consider the issue of a prenup with Jess? Would they ever get to that romantic stage of pondering their inevitable divorce?

When they had first met, it had all been so fun and easy. Neither of them had had any expectations. They had both been equally focused on their careers and social lives, falling out of bars on the weekends and into the office Monday morning. So when had things changed? He thought about how Jess looked at him these days. The withering disappointment. He felt like a puppy who refused to house train. She was climbing the legal ladder while he was clinging on with one hand. Yet they still had a laugh. Sometimes. If they were both drunk enough and both at home and had some spare time and the news wasn't on.

He sighed. Looking around the room as Annie ripped into Rick for his 'misunderstanding of the human race' and 'chauvinistic bordering on psychotic' views on marriage, he couldn't help but feel a bit teary. 'I love you guys,' Mark said, prompting everyone to stop mid-rant and stare at him momentarily like they were playing musical statues Then, like someone had pressed the play button, they resumed their row.

By the end of the night, all of them had undergone the full gamut of drunken emotions. From happy and lively to passionate and argumentative, then thoughtful and finally, morose.

'I mean,' Rick was saying as they all sat down on his vast sofa suite, heads tilted back, 'what's the use of all this money if it doesn't bring happiness?'

'I'm happy,' Holly said, the loudness of her voice betraying the fact that she was also utterly inebriated.

'It's like they say,' Paul philosophised. 'Life's not about having what you want, but wanting what you have.'

'Deep,' Annie replied. Mark wasn't sure if even she knew whether or not she was mocking Paul.

'So,' Holly began with the utmost of seriousness. 'Where does this heavy drinking fit in with your training for the Three Peaks?'

There was a silence as Paul, Rick and Mark mulled this over. The challenge was only a couple of weeks away now. They had been running twice a week and had taken to climbing all 320 stairs at Hampstead Tube Station - interestingly the most stairs of any of the 270 tube stations – at least twice every weekend, much to the amusement and suspicion of the guards. Yet now, here they were, completely, undeniably, unutterably wrecked.

They all looked at each other. Mark was the first to burst out laughing before the rest of them joined in and soon they were all in fits of uncontrollable giggles.

Holly had ordered a cab soon after, shoving a grateful Mark inside and dropping him off at a house that was dark enough to inform him that Jess was either out or asleep. He snuck in like a burglar in a cartoon, all exaggerated creeping but without the required stealth. He bumped into the designer coat rack, tripped over his own shoe and, once upstairs, stubbed his toe on the bedroom door.

'What the hell are you doing?' the lump of duvets which was presumably Jess demanded in a husky just-woken voice.

'Sorry!' Mark yell-whispered. 'Don't mind me.'

The thousand thread count bedsheets sighed dramatically and rearranged themselves. 'Where were you anyway?'

'Out with the guys,' Mark replied, hopping on one unsteady foot as he tried to disrobe.

'The guys' had become instant shorthand for what Jess believed to be his running club. Mark knew that she found his new exercise obsession to be simultaneously encouraging and perplexing. He had never shown such interest in physical fitness before.

In the rare time they had spent together over the past months, she had certainly been impressed with his improved physique – that had definitely been a fun bonus. But she had also been annoyed at his increasingly common excuse for being out late and more often generally. She knew about the charity challenge, but was bewildered by why that meant that he was out in the evenings. Luckily she never questioned his Wednesday afternoon chiropractor sessions/group meetings. Jess knew as well as anyone that a healthy back meant a healthy career.

'Are you drunk?' she asked indignantly. When he was silent, she started moving again, now with purpose. 'I thought you were doing the Three Peaks not the Thousand Pubs,' she said, now sitting up, her usually coiffed hair and an Olivia Von Halle Clemency Silk Eye Mask – yes they made designer eye masks - covering her clearly irate features.

'It was a team building thing,' he slurred defensively. He hated lying. Not least because he was rubbish at it.

'Whatever,' she sighed. 'Are you coming to bed?' And without waiting, she retreated into her cocoon, allowing him to trip and fall his way out of his clothes and into their bed.

The next day at work, Mark couldn't help but regret the decision to go out drinking on a Thursday night. Of course it made no difference to the others – they had no jobs to go to - and Annie had insisted that Thursday was the new Friday, but really. How could he be expected to function with only three hours sleep and a hangover that felt like he had been dragged to work behind the tube train instead of on it?

Opening his desk drawer, he found a packet of paracetamol and downed one after another with his bottle of Evian. It was going to be a long day.

Opening his email folder, Mark searched the messages for any replies to the firm-wide message he'd sent out asking for donations for the Three Peake Challenge, but none were forthcoming. All there had been was an email from Paul with an emoticon showing someone laughing hysterically. He would have to ask him about that later.

He checked his 'Just Giving' page, but it was still at a desultory £250. £50 of that was from mum and dad (he'd have to ask them for more) and the rest was from Lance with a message reading 'Enjoy your little walk. Use this to get yourself something pretty!' Dick.

Nobody in the office had so much as given him a bad excuse let alone a pledge to donate.

Just then, a message popped into his inbox from Georgina Flask. Georgie, as she was known, was a leggy brunette with horsey teeth and a tendency to say 'basically' at the beginning of every sentence. He saw that, like his own, her email had been sent to the entire firm. It read as follows:

'Hi All! As you all know, I have been raising money for my round the world trip to discover myself. Basically, I hope to get a greater understanding of who I am and why we all exist. This has been a long time ambition of mine and I hope that through this self-work I can become a better, more accomplished property litigator. Next week I am going to be cutting six inches off my hair(!) for the cause. I hope you will support me. Any donations would be very welcome. Just go to my Just Giving page xxx'

Almost as fast the email came in, replies followed. Mark counted six in just four minutes amongst which Gwyneth from the property department wrote:

'OMG not your beautiful hair! Donation already there. We'll miss you!'

David from his own department said:

'Live the dream Georgie! We're behind you.'

Even Goodwyn had gotten in on the act:

'I see big things in your future. I've authorised a donation on behalf of the firm. Carpis Dium!'

Mark was astonished. Firstly, did Goodwyn insist on using Latin so frequently when he clearly had no grasp of it? Carpe Diem meant seize the day. Carpis Diem meant seize the carp. A subtle, but not unimportant difference. But more importantly, why were all these people supporting her cause and not his?

Mark looked back at his own, utterly ignored, message. Yes he had mentioned that he was climbing the three largest peaks in the country, a distance of some 24.5 miles. By contrast, Georgie would be travelling downstairs to Toni and Guy. Yes he had mentioned that he was doing it for a good cause and had named Multiple Parent Rescue. He had also given the right details for how to donate.

Completely baffled and somewhat annoyed, he resisted the urge to send an irate reply to Georgie and the rest of the firm and chose instead to vent to his office roommate, Jez.

'Can you believe this?' he said, pointing to his computer. 'Georgie's fundraising. It's ridiculous!'

'I know,' Paul mooed in his heavy Brummy accent. 'Six inches. Her hair is lovely.'

'No, not that, Mark persisted. 'I mean why has everybody clambered to support her poncing around in Fiji and Sydney or whatever else for a haircut and not my cause?' He stopped for a moment and looked suspiciously at Jez. 'Why haven't you?'

Jez's acne covered face looked back at him in surprise. 'Was that a real thing? The Multiples thingy? I thought you were having a laugh.'

'No,' Mark said irritably. 'Why would you think that?'

'Well,' Jez seemed to give this some proper thought. 'Buying more stuff for people who have more than one kid. It's not a proper cause is it? I mean not like helping puppies and horses and inner city kids play the accordion and stuff.'

'And helping Georgina, a twenty five year old from Kent, travel to Mumbai for her summer hols is?'

Jez just shrugged at this and, feeling defeated as well as in need of caffeine, Mark gave up and went to the coffee station.

He was just about to take a sip when he heard the booming voice that haunted his nightmares.

'Ah, Mark,' Goodwyn intoned. 'Glad to see you. Have you donated to Georgie yet? Brave girl. I'm looking for the whole firm to get behind her if you catch my writ.' This terrible law inspired pun was accompanied by an exaggerated wink. Mark knew he should be used to Goodwyn's cringy abuse of the English language – not to mention the Latin one – by now, but it just seemed to get worse and worse.

'Morning,' Mark said. 'I will do. Did I mention that I'm also doing something for charity? I'm climbing the Three Peaks.'

At the mention of this, Goodwyn's expression transformed to the indignant annoyance of a parrot whose cage had been slightly, but not catastrophically, rattled.

'Nobody likes an attention seeker Jones,' he said dismissively before deftly switching subject. 'We have a new client coming in. Jonty Hillcrest. Father died ab intestinum. Needs our help. I'll send you the details.'

129

For a moment, Mark was confused. His Latin was a touch rusty, but he was certain Goodwyn had just said that the man's father had died 'from the intestines'. Surely that wasn't right. Then a light of recognition ignited in his mind.

'Oh, you mean he died ab intestate. Without a will,' Mark clarified.

'Yes,' Goodwyn said, a look of annoyance on his face. 'That's what I said. Pay attention, Jones,' he added, before stalking back to his lair.

For the rest of the morning, Mark sat in his ergonomically gifted chair stewing over the unfairness of it all. How was it that he, with his first in law from Oxford and solid grasp of everything related to trusts and wills was subordinate to a man like Goodwyn? A man who didn't know the difference between seizing the day and fresh water fish? A man who thought a bare trust was a team building exercise? It wasn't right.

He had always wondered how Goodwyn had risen to his current status. They had both been trainees around the same time, both qualified into the same department. And yet, when partnerships were being handed out, it was Goodwyn chosen and not him. Rumours at the time had been rife. Some had said that he was the nephew of Horton Flinch, the firm's aged and generally absent senior partner. Other, more hysterically, had claimed that Goodwyn was his lovechild. Mark's eyes slid to the ominous painting of a skeletal, gargoyle-like Horton Flinch which oversaw their departmental kitchen like a bat hanging from the ceiling. He briefly wondered who the mother would be. It didn't bear thinking about.

CHAPTER 15

Jess was sitting across from Sophie at Claridge's with her usual glass of champagne, trying to maintain a smile while her oldest friend held forth about her latest 'thrilling' life adventure.

'It's a tragedy,' Sophie was saying, shaking her head solemnly. 'A mid-August baby. A summer baby.' She looked up at the ceiling in despair as if her favourite colour lip gloss had been discontinued. She hadn't stopped for breath since announcing the sprog's imminent arrival thirty minutes ago. So far she had discussed everything from baby names – Octavius for a boy, Flavia for a girl - to private hospitals – The Portland was always the only place to go, but in the post-Kate era should I think of St Mary's? - and pre-schools – you have to put their name down at least six months before the birth.

Wasn't she now sharing her lungs with at least one other creature? Shouldn't she conserve?

Jess spent the time that Sophie was speaking assessing her outfit. She was pleased to see that her own ensemble compared favourably. Sophie's dress was this season's Balmain to her own Victoria Beckham. They both wore Stuart Weitzman shoes, but Sophie's bag was Bottega Veneta to her own Birkin. Jess saw with satisfaction that the seams of Sophie's dress were ever so slightly straining already. It was so fun to be able to comfortably compete with her friends on the fashion front. She felt a sense of serenity now that she had the resources to go with her eye for style.

'I was aiming for September,' Sophie was saying, 'but it happened so quickly. Poof! And we were pregnant. I should have realised. You know my body has always been ahead of the curve.' Sophie paused for a minute and Jess thought it might be a chance to change the subject, but then she continued thoughtfully. 'I am doing my pelvic floor exercises religiously though so I'm sure I can hold it in for a couple of weeks.' She seemed satisfied by this thought.

Then, Sophie did something horrific. She leaned forward and put her perfectly manicured - with natural fume-free (for the baby) polish – hand on Jess's chemical ridden talons and simpered, 'It'll happen for you too someday.'

Jess only just managed to stop herself from recoiling in horror. There were two things wrong with this statement. The first was the disgusting pity in Sophie's eyes. Nobody pitied Jess. Admired, feared, reviled, but never pitied.

Second, she had no interest whatsoever in being up the duff or 'expecting' as Sophie so sickeningly put it. Trust Sophie to presume that if someone wasn't at the same life stage as her it was because they weren't trying hard enough. But Jess knew better than to show any kind of disquiet at a statement such as this.

'Oh, thank you,' she replied sweetly instead. 'I guess that for now I'll have to make do with sushi, sleep and being a size eight,' she said, noting with glee the visible reduction in Sophie's glow.

Jess had actually come to meet Sophie for a much needed gossip and to air her latest thoughts about her work. She couldn't talk to Sophie about what she wanted to talk about – William. It wasn't so much that Sophie wouldn't approve. Jess was pretty sure she wouldn't care. Sophie's own moral compass was probably akin to that used by Bloody Mary. It was more that Jess would never admit to Sophie that her life was anything less than perfect.

She would never dream of telling Sophie that her relationship was in the bathroom, let alone down the toilet. Nonetheless it had become increasingly difficult to explain her ongoing relationship with a man whose sole ambition seemed to be running on the spot, at least where his career was concerned. At least he was looking better these days. Her heart did flutter somewhat when she remembered the muscles that now rippled underneath his business suits.

She thought of her clandestine meetings with William, secret not just because of Mark, but also her work. It wouldn't do to be seen cavorting with the father of one of her clients, a client of the firm himself. It just wasn't professional. It was especially bad for a woman. Yes, this was one area where her femininity worked against her. A man could do what he wanted, but women were judged when it came to affairs of the heart, or even just plain old affairs. Nevertheless she had allowed herself this indulgence. She deserved it. She worked hard. Eat your heart out Amal Clooney, she had thought with delight as she had watched her own older man, not a far cry from good old George, seated across from her at The Ivy the other night.

Of course the Force family business – they were the second biggest egg supplier in Europe – left something to be desired in terms of glamour. She tried not to listen whenever he had thrusting conversations which turned out to be about chicken feed or carton shapes. She didn't like to be reminded of the provenance of his profits, but she reasoned that William wore it well. He was so confident, so dynamic, such a *presence*. Everywhere they went people noticed them. They were hard to miss: Him the silver fox to her blond bombshell.

Initially she had kept him at arm's length. Kept things friendly, but business-like, replying to his emails, but not encouraging them. And yet in the past couple of weeks, something had shifted. At first she had allowed him to take her out for coffee, a discreet espresso at a small café in Covent Garden after work. That had paved the way for dinner and then-

She jolted at the thought of that kiss.

Yet it was frustrating in the extreme having nobody to share in her triumph. Her sister was away at some yogic ashram near Bangalore and so was completely incommunicado. And she didn't trust anybody else.

Work, meanwhile, was not offering anything by way of relaxation. Things in the office had become heated ever since the partners had announced that they would be promoting one associate from each department to the position of partner, but that this would be the final such set of partnerships for the foreseeable.

Jess wasn't sure if this was entirely true or whether it was said to provoke the rabid riot of backstabbing panic that inevitably followed, but she couldn't risk it either way. She had to get that partnership. Immediately she recognised that Zane was her main competitor and he knew the same.

It was game fucking on and she was determined to win.

She had needed a sounding board. Somebody with an equally devious mind to her own. Someone on her side. Sophie was supposed to have played that vital role. But apparently Sophie's mind was now less wit and wisdom and more wet around the ears. Undoubtedly she would be the most clued up, fashionable, functioning mummy in the societal suburbs, but that was not a place that Jess planned to be anytime soon.

Nope. She would have to handle this on her own.

That Monday morning, she was first in the office working hard by the time the big cheese, Anthony, strolled in at 8am. She smiled up at him and waved casually as if to say 'it's perfectly normal that I'm here before the cleaners have even finished their work'. But then the smile dropped from her face like a bad western set collapsing mid-scene. Walking just behind him was Zane, holding two cups of coffee and chatting to him animatedly. The two men laughed and, seeing her in her office, Zane lifted up a coffee-clasping hand in greeting, his smile wide and toothy. She forced herself to smile back, but was pretty sure it came out as a grimace.

Shit. If Zane was already sucking up she had some ground to make up. This called for drastic action. But what? Jess looked around her office as if the answer would present itself in amidst the stapler and her Dictaphone. Could she find any dirt on him? Something she could use to smear him? She rolled her eyes internally. She sounded like a bad 1950's detective film. Next thing she'd be setting a honey trap.

Jess decided that a proper plan would have to be devised. Yes she would google Zane on the off chance of finding something juicy that could prove his downfall, but she wouldn't rely on that. She would also have to go old-school. The tried and tested way to gain a partnership in any firm was to bring in the money. And the way to do that was to find new clients. So her work was cut out. If she could bring some real cash into the firm, that couldn't go unnoticed.

Out of the corner of her eye she saw that Sacha, her trainee, was already at her desk. How long had she been there?

'Sacha,' she said tersely, causing the girl to almost jump out of her chair. 'Get me the Sunday Times Rich List and highlight the ones based in London. Focus specifically on those who aren't clients of ours and those on second marriages.' After all, she thought. If it's happened once, it was hardly a giant step to imagine they might divorce again.

Pleased with this, Jess turned back to her work. The DeFornicus case was shaping up nicely. Mrs DeFornicus had managed to uncover some financial statements that made fascinating bedtime reading. It transpired that Mr DeFornicus had been paying a regular sum of money to a woman called Fanny Queen from a credit card his wife knew nothing about. It took Sacha very little time on the web to uncover that Ms Queen was a transsexual dominatrix in Soho with a special attachment to Lindt chocolate balls. Even Jess, who considered herself unflappable, had had to look away from the woman's YouTube videos at certain points.

The only slight downside had been that the firm's computer system had flagged up Sacha's online activities as 'inappropriate' and automatically cut off her internet access. It took a full 24 hours and some rather uncomfortable conversations with the IT department to sort out the mess, but in the meantime Jess had been left without a full functioning trainee, but that was over with and now she had her choice of divorce grounds. Should she go for adultery or unreasonable behaviour? Both were options.

Jess looked at the photograph she had of Fanny Queen lying on a bed of rose petals, her legs splayed in a manner that could be described as gynaecological/gymnastic. Which was more likely to be seen as legally thrusting? She decided on unreasonable behaviour. Much more fun to be had there. She emailed Sacha to instruct her to draft the appropriate court forms before looking at her to do list.

An email popped up on Jess's screen. 'Your Net-A-Porter order is on its way.' She smiled as she thought of the beautifully packaged Mansur Gavriel tote that was on its way to her office. Looking further down the list of emails, she saw the one earlier that week from Mark, asking for donations for his run.

It was so humiliating. The Three Peaks? Couldn't he have done something more fashionable? Lance had just completed the Inca Trail in record time, including a section called the 'Hike of Death.' Walking up a hill in Scotland hardly compared. She knew that Lance and Amelie were laughing behind their backs and it drove her to distraction. She would have to have a word with Mark about this.

CHAPTER 16

It was a week before the challenge and Mark was making his way to Finchley, North London to Branning's house. Branning's wife, Gem was out with her friends and, despite the fact that they were almost six months old, it was Branning's first time alone with all three of his children.

'I need the extra pair of hands,' he had said into the phone. Was that desperation in his voice?

'Won't they be asleep?' Mark had asked. He was due to come round at 8pm. His knowledge of little humans was scant, but surely they had a bedtime.

'Yes,' Branning replied, sounding the very epitome of a dejected dad. 'Yes they should.'

When Branning opened the door that night, Mark's smile dropped off his face so fast it was like an ice cube that had melted in the sun. He couldn't believe the sight that met him. Branning was dressed in a tracksuit that had long since passed the point of elasticity and which was covered in several shades of what Mark guessed was baby sick. He was holding a crying child while further noises could be heard in the near distance, perhaps emanating from the living room. It reminded Mark of hearing seagulls squawk in the unseen distance as he approached the sea as a child.

'What the-,' Mark started before Branning used his free hand to drag him inside.

'Grab a baby,' Branning said in a no-nonsense tone as he rushed back and towards the kitchen.

'What?' Mark asked, still holding a bottle of wine aloft. He had no experience of children. All he knew was that whenever they went to one of Jess's friends' houses and he was asked to hold a new baby, he was desperate to give them back as soon as they were handed to him. 'Mate, I really don't know what I'm doing,' he said nervously.

'You think I do?' Branning said, his hysteria causing his voice to reach a higher pitch than Mark had ever heard. He was now bobbing up and down with a child in each arm in what was presumably a soothing fashion. 'You don't get any instruction manuals with them you know. Consider this your training. Now go and pick up Kate. I think she's got wind.'

Gingerly, in the same way he had approached the tarantula at his eighth birthday party which his mum had thought would be 'so much fun', Mark walked up to the playpen where a bawling Kate was shaking her fist angrily.

'Shouldn't she be in her cot?' Mark asked, peering at her.

'I thought you knew nothing about babies,' Branning hissed. 'Yes she should be in her cot, Mary Poppins. Please can you calm her down so we can do exactly that? They've been screaming for the past hour and Gemma isn't due back 'til eleven. Her instructions said to bob up and down but so far no success. I've fed them, rocked them, changed them and read them everything from The Gruffalo to the cornflakes box, but nothing is working. So unless you have some genius idea just shut up and pick up.' Branning finished his alarming diatribe by motioning to the play pen.

Gingerly, Mark reached down and picked up Kate from under her armpits, lifting her up and examining her face. The moment he did this, Kate stopped crying. Then, as if shocked by this development or awaiting instructions, her brother and sister ceased their bawling as well.

There was silence. Sweet, unadulterated peace. Mark had never appreciated it so much before. When the three of them were yelling it was impossible to string together a thought let alone a plan.

Branning stopped bobbing and they all stood stock still. It was like a scene from a World War II film. One where the soldiers are creeping through fields and one of them holds up their arm in a 'wait' gesture. They were all uncertain of what to do next.

Mark and Kate surveyed each other, Kate's pudgy face pure perfection in its disgruntled gaze. She was assessing her adversary. Plotting her next move. Mark could respect that. Her eyelids drooped slightly igniting the hope that she might be falling asleep. He smiled at her. She really was very sweet. But instantly he knew he had made a mistake. Kate's eyes widened in alarm as though she was thinking, 'who the hell is this?' Then her face crumpled into itself and she let out a shriek louder than any Mark had heard before. Enemy fire.

On cue, her siblings, Cara and Jack joined in while Branning resumed his frantic bobs.

'This isn't working,' Mark yelled over the din. 'What else have you got?'

And so, for the next hour and a half, they experimented with the world of infant sleep techniques. They tried rocking, swaying, bobbing, walking round in circles, singing, humming and walking them in a buggy up and down the road.

Both Mark and Branning lost it at several points in the procedure, not least when two of the children seemed to be nodding off only for the third to wake them with a well-timed screech.

When they had finally given up hope, they alighted on the television. 'Gem's going to kill me if she finds out,' Branning said as they sat in the flickering light of the TV screen, a colourful cartoon world before them. The moment they had turned it on, it had been like magic. All three children's pupils had dilated and they had, as one, been silenced. There had been murmurs of discontent when choosing the right programme. Kate preferred Baby TV while Cara liked BBC News 24 – Mark made a note to keep an eye on her. None of them liked Channel 4. In the end, they had settled for the satire of the dark comedy of *Family Guy*. There was a marathon of the show on some obscure satellite channel.

It took three attempts, but in the end they managed to get all three babies in their cots before they heard Gemma's key in the door.

'Hi Mark,' Gemma said breezily, a pleasant smile on her face.

After a quick chat, Gemma went upstairs and Branning led Mark into their garage, where he had set up what could only be described as a big boy's fort. There was a football table, an old TV and a fridge which it turned out held a decent stock of Coronas.

They sat and started drinking, talking about work and old times, Branning telling him how hard it had been over the past few months. But overall, despite being exhausted and unshaven and frazzled, Branning looked happy. Miserable, but happy. Somehow that was the most accurate description of his friend at that moment. Mark was struck by the fact that he wished he had been more involved with his friend's struggles with fatherhood.

'I feel like we never see each other anymore,' Mark said wistfully.

'I know. It's been hard lately,' Branning said, taking a swig from his beer. He was already slurring slightly. 'We never get out because we haven't got a babysitter and we're too exhausted most of the time. Gemma only went tonight cos it was her friend's fortieth and even then I couldn't go without a babysitter. Even our parents are still too scared to do it.'

'Jess and I could come to you and we could all have a night in. Get a takeaway. Maybe a film.' Mark couldn't help but notice that he too was struggling to get his words out. He wasn't sure if it was exhaustion or the effects of his third beer.

'Mmm,' Branning's response was non-committal.

'What?' Mark knew his friend all too well.

'No, it's a great idea. We'll definitely do that,' Branning said quickly.

'No, come on,' Mark said, turning to look at him. 'What is it? You were going to say something.'

'It's nothing,' Branning replied. 'I wouldn't know how to say it,' he said dismissively.

'You sound like you're trying to ask me out to prom,' Mark said laughing. 'Out with it. You never know. I might say yes.'

This seemed to be the cue Branning was waiting for.

'It's Gem,' he said.

'Oh god, is this about the stag do?' Mark asked. 'I said I was sorry and I had no idea they would lock you in that room with her. And anyway, nothing happened.'

'No, no, she's over that. Sort of. It's more about Jess.'

'Jess?' Mark managed to ask, dreading whatever was coming next.

'She sort of. Well, she sort of um. Terrifies her,' The last two words were blurted out. Then, as if realising what he'd done, he froze. And Mark froze. They seemed to sit there for an age, silent and unmoving.

Then, to his surprise, Mark began to laugh. It started as a silent chuckle but was soon a stomach clenching, tear jerking, pant inducing laugh of fall about proportions. They were both doing it. Mark wasn't sure when Branning had joined in, but there they were, grabbing onto the sides of their plastic garden chairs and rocking with the force of it.

Just as they were calming down, Mark said, 'Gemma is scared of Jess.' Like the triplets starting a new wave of crying, the two men collapsed into another helpless fit of giggles. How drunk *were* they? It was probably the mix of beer and post-trauma relief, but at that moment, Mark felt a sense of such brotherhood, of camaraderie with his old friend. He was lucky to call him a mate.

'I'm terrified of her too,' Mark found himself saying in gasps. 'Do you know,' he wheezed, 'she won't let me tell anyone I've won the lottery?'

That was it. The laughter was unstoppable now.

'Ten million,' he said, wiping tears from the sides of his eyes.

It took several minutes for them to calm down. Their breathing only eventually slowed and their faces straightened. They sat in their garden chairs, holding onto their beer bottles and looking into space.

Bloody hell,' Branning finally said simply. 'So that's why you've started dressing like a 1980's pop star.'

'Yep.'

'Should've known. Want to stay in the spare room?'

'Yes please.'

Waking up in Branning's home office the next day, Mark was beset by the buzzing of his phone. Thinking it must be Jess wondering where he was, he groped around, picking it up from the floor and only just managed to answer.

'Mark Jones? Mary Stoppard here from the Daily Mail,' said a pleasant, but business-like tone. 'What do you say to people who accuse you of being the very epitome of everything that's wrong with the world?'

What? Mark blinked. What was happening?

'Mr Jones, we really want to tell your side of the story. This has gotten out of hand and you need to get out there with your best foot forward.'

Something about feet. Wiping some drool which had escaped from the side of his mouth, he tried to come to grips with what was being hurled at him, but instead he fumbled and accidentally disconnected the call.

He was still lying prostrate when it rang again. This time, he checked the caller ID and was relieved to find that it was Jess.

'You won't believe what some crazy woman just said to me-,' he began.

'What the hell have you done?' Jess was yell-whispering at him. Mark stared at the phone again, just to check it was indeed his girlfriend on the other line.

'Huh?' His addled brain sifted through possibilities. She could be referring to anything. Most of what Mark did was a matter of disapproval for Jess. Had she been worried when he hadn't come home last night? 'Sorry.' This seemed to be the only safe reply.

'We have journalists on our doorstep, Mark. There are camera flashbulbs and fat guys in leathers having coffee outside our home,' she said, the controlled nature of her tone only underlining her anger. Jess was never more dangerous than when she was holding back. It was like talking to a coiled snake, ready to pounce. 'And I haven't had my hair done!'

'Why would they be there? Are you sure it's not for two doors down?' That was where a TV chef lived with his glamorous wife and three children. She was frequently seen striding up and down Hampstead High Street with a stroller while a cameraman followed her as though she was on a catwalk.

'You. Tell. Me,' she enunciated and Mark detected a definite undercurrent of boiling rage.

'Hold on,' Mark said as his phone buzzed. He looked at it. He could see that there were several messages, one from his mum:

'Call me!!! :)'

Others were from members of the lottery group. The words swam before his eyes. He couldn't make sense of anything. He needed coffee. His head as hurting and he was pretty sure he's been lying on a – yes, it was a beer bottle.

'Jess, I've got a call on my other line. Let me see what it is,' he said and, while she was still protesting into the receiver, he switched calls.

'I am so sorry mate.' It was Paul. 'Dina did it. I had no idea.'

Mark was glad to hear his friend's voice, but couldn't understand the substance of what he was saying. 'Did what?' he asked.

'Oh shit, you haven't seen.' There was a pause. 'Dina told *OK!* about our charity challenge and, um, about the group. She thought it would be good column fodder. It came out this morning.'

Mark tried to compute what Paul was saying. 'So, everyone knows about the lottery group.'

'Yes.'

'And that we're in it.'

'Correct.'

'And that we're doing the Three Peaks.'

'All right so far,' Paul confirmed slowly.

Mark ran his finger through his hair. It was taking his mind an inordinate amount of time to analyse the exact ramifications of this. He tried to hurry it along. Ok, so everyone would know. Friends. Family. Work. He couldn't decide if this was a good or a bad thing. On the one hand, what a relief. No more lying. No more obfuscation. He could just be honest with everyone. It was like a weight being lifted.

On the other...

'I've got cameras outside my house,' he told Paul.

'Yeah, me too,' Paul commiserated. 'Been there all morning the bastards. Dina keeps bringing them coffee.' He paused. 'Look I'm really sorry, I know you were anonymous. I feel terrible.'

For some reason, it was this last statement that made Mark realise that his parents might have found out about it. And he hadn't been the one to tell them. His mum loved the papers, especially those that specialised in gossip and human-interest stories. Had she read about it already?

Just then, Mark saw Branning out of the corner of his eye. His friend had come in with a coffee and his iPad. He laid the tablet on Mark's lap and pointed to the screen. It was on the homepage of the *Daily Mail*, which read *'Moaning Millionaires Plan Climb to the Top'*. There was a photo of Dina and Paul from *OK!* along with one of Rick from when he accepted his lottery cheque. And there it was. A photo of him chugging from a giant yard long beer glass while his drunken mates cheered him on. He looked like a lager lout let out on parole. He knew immediately where they had got it. He recognised it from Branning's stag do photos, which festooned his friend's Facebook page.

143

'Don't worry,' he said into the phone, although he for one was not following that particular piece of advice. As he accepted the coffee from Branning, Mark skimmed the bullet points of the article. It said things like 'Lottery funds paying for winners' weekly meet ups to whinge about winning' and 'the thrill-seeking threesome all hail from a wealthy suburb in North London.'

It seemed to have everything: How much each of them had won, their previous (and in his case current) occupations and even some of the things they spent their money on. Yet, rather than focus on how they were raising money for charity, it made it sound like they were lazy layabouts trying to fill their days.

Flicking to the comments section didn't make him feel any better.

'What do these F&%$ers need a support group for? They've won the f&$@ing lottery! Makes me sick' SPEAKZ TA TRUTH UK

'I for one am tired of generation me. I want this I want that and I'm not happy when I get it. Bring back conscription.' London Lady 45

Branning looked at him dubiously. 'Mate,' he said, shaking his head.

'I know,' Mark replied. What was he going to do? He couldn't just sit there. For one thing, he thought, looking at his watch, he had to be at work in an hour. Then there was the matter of Jess, trapped in their home, a prisoner of the paparazzi.

He had to act. Luckily, he had failed to remove so much as his shoes before falling asleep last night so he was ready for action. He downed his coffee, thanked Branning and yelled a hello/goodbye/sorry to Gemma as he ran through the house and out to his car.

Like a Hasslehoffian hero in his own Kitt from *Knight Rider* or Kevin Costner in *The Bodyguard*, Mark dialled Jess and spoke urgently.

'I'm coming to get you,' he said. Unfortunately, she didn't seem all too impressed.

'That's just great,' she grumbled 'I'm late for work.'

By the time he had reached their house, the paps were restricted to the pavement, a couple of police officers who Jess must have called standing by the door. When they realised he was opening the garage to get into the house, they all started shouting and banging on his windows as he passed. It was like being in the monkey enclosure of Windsor Safari Park. But finally, he managed to manoeuvre the Porsche into the safety of the garage where Jess was waiting for him, arms crossed.

'You joined a *support* group?' she said, only part question. It was actually more of a dumbfounded statement. Mark couldn't help but notice that Jess said "support group" much as someone else would have said murderous cult, but he couldn't blame her.

'It's just a group. The support bit is incidental,' he defended.

'Oh my god, do you know what you've done?' she raged. 'Everybody knows. Everybody.' Her eyes were as wide as saucers. 'I've had calls from my mum asking why I didn't tell her and from my office asking if I'm coming in today and from my primary school headmistress asking for a donation for fucking whiteboards.'

'That sounds like a worthy thing to do-,'

'Mark!' She was properly yelling now. 'So, when you were at running club you were actually meeting up with a group of saddos to do what? Cry about winning the lottery?'

'No,' Mark said patiently, trying to keep his mind on the task of driving. 'When I said I was at running club I was training. We're doing the Three Peaks, remember? It's just that I was training with some of the other members. I went to the group meetings instead of the chiropractor.'

This seemed almost worse in Jess's eyes. 'During work hours? Are you *trying* not to get promoted?'

'I think you're missing the point here,' he said, trying to sound reasonable.

'You're the one missing the point,' she snapped. 'Christ, Mark. It was bad enough when you were a lazy bastard who didn't try. Now you're a famous one.'

There was no way to respond to that. He tried, really he did, but his mouth just flapped in silent uselessness.

'Where were you anyway?' she asked, now slightly calmer.

'Branning's. I fell asleep. I sent you a text,' he said.

'Ah, yes, you mean the one that said,' she pulled out her phone and started reading 'Studying a bra nod black tornado.'

Bloody predictive text.

'I'm pretty sure that said staying at Branning back tomorrow,' he mumbled.

'Of course.'

'Look,' he said, keen to move on. 'It's done now. Shall we just go to work? We're already late.'

A dark silence carried them the rest of the way. Fortunately their offices weren't too far from each other's and it appeared that no photographers were camped outside either one so they both made their ways to work unmolested. Mark breathed a sigh of relief as he negotiated the rotating door to his office building.

It was here that he realised he may have underestimated the effects of the media attention. As he entered the lobby, the security guard put down his paper and presented him with a manic smile. Usually, he greeted him with a quick, curt nod, but not today.

'Morning Mr Jones, lovely to see you,' he said loudly in his Estuary accent.

Things got even weirder in the office. The moment he arrived, all eyes were on him. He felt like the last person in a horror film not to be taken over by the pod people: conspicuous. Everyone bore wide-eyed expressions, some filled with shock, others with wonder and, most terrifyingly, a few of lust.

'Jones can I see you in my office,' barked Goodwyn before Mark had even managed to take his jacket off.

'So,' Goodwyn said once they were sitting across from one another, Goodwyn's hands clasped together thoughtfully. Mark couldn't help but glance as he always did at the photos of Goodwyn around his office. They weren't, as so many people's were, of family or loved ones. Instead, Goodwyn surrounded himself with his own image. Goodwyn cycling across a finish line, Goodwyn alone on a beach. It was enough to make Narcissus blush. 'I don't know what's been going on, but I won't have you disrupting the firm.'

'Yes, sorry, I had some trouble getting in,' Mark said, internally congratulating himself on the understatement of the century.

'Jones,' Goodwyn said, much in the manner of a headmaster trying to reason with the boy who tried to eat the class pet. 'Here at Porpoise, Fielding and Smudge, we pride ourselves on providing a professional service.' He paused then added sombrely, 'A prostitutio ministerium.'

Mark blinked. His boss had just told him they ran a prostitution ministry in Latin. Had he meant professional? There was no time to dwell on this because Goodwyn wasn't finished.

146

'It is one built on a values-based ethos of actioned thinking and proactive movements,' he continued determinedly. 'I need team players. We cannot have our associates cavorting around in the national press for winning the lottery. It is simply not the Porpoise way.'

'Right, well,' Mark said in as professional a manner as he could muster. Stay calm, he told himself. 'I'm terribly sorry if I've caused any disruption,' he said. 'I'll do my best not to let it happen again.'

Goodwyn's face now contorted in a way which Mark couldn't interpret. It was like it couldn't decide which way to go.

'Is that everything?' Mark finally asked.

'Um,' Goodwyn was clearly trying to form a sentence which simply wouldn't emerge and his face was bearing the brunt. Any moment now Mark feared it would split into two. Finally, his boss muttered, 'Yes Jones. That's it. Back to your office.'

'Ok, then,' Mark said, part relieved, part decisive as he gingerly got up. He had a feeling Goodwyn had been desperate to say something about the news stories, but didn't know how.

As he left Goodwyn behind to stew, he felt an entire City firm screech to a halt to stare at him as he walked back to his office. It was only when he shut his door that everything started up again in earnest. As soon as the latch clicked, it was like the mute button had been pressed again, allowing sound back in. Phones started ringing again, keyboards were tapped, conversations continued.

His office roommate, Jez, was at his desk as Mark entered. Never one known for his subtlety, nor his work ethic, Jez stopped working and languidly came to sit at the chair by Mark's desk.

'So,' he said, his Brummy tone drawing the word out in exaggerated nonchalance. 'What's new?'

'Whatever do you mean?' Mark asked, eyes firmly on his computer screen.

'Rumour round the photocopier and, well, the world, is that you've come into a bit of money.' Jez had his hands clasped together, two fingers tapping against each other in his 'means business' pose.

'Yes,' Mark said levelly, still appearing to concentrate on his computer, which hadn't even logged on yet.

'So what the hell are you still doing here?' Jez's excitement forced Mark to look up to see his colleague's incredulous gawp. 'I mean, ten mil? I'd be halfway to Fiji by now with a bevy of gorgeous women on a decent sized yacht.' He looked wistfully off into the middle distance.

'Well, we decided to go more low key. And I have a girlfriend.'

'Oh my god. I mean. This is huge. We should go out and celebrate,' Jez was saying. He was now pacing around like a ball of pent up energy.

Mark couldn't help but smile at his colleague's excitement. He wished he felt as thrilled about it as Jez clearly would have had he won. He had the sudden urge to just give Jez all the money. This wasn't the first time he'd felt like this. In the months since he'd won, there had been several occasions when he'd thought of impulsively transferring the funds to a random bank account or just handing a massive wad of cash to a person on the street. It was just such a huge sum that sometimes it felt easier to let someone else carry the burden. There was a very thin line stopping him on those occasions and it was only just about there now.

Maybe Jez wouldn't have been as excited if he'd actually won. After all, Mark had, like everyone else, thought he'd known exactly how he'd feel if the unlikely happened. But then, when it did, his brain had taken a sharp turn in a direction he couldn't rationalise. It was like winning had compromised his thinking.

'Tell you what mate,' he said to Jez, 'Let's go to The Stag later this week,' he suggested, naming the firm's favoured pub. 'We'll have some drinks and I'll tell you all about it.'

'Deal,' Jez said smiling. Then, in what reminded Mark of a guy who's just been asked out on a date by the prettiest girl in the class, Jez let out a little giggle and added, 'Drinks on you!' before sitting back down.

For the next few hours, everything felt refreshingly normal. He stayed off the phone and spent his time drafting wills and checking some figures. There was also a research article he'd been putting off which he finally completed. It was so easy to just ignore the world. Even if his office had become like the London Aquarium equivalent of fishbowls, with people constantly trying to peep through the shutters to catch a glimpse of the giant lottery whale in their midst.

It was only when he checked his phone and found 132 missed calls, one of them from his mum and another from his dad that he knew he would have to resurface. They must know, he thought. They never phoned in the middle of the day on a weekday for no reason.

'Oh, hello love,' his mother said on the phone a few minutes later after he's started with the traditional 'hi mum, it's me'. She sounded exactly the same as she always did.

'Did you ring?'

'Oh, yes,' his mother began. 'I was chatting to Mrs Finnegan and she said that her daughter's also a lawyer in the city. Her name's Lucy. I can't remember her surname because she's married now. Do you know her?'

'Mum that is ridiculous, how would I-,' Mark stopped. He knew there was never any point in trying to reason his way out of these conversational cul-de-sacs. 'No mum, I don't think I do.'

'Oh and Judy said she saw you in the papers,' his mum jabbered. Mark could just picture her drying a dish with a towel as she spoke. 'Silly woman started going on about how you'd won the lottery. Honestly that woman can be a gossip sometimes. I was half tempted to tell her she should take her medication only I'm not supposed to know about that and I promised Jane I wouldn't say anything-,'

'Mum haven't you read the papers today?' Mark interrupted.

'Not yet,' his mum said indignantly. 'I'm busy. I've been out to Pilates. Oh you should see what we do, it's fantastic. I've never felt better. Do you exercise?'

Mark rubbed his hand over his face, wondering what to say next. How could he have let it get to this?

'Mum its true.'

'What is darling?' His mother asked, the clatter of dishes being stacked on a shelf in the background.

'What Judy said,' he replied. All sounds of crockery being moved ceased. 'Mum, I won the lottery.'

'Oh, right,' his mum said brightly. 'That's lovely dear. How much did you win?'

It was after Mark told her that the very distinctive noise of Denby plate smashing into porcelain floor echoed loudly down the line.

CHAPTER 17

'So you're here to seek my services,' Mick Crawford said, his beady eyes and thin lips spread into a smile that was more lizard-like than likeable. He joined his bony fingers together in an arc and swivelled his chair slightly to the right, allowing him a full view of his window and the London skyline beyond it. 'I can see your problem,' he said thoughtfully. 'People want to believe that they're going to win the lottery. You've taken what they believe is rightfully theirs. And now you want to complain about it too.' He shook his head and tutted.

Mark saw his point, but was in no mood to admit it. He looked at Mick Crawford. Yes he had a certain reptilian repulsiveness, but his record as the number one PR man for any public figure in trouble spoke for itself. It had been Mick who had turned around public opinion when one particular football club's players were caught holding a festively themed 'Santa claws and bitches' Christmas do one year. There had been so many public apologies and family spreads of the players in question in OK! that, by the time he had finished, the men in question were being lauded as feminists.

But nevertheless, this was a dubious step. Did they really want – or perhaps need – to get him involved? Mark thought back to when the suggestion had first been mooted. It had been at Holly's house the week before.

'Why the hell do they need a support group?' One man had yelled over the radio waves in his strong Welsh accent. 'Isn't it enough that they've won millions? It's disgusting. I tell you I support my seven children and my wife myself without anybody else on a postman's salary. Where's my support group?' The voice was tinny but the aggression was clear.

'Thank you Bryn from Cardiff. Sonia, you're on next. What do you want to say?'

'Nikki I think we're all forgetting that, yes they're millionaires, but they're people too,' a woman's Scottish accented voice crooned. 'And they were doing this charity event for a good cause. I think we should cut them a break.'

'Ooh, Sonia,' Nikki Campbell said teasingly in his deepest, smoothest tone. 'You're a lone voice from what we've had this morning. Most of our listeners here on 5live are incensed. Aren't you? This group, this ungrateful lot have won a massive £128 million between them, but they're still not happy,' he said with the fervour of a TV evangelist. 'They want our sympathy now as well. They *need* support.' He put a great deal of emphasis on the word 'need'. 'And Avalon is footing the bill!'

'Well,' Sonia said, sounding a lot less certain.

'A lot of people have compared them to benefit scroungers, Sonia. Getting something for nothing. You don't like scroungers, do you? Would you be in favour of a support group for benefit scroungers?'

At this point, Paul had switched off the radio. 'It's been like that for days,' he'd moaned as they all sat in Holly's living room that Wednesday afternoon for their meeting. They had stopped going to the church hall as its location had been leaked online, meaning that there was a constant supply of photographers hovering nearby just waiting for one of the members of the 'whining winners' – the moniker given to them by the tabloid press – to turn up.

'That's nothing,' Holly had said. 'Apparently the teachers' unions are going on strike to protest lottery funds being spent on frivolous things instead of on whiteboards.'

'I'm pretty sure the socialist party have joined in with that,' Paul said miserably. 'Something about the capitalist state and repressing the working people.' He stopped and his face darkened. 'I *am* a working man. Worked all my life on building sites. What the hell are they talking about?'

'I heard there was an online petition for lottery wins to be taxed at 50%,' Derek said.

'Yeah, I heard that one,' Mark said. 'It was in the papers today. 20,000 signatures so far.'

'This is getting out of control,' Mark had concluded to nods all round.

And that was when Annie had suggested Mick Crawford.

'Just hear me out,' she had said, index finger lifted, said as Rick prepared to shout her down. 'Everyone is against us right now. We just want someone to put forward our point of view. Get our side across.'

None of them had been particularly excited at the prospect, but Annie had convinced them to at least meet with him. And that's where they were now.

'What you need are some press appearances,' Mick was saying, his eyes gleaming like a man who's discovered a tomato shaped in the image of the Lord. Then he just started listing TV shows excitedly. *This Morning, Loose Women, The One Show, Come Dine with Me, Escape to the Country, Jeremy Kyle.*'

'We've won the lottery not slept with our entire family. What would we do on Jeremy Kyle?' Paul had queried, but nobody seemed to notice.

'You go on, tell your side, look like passable human beings and milk the human-interest side. Tell them how you've helped your gran or done stuff for charity or moved out of your council estate.' He paused here. 'Have any of you got a life-threatening illness?' Silence. 'Can any of you sing?' When this too was met with nothing he waved it away. 'We'll find things.'

'Do all of us have to do it?' Derek asked nervously.

'The more of you the better,' Mick had said shortly before looking at Derek again. 'Probably not you. Let me see which of you the media want. You I can definitely work with,' he said to Annie. 'And you, with your young mum thing. You're made for daytime screens,' he said to Holly.

And so they had agreed a trial of Mick Crawford's services. As such, Annie had found herself looking into the doe eyes of Holly Willoughby and Phil Scofield as she told her sad story of growing up on the mean streets of Archway, while their own Holly had been embraced by the gaggle of Loose Women in which she laughed along and debated such hot mummy topics as public breastfeeding and mum/baby parking spaces. Even Derek found himself a guest slot on *The Antiques Roadshow*, explaining why the train set an old biddy had found in her attic was more pound shop than priceless.

Mark was pleased that he had gotten away with nothing more than having to write an article in *The Guardian* about charitable giving amongst the uber rich. It was a sort of millionaire's mea culpa. A subtle apology for his newly found wealth entitled *'Why I can Never Give Enough'*.

And people had responded. The papers had visibly reduced the column inches they had previously devoted to winner bashing. The radios fell silent on the issues of ungrateful riches. And Channel 4 had stopped showing that horrid documentary about how the lottery was rigged, replacing it with an ode to fallen lottery winners.

All in all it felt like things were on the up, even at home. At first, Jess had been somewhat reticent. Furious was probably a more accurate description. It wasn't just that he had joined a support group or that he had done it behind her back. As all of the details of the group's activities emerged she seemed completely incapable of grasping what kind of bond he could feel to this contrasting collection of people.

'So that guy on the Heath with that horrendous pile on Bishops Avenue is in your little group then,' she had said, mid rant the night after the revelations had hit the press. She'd shaken her head. 'It says here he's a builder from Essex. What the hell do you have in common with a builder from Essex? And why would you tell him our private business?'

'I wasn't sharing military secrets,' Mark sighed. 'We just talked about life and stuff.'

Jess had rolled her eyes and shaken her head. She had been frosty for days. But then, one day, she had come home early, a bottle of Pinot Grigio in hand and kissed him on the cheek.

'What's this in aid of?' he had asked, now holding the bottle.

'Oh nothing,' she had breezed.

In fact, he had finally managed, after a few glasses, to get her to confess that the lottery win had brought her some positive publicity. So much so that she'd been able to attract numerous new well-heeled clients.

'Turns out,' she said, 'That money likes money. One of them actually called me 'One of us',' she said jubilantly. 'They love that I have money. They think it means I won't try to shaft them.'

She had clinked Mark's glass with her own and smiled smugly at the screen as that night's episode of Question Time started.

153

'The first question,' Dimbelby announced as he studied his notes. 'Should the media publicly apologize to the members of the lottery support group for their appalling treatment at their hands?'

Well done Mick, Mark thought. Worth every penny.

CHAPTER 18

Jess was practically humming as she tip tapped on her keyboard, so pleased was she with her latest venture. It had been bold, yes. Possibly even ruthless, but undoubtedly pure genius.

Not only had she been pulling in new clients off the streets of Knightsbridge by the limousine load, not only had she manged to turn Mark's ridiculous lottery win into a professional one for herself, but she had also undertaken her very own one woman mission to take down that smug bastard, Zane. She had concocted it the other night at a firm cocktail event as she watched one of the older female partners, Georgina Holt, flirt up a storm with him.

Pinot Noir in hand and in her red ruched Donna Karan dress which she knew only a toned figure such as hers could pull off, Jess had studied him. There he was, on her patch, smiling and laughing along with Georgina. Possibly about to take her partnership. The partnership she had worked so hard for. And all because he looked good in a Gucci suit. She watched as he threw his head back in an exaggerated laugh in response to a comment of Georgina's. It made her sick.

And that had set her thinking. Zane had been hired as some sort of eye candy for the ladies, but what if that became a liability? What if, rather than charming them, he actually upset one of their more important female clients? What if there was incontrovertible proof that he had done so?

She had enjoyed the plotting, the scheming. It was what she was built for. In the end she had picked Doris Fingernut-Schultz. At 89 years of age, Doris was not only the firm's longest-standing client, but also one of their most valued. She had married into the Schultz bakery dynasty at the age of 24 and had been a strong, leading light in propelling that business into the twentieth and twenty-first centuries respectively. She was tough, smart and savvy. She also had an iron will and the ferocity a Doberman would die for. Doris was not one to be trifled with.

Jess had been furious when Anthony had asked Zane and not her to assist with Doris's daughter's divorce. Doris's four girls were fond of divorcing their husbands. It was what they did in between rounds of Botox. In the past, Jess had always been Anthony's go-to-solicitor of choice. So why had he picked Zane? It had been the last straw.

Last night, when Zane had gone to fetch his usual 9:03pm coffee from the kitchen, Jess had acted. She'd had to be quick. He always took exactly nine minutes to go to the loo, prepare his drink, have a quick chat with the night porter and return. She ran into his room and moved the mouse erratically. She had to get to the computer before it locked. She had no idea what his password was so she needed it to be open. Then she used her phone to email him the message she had prepared, copied and pasted it into a new message and sent it to Doris's email address. This hadn't been her first secret foray into Zane's room, but it was her final, master touch. She took one last look at the message:

'Dear Doris

I am terribly sorry to disturb you. I know that things have been tough with Lizzy's divorce and I wanted to let you know that I am here if you need a shoulder to cry on, or anything else.

Please forgive my impertinence. I have been watching you from afar and I so admire both your work and you as a woman. I have always felt that I have an affinity with the more mature woman, but I sense we have a connection and one that I hope can flourish into so much more.

Yours, if you'll have me,

Zane'

She jolted her head up at the sound of approaching footsteps. Quickly, she double deleted her message to Zane from his email inbox, making sure to get rid of it entirely and locked his computer, ensuring not to leave even a clue she had been there.

Having managed to exit unnoticed, she returned to her room and started packing up. Her work was done after all. Things would get better soon.

Now, on the dull rainy morning of that February day, Jess knew she wouldn't have to wait for long. She imagined how Doris's eyes would bulge in disgust as she read the message. How Zane would be called into Anthony's office.

'We've had a complaint,' Anthony would say, concern etched onto his grave face. He would be confused. He would expect Zane to deny it and would be grateful when he did. He would excuse it as inappropriate prankery and set up an investigation to check who had done this to his golden boy. The only thing is, the investigation would uncover some rather unsavoury truths – sort of.

For, when they went through Zane's computer, they would find that every evening at about 9:05pm, he logged into his regular accounts at toyboytrash.com and sugarmummiesforyou.co.uk to continue his rather forward flirtations with women of a more mature vintage. There were also the unexpectedly bold photos of his conquests to be found in a secret folder simply titled 'Mutton'. Jess was especially proud of this. After all, nobody would believe that a young handsome guy like Zane would just suddenly letch onto an elderly lady. Not unless he had a history of such things. It had taken military like precision, a gag reflex of steel and quite a bit of imagination to juggle as many 'cougars' as she had done for Zane of late.

There would be hushed horror, embarrassing meetings and, finally, a discreet conclusion to Zane's employment at Drakers LLP.

She looked at her watch and up across the hall where Zane was on the phone, absentmindedly swivelling in his chair as he spoke. It was almost lunchtime. Surely Doris had checked her emails by now. And yet nothing. Never mind. It would happen. And when it did she would have a front row seat.

She looked at her screen where she was working on the Feign divorce when an email popped up in the corner of her screen. It was from Sir William. Somehow the whole lottery story had completely passed him by. Of course, he was in the middle of a particularly tetchy takeover of a large chicken farm somewhere up north. Apparently their egg laying capabilities would help them crack the US market. Whatever the numbers, it meant that stories about lottery winners were small fry to him at the moment. She read his message.
'Hey gorgeous. Dinner?'

She smiled and bit her lip, starting to type immediately, 'Just thinking of you.' It was true enough. She had just been thinking of his daughter's divorce. Then she stopped. Could she do dinner that night? She racked her brain as to her evening plans. She hadn't eaten dinner with Mark in so long now it felt like they were ships passing in the night. He had said he would be home that night. And, while she did hope that William might provide an excellent alternative to Mark in the long run, she certainly didn't want to count her chickens, so to speak.

'Can't do tonight I'm afraid. Rain check?'

She tried to leave it vague. Non-committal. Pressing send she emailed her secretary to request that she bring up her usual lunch and then turned back to her work.

She was pleased when, that evening, Mark was not only home, but greeted her with a bottle of red and a takeaway.

'Hello stranger,' he called out as she entered their large kitchen/back room extension. The designer lighting was set to a perfect mixture of dimmed in the seating areas and bright and inviting in the kitchen, creating a cosy yet vibrant feel. This was enhanced by the streams of fairy lights in the garden visible through the seemingly infinite expanse of glass which made up the back of the house. It was like the stars had come down to earth, she thought briefly. Or at least that was how Elle Interiors magazine had described the effect from the photos she had copied.

'Hello,' she said, putting her bag down on one of the sofas by the door. 'What's this in aid of?'

'This is my way of saying I'm sorry. I'm sorry for being out so much and for accidentally outing us in the national press. I know it's been a huge headache and I'm proud that you've turned it into a positive at work.'

Jess sighed and accepted the drink. 'Cheers to that,' she said.

They spent the evening doing the things they hadn't in ages. They talked, they laughed and they drank. Drinking was heavily involved. In fact, two bottles down and the laughter had turned from convivial and heartfelt to slightly hysterical in nature. Nevertheless, it was a good night. And then they did something else they hadn't done in a while.

The next day, Jess walked into the office with a mixture of a very sore head and a sense of confusion. Had she been too quick to dismiss Mark out of hand? No, he wasn't ambitious nor was he headed in the stratospheric upwards trajectory that her own career promised, but did she really need that? After all, wasn't one supremely successful person enough for any couple?

She decided to ignore this and focus on her work. She could deal with it all later. At around 11am, she saw Anthony Guild stop outside Zane's office and pop his head in. This was it, she thought with glee. This was the moment. She watched surreptitiously as Anthony and Zane chatted. She couldn't see either of their faces. Was their body language agitated? She saw Zane lift his hand in a salutary wave of goodbye and Anthony started to turn away.

What was happening? Jess looked studiously at her computer, making sure she wasn't seen watching.

It was then that she heard a knock on her door. Looking up, she saw Anthony smiling benignly from the doorway. She thought quickly of the Feign file. He had wanted an update on it this afternoon, but it wouldn't be unusual for him to check in early. She put on her brightest professional smile as he entered.

'Jess, could I have a quick word?' he asked.

'Of course,' she said. 'Come in.'

'I was hoping you'd come into my office,' he said. 'It's rather important.'

Jess froze. Something important. Was this it? Was he going to offer her partnership?

'Of course,' she said, standing up and smoothing down her skirt. Her extremities felt cold as blood rushed to her head and she was fighting to remain upright as the world spun around her. She was even more excited as she saw a couple of the other partners in Anthony's room. She recognised the paunch and dour face of Bob Fullerton and the straight-backed figure of Georgina Holt.

This was it. All her hard work would finally pay off.

After she had greeted everybody and sat down, Anthony began.

'Jess, for a long time now you've served the firm well,' he mused, staring her straight in the eyes. She did her best to meet his glare. 'You've brought in lots of good clients and you've done good work.'

Jess beamed, but also silently urged him onwards. What was taking so long?

While she waited, she silently planned her Instagram status for that afternoon. Maybe a photo of a handshake or a glass of champagne. Champagne was definitely required. She could taste the bubbles now.

'Which is why I am shocked and *appalled*,' Anthony continued, 'to learn that you have been cavorting in the way you have with one of our most prominent clients.'

Hold on. What?

Anthony's face was now thunderous. 'Would you like to explain these?' He was holding out a pile of papers. They looked like email printouts.

With a shaking hand, Jess took the proffered documents and started flicking through. It was hard to focus on the content, but snippets did occasionally pierce her mind fog. She saw enough to know that there, in black and white, was her entire email relationship with William Force. All of it.

And yet there was something not quite right. She forced herself to focus. Yes, she saw it now. Some of the messages were purportedly from her email address, but she definitely didn't recognise them. Messages that she had supposedly sent to William last night. Moreover, these latest missives included several suggestions that they try some pretty spicy bedroom activities. Jess gulped involuntarily as she skimmed them. They ranged from light spanking to the kind of antics that would make even Max Mosley blush. Amongst the phrases that rushed out at Jess were 'leather whips', 'legal briefs' and 'give your eggs a decent handling'. In response, William's tone, which started off as flirty, went from dubious to disgusted as 'she' listed an ever more lascivious list of potential activities. By the end he had suggested that they 'take time to reconsider things.'

It didn't make sense. She hadn't written these. It must be a mistake. Jess tasted a sharp metallic tang and realised she had bitten her lip right through, drawing blood.

'It's not true,' she said, looking around at the stony faces. But she needed time to frame her argument. Because it *was* partly true.

'Look,' Anthony said, hands clasped, elbows on his desk. Whilst our firm's rules state that there's to be no client/solicitor shenanigans, we do accept that it happens. I mean,' he laughed and looked around at his colleagues. 'Who hasn't had the odd dalliance with a divorcee? Look at Zane,' he said. 'Apparently he's doing stellar work with Doris. Not sure I could do what he's done to keep the old bat purring, but he's taken one for the team. Now that's going above and beyond for the firm I would say.'

Bob laughed and retorted, 'Yes well, I'm pretty sure we'd have no clients left if we had to chuck out everyone who had slept with one of our people.'

'Indeed,' replied Anthony. And the two men laughed conspiratorially and sighed as if remembering good times.

This was salvageable, thought Jess. Everybody messed about with clients. They had just said so. It would be okay. But then Anthony's expression morphed to one of anger.

'But what I will not have is one of my associates upsetting one of our most prestigious and profitable clients,' he barked. 'Let alone allow her to badmouth our firm.'

'What?' Jess hadn't meant the crass question to escape her lips, but this was news. 'I didn't-,'

Anthony's gaze lowered to his own stash of paperwork. 'I'm so glad I met you before I left this cesspit,' he read in a monotone. 'I hope you'll come with me when I finally move.'

'I didn't write that.' Jess rapidly shuffled the papers to find the offending prose.

Anthony appeared not to have heard her.

'This will remain discreet,' he stated coldly. 'Fortunately, Sir William has been very reasonable so we can afford to keep this quiet and you can leave our cesspit,' he paused meaningfully. 'With a decent reference.'

Stunned, Jess grappled for a foothold. 'My clients-,'

'Will transfer to Zane.'

It was like an avalanche; a complete surprise that pinned her in place. What had just happened? Were they telling her to leave? For good? The facts wouldn't stick in her mind. All she could do was stare at the pages in her hand.

'We'll expect your resignation by the end of the day,' Georgina said. Her expression was especially vitriolic and Jess knew why. It had something to do with the fact that Georgina had always seen Jess as her protégé, as a good example of a strong, hardworking woman.

She had to fight her corner.

'I didn't do this,' she tried to say. The words came out as a squeak.

Anthony just shook his head. 'I wish you wouldn't make it worse,' he said. 'We've checked your computer. We found the, um, materials,' he croaked.

'Materials?' Jess asked. What was he talking about?

'Naughtyspankysluts.com?' Bob said. Jess could tell he felt a certain frisson at being able to utter such words in the office.

'What?' Jess cried. 'I didn't. I would never.' But she could see it was too late. She wracked her brain trying to comprehend how such things had ended up on her system. She was meticulous about logging off from her computer. The only times she hadn't were-

No.

She thought back to how hurriedly she always had to sneak to Zane's desk when he was away from it. She always had to pounce up, leaving her desk at a moment's notice. Was it possible that, while she was at his desk, he had been at hers? Surely not. And yet, she had been so busy with her own plan, she may well have missed his.

'I'll have Bess come and help you clear your desk,' Anthony said, referring to his trusty secretary. 'Unless there's anything there that we wouldn't want her to see?' He asked this with a raised eyebrow. 'Bess is seventy after all. I wouldn't want her to see anything. Untoward.'

At this, Jess just shook her head, her mouth still wide open. Dazedly, she made her way back to her desk. It was as she sat down on her chair, her legs having caved in, that she caught a glimpse of Zane across the hallway. He was on the phone, coffee in hand. When he saw her he gave a bright smile and lifted his mug in a 'cheers' gesture. Then he put the drink down, pointed at his phone and mouthed 'Doris' at her with a wink.

CHAPTER 19

As his eyes skimmed the ratty pages of the free newspaper, Graham was in a state of feverish excitement. Had he found them? Were these the ones he was to save?

He had searched for so long, looking for someone who needed his help. At first he had scoured the net, looking to see if he found any stories that caught his eye. There were people who had lost it all, people who couldn't find their way and those who didn't seem to realise they were lost at all, but were any of them right? He knew it had to be something that spoke to him. He imagined that when he found the right one – or ones – he would just know.

Over the weeks and months that followed, it had become an obsession. He had to find them. They were waiting for him. He even started looking at homeless people in the street, wondering whether the answer was in front of him, but never felt anything. How was he supposed to decide who was the most needy and most deserving?

He had reached a point of futile despair. Maybe, he had thought, staring at his computer screen, this wasn't meant to be. Perhaps he should find a hobby. His mother was always saying that. He'd considered model trains, but one look at the message boards had put him off. That lot were off the rails. Or maybe something more sedate. Stamp collecting? He certainly wasn't cut out for cat shows. He'd learned that the hard way, he had thought, looking at the scratches still running down his arm.

And that's when he heard sounds emanating from the kitchen behind him.

'This isn't good,' Smith was saying. 'Heads are gonna roll.'

Graham had seen him follow Liz to the kitchen, where some of the others were making their usual 10am cuppas. He was always trying to corner her over the biscuit tin.

'But didn't they already cut that winner's support group from the budget?' Liz had asked, making her usual slurping noise as she sipped her Diet Coke. 'I thought Emily had done that.'

'Yes, but not soon enough. And now it's ended up like this...' Smith had trailed off. The air in the room practically moved with the force of so many heads shaking at once. What had happened? Another death? Another lottery-related suicide? What?

Soon thereafter, Smith had returned to his desk, but not before absent-mindedly leaving his copy of *Metro* on Graham's desk. At first Graham had angrily lamented the fact that his desk was always treated like a rubbish tip just because it was by the kitchen. He should email Gwyneth. He would email her. Right now. She was supposed to be the office manager for Christ's sake, but she never stopped people from leaving their rubbish in his cubicle. Why wasn't she doing anything about it? But then the headline had caught his eye.

"*Whining the Lottery: Avalon in Support Group Sham,*" the front page yelled, alongside a photo of a familiar fat couple holding a large cheque. Graham turned to the middle spread and read on.

'Avalon Plc, the group responsible for The National Lottery has come under fire today for spending potential charitable cash on maintaining a lottery winners' support group. Held in the well-heeled area of Hampstead, North London where the average house price is £2,218,846, the group counts several moaning multi-millionaires amongst its members. According to an official flyer which Metro has managed to obtain, all lottery winners are invited to join and encouraged to 'share their feelings and worries' about winning.

'The story came to light when Dina Baker, who together with her husband Paul, won £30 million two years ago, wrote about it in her weekly column for OK!. Now a self-proclaimed 'lottery lady about town', Dina detailed how her husband attends these weekly meetings with several other lottery winners to 'basically have a good old moan'.

'Mrs Baker, who has invested heavily in plastic surgery and a vast mansion on The Bishops Avenue – known as Millionaire's Row - since her windfall, wrote, 'Winning's been great. We can send the girls to the right schools, keep up with the latest fashions and even the Kardashians! I don't know why Paul's so down on it all, but maybe this charity thing will help.'

Graham was electrified as he read how this Paul Baker along with two other lottery winners, Mark Jones and Rick Gordon were planning on climbing the Three Peaks to raise money for charity.

The support group. *His* support group.

He looked again at the photographs of the men in question. Yes, he remembered the fat one. And he thought he recalled the other two.

They were his. They had come to him. They had been in his office, had taken the flyers and gone to those meetings. He had brought them together. And now they had been sent to him again. They needed his help.

'Er, Graham?' It was Liz's voice. He looked up to see her head over the cubicle partition.

'Could you answer your phone? It's been ringing for, like, ever.'

Graham looked at Liz for a second before directing his gaze at his phone. How long had it been ringing?

He picked it up and didn't have to say a word before the line exploded with noise.

'Hi!' chirped a cheerful voice. 'This is Brian Glossup. They told me to speak to you about my *lottery* win? I won!'

Graham took one last glance at the newspaper before sighing, folding it up and placing it in his desk drawer. He'd have to come back to it later.

'Congratulations,' Graham said with as much enthusiasm as he could muster. 'You've won,' he checked his list, '£2.8 million.'

CHAPTER 20

'Alright, so. Remember. Keep hydrated, keep away from edges and stay alert!' declared the enthusiastic foetus of an instructor who had introduced himself as Todd. This alarmingly brief statement apparently passed for a safety briefing. With floppy, sandy blond hair and teeth that would make a Hollywood starlet look like Austen Powers, he was preposterously chipper and even more preposterously ill-equipped of life to be leading them on this trek. It was like being prepped for battle by Justin Bieber.

'Is that it?' Mark asked.

'What were you expecting?' Paul muttered. 'It's climbing. We go up.' He illustrated an upward motion with one of his walking poles.

'But aren't there,' Mark searched, looking around the welcome centre like it might provide the answers. 'Techniques? Altitude training? Is this all we get?'

'It's Ben Nevis not Everest,' Rick offered, quite unhelpfully.

They were at the meeting point in a hut at the foot of Ben Nevis. It was a clear day, allowing them to see much of what lay ahead in that first challenge. Todd had nonchalantly informed them that they would be hiking some 24.5 miles, of which this first mountain would form 10.5. Mark was already seeing the error of his way. What had he been thinking? Climb the Three Peaks. Do it for charity. It'll be fun. Fulfilling.

Idiot.

It wouldn't be fun. What was fun about the map, compass, gloves, hat, waterproofs, rain cover, spare socks and pants, full first aid kit, head torch and other survival gear that were currently weighing him down in his rucksack? And what about the hours of bus journeys? For some reason, it hadn't occurred to him that the three highest peaks of England, Scotland and Wales weren't exactly next to each other. It would take some six hours just to get from Ben Nevis to their next stop, Scafell Pike.

'What the hell are you wearing by the way?' Mark asked Rick by way of repost, surveying him warily.

'It's the latest in pro-human application engineering,' Rick said indignantly. 'And it looks good.'

'It looks ridiculous,' Paul said, voicing the painfully obvious.

'Why?' Rick asked, obstinately unperturbed.

'Well the full camouflage, for a start,' Mark said. 'This isn't Vietnam.'

'It's breathable and measures my heart rate and it's the new season in hi-tech outdoor active gear.'

You look like the lovechild of military Barbie and the Terminator,' Mark said, to a guffaw from Paul. 'What's that on your sunglasses?' he added, peering at the silver and black contraption which obscured much of Rick's face.

'Ah, now this has Bluetooth and GPS as well as a tiny microcomputer which-'

'Save your energies fellas,' Todd said cheerily as he returned with some badges for them to wear. 'It's time to go.'

As they started the walk, Mark's spirits lifted again. This wasn't too bad. The fresh air, the singing birds, the clear skies. Here he was, with his two friends, in nature, enjoying a brisk hike. This was fantastic. And they were raising money to boot. Perfect.

In fact, the one upside of all the publicity was that money had been flowing steadily into their Just Giving page. Their meagre £250 had multiplied into £4,000 and was growing by the day.

He could do this. They all could. And they would do so with a smile. They had chatted amiably about a range of subjects, asking Todd about his work and talking about their surroundings.

This positive feeling lasted for at least two hours. Or was it three? Yes, three hours, he would recall later. That's when the mood had shifted for the first time. Mark remembered the moment because it coincided with when Rick pulled out his Handspresso machine and offered him a cup.

'Is that a portable espresso machine?' Paul had asked in disbelief.

'What is the matter with you?' Mark had gawped, appalled.

'What? It's good to be prepared,' Rick defended.

'I'll have a cup if he won't,' Paul had said, reaching out for his brew.

That's when a large drop of rain plopped its way into the coffee. Mark had hoped it was bird poo. It would serve Rick right for being such a ponce. And Paul for encouraging him. But no. As another drop was followed by another and then an entire deluge of the bastards, Mark felt his mood dampen.

'So how do you guys know each other?' asked Todd, still happy and full of breath as he led them up yet another path, the rain only making him seem more like a glistening superhero and not like the wet rat Mark was sure he resembled by contrast.

Rick and Mark exchanged glances. Did he not know? Paul shrugged at Mark as if to say, I guess not.

'Running group,' said Mark, letting the subject slide away, much like Rick's sunglasses a few minutes later. He was attempting to take a shot of them when his selfie stick clashed with his head, allowing the sunglasses to fall down one extremely precipitous cliff.

'Did you say they had GPS?' Paul asked as they peered at the glasses' downward trajectory.

'Yeah.'

The rest of the climb was very much an uphill struggle in every sense of the phrase, but they had made it. And they had done so with relative dignity. Paul had had one moment of weakness at a false summit when he had considered throwing Todd off the edge. To be fair, he'd have had it coming.

'This. Is. Only. The. First. Peak,' Paul had panted, anorak-covered head down upon realising there was still a fair way to go. 'And we're not even there yet.'

'Come on guys!' Todd had said cheerily in response, showing zero signs of physical exertion. 'You can do it. We're almost there.'

Rick and Mark had seen the murderous intent in Paul's eyes.

'If you chuck him over, we won't know our way down,' Mark had muttered to him. He'd given this some thought himself. Paul emitted a small growl.

But they made it. They actually bloody made it up to the peak. And looking over the unspoiled landscape around them, the river glinting below, Mark had a sense he could keep climbing forever. Even Paul looked pleased. Whether it was the feeling of achievement, the espresso kicking in or the magnificent views, they were all smiling wistfully as they took it all in.

They even posed for Todd as he took their photo, each of them bearing wide grins. Rick was first to post it onto Facebook.

'How on earth do you have service up here?' Paul said, moving his phone around like he was trying to tune an old-fashioned TV aerial.

'Shouldn't say,' Rick muttered conspiratorially. 'It's the latest in military technology.'

'Let's go lads,' Todd announced.

It must have been exhilaration that propelled them back into their minibus because Mark remembered nothing from the ascent. They collapsed into their seats and breathed sighs of relief. It was perhaps at this point that the reality of the situation started to sink in.

Slowly consuming the sandwiches in the bright light of 3pm on a drizzling afternoon, they all looked out of the steamed-up windows. Mark was exhausted. Shattered. He already had a feeling that he had completed something. It seemed unreal that he was barely a third of the way through his task. They were now set for a six-hour drive before they would basically have to do it all again. And then again.

By the time they reached Scafell Pike, it was 10pm and pitch black. The seats of the minibus had long since passed the point of comfortable and they were all groggy from sleep.

'Alright everyone.' Todd was still bright and bloody perky as he donned his ridiculous looking helmet with inbuilt light. 'One mountain down, two to go!'

Unable to muster the energy to answer with so much as a groan, the three of them had followed him unquestioningly. It took at least two hours before anyone uttered a word.

'Is this really happening?' Paul asked into the darkness.

Rick had groaned in answer and Mark had exercised his right to silence. He needed his concentration. Even with his headlamp, it was hard to see anything and with every step he feared a fall. It was also the point in the climb when he had decided that, if he just powered through silently, stoically, it would all go by quickly. Like meditation. Or a prostate exam. But any zen he possessed lasted mere minutes.

In addition to the overwhelming fatigue and bitter cold, there was the occasional startling realisation that they were climbing higher and higher in dark, wet conditions. There were several points at which Mark had to stop, just to steady himself.

This was ridiculous. More than that, it was dangerous. They didn't need to do this. They could stop. They could just give the money to the charity themselves and go home. Have a cup of tea.

'This doesn't feel safe,' he ventured to nobody in particular. He was too much of a chicken to actually suggest that they quit, but maybe somebody else would. They didn't.

Chickens.

'You're doing great guys!' Todd belted out.

'Are we going to die?' Paul had asked at one point, although his voice was so meek and high pitched, Mark had had to check it was really him talking.

Reaching the second peak wasn't so much marked by celebration as cynicism. Like disillusioned youth walking by yet another classroom mugging, they simply took an exhausted, mandatory selfie and trudged back to the bus.

It was at the bottom of Snowdon that they hit their lowest point yet. Having completed Scafell at a ridiculous 2am, all three of them had fallen into comas on the four-hour drive over. Mark must have been dreaming because he felt like he had been swatting away at a fly or a bee; something annoying and persistent when he awoke in the dim lighting of the bus.

'Mark, wake up,' Rick said, prodding him in the shoulder. As his friend came into focus, Rick said. 'It's not good.'

Disorientation initially shielded Mark from reality. The first sensation that engulfed him was pain, followed by extreme discomfort. He must have slept in a bad position, at least if the sharp pangs in his back were anything to go by, and his legs felt like lead weights. And even though the inside of the minibus was stultifying in its heat, he felt cold, almost certainly brought on by exhaustion. Sitting up didn't help.

'Wakey wakey sleepy head.'

Todd. Fucking Todd.

Ah shit. This was the coach.

'Please say it's over,' he heard himself say. It had to be. He couldn't move an inch. He tried to remember how many peaks they'd climbed already. Could it be three?

'Just one more to go,' was Todd's reply.

Mark's eyes were drawn to the windows. Beyond the steam, he saw flashing lights. It was still dark outside and the erratic illuminations added to the general surrealistic feeling. Why the lights? An AA van? Had they broken down?

Using the sleeve of his jumper, Mark rubbed away at the misty glass, revealing a circle of clarity.

Told you it wasn't good,' Rick grumbled. 'They found us.'

'They' were the paparazzi, standing outside, their cameras flashing. They were jostling and yelling things, although it was hard to hear the words.

'There's just two of them,' Paul said, unimpressed.

Mark stared at the two blokes vying for best position by their bus window. One was large and bald, the other short with curly black hair in a ponytail. He recognised both of them from his doorstep. Had they really followed them here?

'What do we do?' Rick asked.

'Dunno,' Paul said.

'I think we go and climb a mountain,' Mark said.

'Jones,' the larger one of them said conversationally as he stepped off the bus. 'What took you so long?'

'How did you find us?' Mark asked.

'Followed you from home, didn't we,' the smaller one said matter of fact. 'You're not exactly Houdini,' he added, guffawing. For some reason, Mark felt annoyed, not by the fact that they'd followed him, but by the assertion that he didn't cover his tracks. He hadn't been trying, but still.

171

'Go on guys,' the bald one now said. 'Give us a group shot.'

Obligingly, probably because none of them had he energy to resist, they all stood in a huddle while the two men photographed them. Todd, who seemed completely unfazed by the arrival of professional photographers, joined them for the pose.

'You're not going to follow us all the way up, are you?' Mark asked, dread overtaking him. If there was one way to make this day harder, that would be it.

'No way!' the smaller one said.

'We'll leave the heroics to you lot. See you at the bottom,' the bald one added, sipping what looked like a Starbucks.

Undeterred by their audience, Todd began what might have been a pep talk.

'Alright guys, it's the last one. The final peak. The –,'

They all turned at the sound of the Star Wars soundtrack coming from Rick's direction. Legs apart, one hand on his hip, he had his wireless speaker in his other hand, which was extended in a determinedly outstretched arm.

'Let's just go,' Paul grumbled.

The first hour of the trek was completed in almost total silence except for the trudging of boots, with each one of them lost in their own thoughts. It was Rick who spoke first.

'Where did I go wrong?' he asked. 'I just wanted someone to love me.'

'If I recall correctly,' Paul huffed, 'You wanted everyone to love you. That was part of the problem.'

Now past the point of caring about whether or not it counted as prying, Mark had to ask. 'So, what? Did you cheat on your wives?'

Paul scoffed.

'It was,' Rick said in between pants, 'Complicated. It was an addiction. A,' puff, 'Sex,' puff, 'addiction.'

'That was a yes,' Paul interpreted.

'It's a proper problem,' Rick insisted. 'Michael Douglas has it.'

'Oh well, if Michael Douglas has it,' Paul replied.

From then on, they developed a pattern of long stints of silence, peppered with short bouts of increasingly non-chatter. Paul was next to fall off the sanity wagon.

'It's so beautiful here,' Mark had been musing, trying to pretend he cared about scenery when his legs were about to fall off.

'Is it wrong to end a marriage by text?' Paul asked, achieving the conversational equivalent of a hand break turn. So abrupt was the change of topic that Todd had to grab Rick's arm to prevent him falling down a particularly steep ridge.

'Are you mad?' Mark asked him.

'Well, I just can't face telling her,' Paul said in a whinge. 'But I've decided. This is it. I'm leaving.'

'So you're going to text and say what? Goodbye thanks for over a decade of marriage, I'm off with the cleaner?' Rick said.

'So, what, a video message?' Paul asked, clearly desperate.

'Isn't there any hope?' Mark asked.

'I dunno,' Paul grumped, and they stopped talking again. The next sound was not in the form of words, but humming. It was the *Minder* theme tune and it was coming from Rick. Paul joined in, then Mark, prompting a huffy and virtually tuneless hike down memory lane in the form of a medley of old TV shows. This ceased after a rendition of the song from Dad's Army.

Time meant nothing now. All Mark knew was the trudging endlessness of putting one foot in front of another and hearing the sound of his breath. He was a zombie. This would never end.

'Almost there, guys.'

Huh? Had he crossed into hallucinations? Had Todd really just said those words? And what did they mean?

'How. Long?' Somebody said this. It might have been Mark, it might have been the tooth fairy.

'Ten minutes give or take.'

Mark wanted to believe, Really he did. But he couldn't handle a false dawn. They were very high up now. Could they really be nearing the end? He didn't know. Trust no one. Especially Todd.

So, despite these words, despite the increasingly far stretching views and the signs that they were near the top, it was still a shock to finally get there. To see the ghost town of the summit visitor centre.

'Ha!' Rick yelled, falling to his knees and looking heavenwards in an unnecessarily dramatic pose. 'We did it!'

Mark felt a massive smile spreading across his lips. He had no energy left so this was surely an instinctual thing. He saw it mirrored in the faces of Paul and Rick. Paul had his hands on his head.

'Welcome to the peak,' Todd said proudly, 'Well done! Take it in. Take a look around guys.'

'Hold on,' Paul said. 'Is this really it?'

'Well there's a few stairs over there you can climb for a photo. That's the 'official' peak,' Todd said, with finger quotes around the word official.

They all stopped and looked in various directions, uncertain of what to do to mark this momentous occasion.

'Photo?' Todd suggested. Dropping their bags down where they stood, they all walked towards one of the edges and put their arms around each other. Todd handed them a banner which read 'We completed the Three Peaks', which they held aloft. As Todd clicked away with first a camera and then each of their phones, Mark allowed the sense of achievement to take hold.

'Shove it, world!' Rick yelled as the flash went for the final time.

This was like the perfect antidote to the lottery win. A real, achievement, both for himself and for charity.

'I'll see you in there,' Todd said, pointing to the visitor centre before going inside.

'It's so quiet,' Mark said once he was gone. 'I thought this place got crazy at the top. A tourist hub.'

'It's not the season yet is it,' Rick said. 'We've come early. Train doesn't even come up here yet. Not 'til mid-March.'

They started walking around, looking at the views and enjoying their achievement. They stumbled along, their legs numb and their eyes disbelieving.

'I can't believe we've done this,' marvelled Paul as he and Mark looked together, smiling into the distance.

Just then, as if from nowhere, there was a Tarzan like yodel and a quick high-pitched shriek. They both turned around simultaneously just as Rick yelled, 'What the hell are you doing?'

The vision before them was not one which either man was expecting. Rick was clutching onto a pole, a look of terror on his face. A short skinny man with grey hair and a face with pinched features and a sour expression stood a short distance away from him. He appeared to have adopted what was an approximation of a Haka pose, legs astride, squatting, arms apart from his body.

'He just tried to push me over the edge!' Rick yelled, his voice breaking in pure hysteria as Paul and Mark approached.

'No I didn't. I was just walking past,' the man said in a nasal tone.

'No way,' Paul said.

'Yes, yes you did. You yelled and then you ran at me.' Rick was almost shrieking by this point.

Paul looked beyond Rick. 'What edge?' he asked. 'There isn't one.'

What edge indeed. For, while it was a mountain peak, nobody could call the top of Snowdon even mildly steep. There wasn't a cliff in sight.

'For g-d's sake are you going to argue with me over angles?' Rick said, now dismounting from the pole. 'He could have killed me!'

'What, by rolling you down that slightly steep hill?' Mark asked. 'Hardly.'

'Well, there would have been some chance of death,' the sour man said, now sounding indignant. On hearing the sound of his voice again, Mark couldn't help but feel a sense of déjà vu. He examined the speaker more closely.

'Do I know you?' Mark asked. There was definitely something familiar about the man.

'No,' the man said, in a defensive tone that implied exactly the opposite.

'Yes, I think I know him too,' Paul said.

'Do you work in Hampstead tube?' Mark asked.

'Or maybe the off licence on the High Road?' Paul offered.

'Guys I think you're missing the point here,' Rick said, 'He just tried to kill me. And besides, he looks like that tramp on Heath Street.'

They started to argue the point when a loud yell pierced the din.

'I am Graham Gill!' The man loudly and quite unexpectedly snapped, his voice breaking with the effort. He sounded like an angry Yorkshire terrier: Furious but ineffectual. His tone then went down a few octaves. 'I am a lottery liaison executive at Avalon Plc and I gave you – each and every one of you – your winnings.' He spat the works, looking dignified if deranged.

'Oh,' they all said simultaneously in realisation.

'So why are you trying to kill me?' Rick asked.

Graham shook his head. 'No, no, no,' he said soothingly. 'I'm not trying to kill you. Not just you, anyway. I'm here for all of you. I'm *helping* you.'

All three men must have looked equally confused because Graham carried on. With a look in his eye that Mark could only describe as unhinged, he addressed them all.

'You were sent to me,' he said excitedly, inching nearer to them furtively like a squirrel nearing a nut. 'I think you were sent to my office so I could help you.' When they all looked dubious he carried on, even more excitedly. 'Are any of you happy since you won? Has it made your lives complete?'

None of them had an answer to this. Or they did, but they didn't want to admit it. Rick spoke first.

'What's your point, friend?' he asked warily.

'I know what it's like,' Graham appealed desperately. 'I *know* how hard it is to go day in, day out without an answer. Knowing that there's no reason to carry on.'

'Is this a wind up?' Paul asked, looking around presumably for a camera.

'Let me help you,' Graham was saying, his arms now lifting in the air like he was a ballerina or someone trying to summon lightning. 'I can make the pain go away.'

'He's a nut ball,' Mark said, disgust and horror tinging every word.

It was in that moment that Graham seemed to come back to life. He started another sprint and Mark found that this crazed little man was running directly at him. Instinctively, Mark jumped out of the way, but Graham made a sort of netball pivot to follow him. Paul and Rick started running too and soon all three men were in a sort of 'it' game across the rocky terrain, Mark then Graham and the two other men. When he reached a middle ground far away from the edge, Mark turned and attempted to catch Graham.

The two men stopped and stared at each other.

'Get help,' Mark yelled at Rick. They were right at the brink of the mountain, far from the visitor centre. Mark hadn't realised quite how far they had walked but he knew it was too far to yell for help, especially with the wind now picking up. Rick gave him a quick salute in response before running towards the visitor centre.

Knowing that the other two men were behind him, Graham turned in a third direction, heading towards a different edge. There they had a sort of Thelma and Louise moment. Graham was standing with the horizon behind him, wispy grey tufts blowing in the wind as he was beset by Paul and Mark.

'Look,' Mark said reasonably, 'Why don't you come in, have a cup of tea and we can chat about this?'

'Yes, you could scrape a knee if you fall,' Paul said with a sneer before Mark shot him a warning glance.

Graham's eyes were wild. He looked like he was at the very pinnacle of a fight or flight decision. He looked from Paul to Mark.

'You don't know what it's like,' he began in a trance like state. 'Day after day you lot come in. With your winning tickets and your problems,' he spat at them before he changed his tone to a high pitched whine. 'How much do I give to family? Why do I have to split my win?' Annoyance spread its way across his face like a stain. 'And then there's Smith and Perkins and Hammond,' he added, looking down resentfully. He had started walking along the edge now and they followed him like a procession.

'Who?' Mark mouthed at Paul who shrugged back with his mouth curled downwards as if to say 'no idea'.

'Always moaning over their coffees. But does anyone want to know what I think? Oh no,' Graham barrelled on, apparently not needing an audience. 'Well, I have seen it all. I watch from afar. I know what needs to happen. I *know* what will make you happy.'

'What?' Paul asked, slightly entranced by Graham's voice.

'Nothing,' Graham replied simply, lifting his arms slightly before dropping them by his sides in defeat. 'Nothing will make you happy. So why bother?'

The man stopped and all three of them stood still again. Some of the fight, the tension, had gone out of them at these words. Was there truth in this? Was it true that if winning the lottery couldn't make you happy, nothing could? It wasn't a bad point, surely.

Seeing that he had their attention, the man pushed his advantage. 'I'm giving you a way out,' he said and started walking towards them.

The next sequence happened in slow motion. No. Really. Or at least that was how Mark would later remember it.

Mark saw Todd and Rick running over from the visitor centre, a couple of security guards in tow, but Graham didn't. With his back to the approaching men, he had noticed that they were distracted and made one last desperate lunge towards Paul, who was now not far from the edge. Like James before him, Paul managed a quick sidestep, but Graham was clearly not as prepared as he had been. For, instead of turning and trying again, he wasn't able to stop, his trajectory locked as he simply kept going.

One of his feet crossed a line. It was definitely a sudden line. It seemed to appear from nowhere. Mark would later swear that the man had been suspended in mid-air for a moment, a look of sheer surprise on his face before he abruptly disappeared. In a second he was gone.

The men all stood there, mouths gaping open.

'Bloody hell,' Paul said.

Then the silence took over, the wind the only sound to be heard.

CHAPTER 21

As Graham felt the wind on his face, he reflected on how things had not turned out the way he had expected. But wasn't that always the way?

He had always scoffed when his mother had said, in her most superstitious tones, 'If you want to make G-d laugh, make plans,' as she and her friends played bridge over cups of dark tea.

But perhaps the real problem was, he hadn't planned well enough. It had seemed so simple there hadn't been any need for elaborate strategy. How hard could it be to push a tired man over a mountain edge? Surely even three wouldn't be too hard. Especially given that he'd have the element of surprise.

He could kick himself for his lack of foresight. Yes he had checked when they were coming. He had followed their progress and made sure he was at Snowdon before they were. That was where he planned to strike. He wanted to give them the chance to complete their mission and then, at its very peak, he would send them off happy. But he had been too hasty and let things slide.

First there was the matter of actually getting up the mountain. He had heard that there were trains that reached the top, but when he got there it transpired it was too early in the season. They weren't running yet. They did run to almost the top, but there was still a fair way to go.

No problem, he would walk the rest of the way. He would just have to set off in enough time before them and, by the time they reached the top, he'd be ready. He bought some hiking boots and supplies from a shop nearby.

'You're climbing Snowdon?' the dubious looking woman at the till had asked him in her Welsh sing song as she rang through the purchases. 'You know it can be quite tough out of season. And for a novice.'

'Yes, yes' he had replied disinterestedly.

When she heard his accent, her expression changed immediately from slightly worried to completely carefree.

'Ah, you're English,' she said jovially, all worry having evaporated. 'Go on then.'

Everything had gone well. He had disembarked from the train and noted with satisfaction the number of precipitous drops in all directions. It was only at the end that he realised his error. For, while Snowdon was filled with long, endless drops, its peak was not. It actually looked quite safe, with its large visitor centre and flat expanses. There was some potential for spraining an ankle, what with the rocky ground, but that was about it.

When he went into the café for a drink, the teenage barista looked him up and down. 'What will I get you,' he asked in a deadpan monotone.

'Just a coffee please,' Graham had said. 'And a croissant,' he added. He really was quite hungry. When the teen had grudgingly brought him his order, Graham decided it was a good opportunity to obtain much needed intel.

'Have there ever been any deaths off Snowdon?' he asked, trying to sound nonchalant so as not to arouse suspicion. He needn't have bothered.

'Oh yeah,' the teen had said. 'Loads.'

Graham had brightened at this. There was potential.

'Not off the top of course,' the young man had added, saying it like nobody in their right mind would consider such a thing. 'There are parts where people...you know. Go.' He said this last bit in a ghoulish moo.

Another employee sidled over at this point, clearly attracted by the macabre topic. 'There was an article just the other day,' she said. 'Said Snowdon was the safest peak in Europe. Virtually impossible to fall off the top.'

Disgruntled, but not deterred, Graham had considered asking them where the steeper parts were. But it would be no use, he had reasoned. For one thing, he didn't know which route the team were taking. Apparently they hadn't decided yet and were waiting to choose on the day depending on the weather and their levels of energy. That's was another reason he was waiting at the top.

He decided to walk around and check the area. There must be somewhere reasonably steep on Wales's highest peak. He had just been pondering a particularly rocky patch when he had seen Rick. He should have waited. He knew that now. He should have bided his time.

But after weeks of clutching the well-worn article and devouring everything he could learn about him online, the sight of this man in person was so thrilling, so exciting that Graham lost his train of thought. Without a moment's hesitation, he had lunged at him.

Of course, he knew he was in trouble when the other two had arrived. No more surprise, he thought in desperation.

He had almost had them at one point. With his speech. Had they not cornered him, given him any other choice, he'd have succeeded. He could see it in their eyes. They knew he was right, he thought smugly.

He noted that ground was nearing quite quickly now and wondered why his life wasn't flashing before his eyes. Wasn't it supposed to? He closed his eyes and tried to summon some picturesque flashbacks, but it was more of a trudge. He remembered the ring road. That bloody Watford ring road. Who had designed that thing? He considered his cat. Who would take Dave now? Probably Smith, he thought in annoyance. He'll probably use it to impress Liz.

And that's how his thoughts turned to the office. Wait until Smith, Hammond and Perkins hear, he thought in satisfaction. Wait until they find out that –

Oh look, a rock.

CHAPTER 22

'So, Mark, what was it like do the Three Peaks?'

'How much have you raised for charity?'

'What have you and the club got planned next?'

The police and ambulance came just as the four men reached the bottom of the mountain, but they couldn't reach Mark, Paul, Rick or even Todd for several minutes due to the onslaught of journalists awaiting their arrival.

Staggering like the survivors at the end of a slasher movie, the four men walked the final steps to ground level before standing mute as the microphones hovered beneath chins.

'What do you make of Simon Cowell's comments that you couldn't climb a mountain if your life depended on it?' one journalist yelled out.

'Rick, what are you wearing?' another shouted.

Finally, a couple of officers pulled them away from the throng and into the minibus, where their bemused driver was waiting.

It was an hour or so later when they found themselves in Snowdon Police Station each being asked the same questions separately. The tapes, later leaked to a journalist for the Daily Mail, included the following gems.

Police Officer: 'So, who was this man?'

Paul: 'Dunno. Worked for Avalon apparently.'

Mark: 'The guy who handed out the winnings.'

Rick: 'A lunatic?'

Police Officer: 'And why would he want to kill you?'

Paul: 'Jealousy. Everybody's jealous. Well, let me tell you-.'

Mark: 'Not sure.'

Rick: 'He's a crazy person. Obviously.'
Police Officer: 'And what was his name?'
Paul: 'Erm...'
Mark: 'Er...'
Rick: 'Um...'
They were soon let out and told they could go home. It helped that one of the café staff at the Snowdon Visitors' Centre had caught it all on their iPhone and that Graham had left a note on his desk.

The papers had handled it with their customary brand of tact. Indeed, some of the articles had had a definite ring of glee to them. 'Snowdon Murderer Dives to His Death', 'Lottery Killer in Unlikely Death Lunge', 'Snow Done It?' and 'Snowdon Psycho Suicide Mystery' were just four of the headlines out the next morning.

Nobody could quite understand how Graham had expected to kill the lottery winners, why he had done it, nor, most importantly, how he managed to succeed in ending his own life in this way. Through sheer luck he had found – stumbled upon – possibly the only life threatening ledge on the peak of Snowdon.

'It's really quite extraordinary,' Alwyn Thomas, head of the Snowdon Climbing Society had been quoted as saying. 'We still have no idea how he managed it, even after several reconstructions. It's really very impressive when you think about it.'

'My dog once turned a paw on Snowdon,' Clive Edgerly from Cumbria said to a *Daily Mail* journalist. 'Almost had to take him to the vet.'

'He hadn't even eaten his croissant,' Darren Bleak, barista at the Snowdon Visitor Centre had told *The Sun*.

Indeed, so unlikely was the death of anyone by such a fall in such weather that conspiracy theories started to circulate, some of them quite hysterically.

'How On Earth Did he Die?' The front of *The Mirror* screamed several days after the incident. They had taken the liberty of consulting some of the world's most experienced climbers as well as compiling mortality statistics from Snowdon's history. And, while parts of the mountain, notably one called Crib Goch, had suitably sheer drops and the kind of terrifying edges one would sensibly stay away from, the top of the mountain was mostly described in much less extreme language.

National Climber Magazine had drawn out the peak of Snowdon and the part where Graham had fallen and had calculated that in the relatively calm conditions recorded that day, he had had a less that 0.05% chance of dying, even if he tried.

The reasons for his actions were much less clear. The most popular line of thinking was that he had been driven mad by the fact that he could never win and therefore wanted to kill those who had. This definitely seemed plausible. But newspapers and TV news anchors spent many an hour and column inch trying to decipher his now infamous final note.

'What do you make of the 'I knew of their pain' section?' Emily Maitliss had asked two psychologists on Newsnight. Graham's whole message was up on a giant screen behind them.

'You see, the bit I find most interesting,' the leggy redhead with large anime eyes answered as her name, Christa Pond, flashed up on the screen, 'Most revealing if you will,' she added, just as an extra bit of leg protruded from under her tight black suit skirt, 'Is the part where he asks for his cat to be fed.'

The other psychologist nodded sombrely at this.

'This is not a man who thinks he will survive, but is he an evil man?' she asked nobody in particular.

'Now I don't think we can doubt he's evil,' the other psychologist interjected in a Scottish accent. He was a lanky, thin faced man with a prominent bald spot. 'The question is, why did he have a cat in the first place?'

The conversation had deteriorated into an argument about whether it was the lottery culture or the pressures of pet ownership that caused his mental demise.

There were some very unusual ideas on the Internet. Many blamed the government. Others MI5. Some had pontificated that it was terrorism, but that was really more of a fringe theory. None of the larger or even smaller terrorist organisations were taking credit for this one.

'Do we look crazy to you?' one Al-Qaeda operative had responded indignantly when a journalist had asked them the question straight out.

It had taken several weeks for the story to die down, during which Mark, Paul and Rick as well as the other lottery group members had had to endure numerous interviews and TV appearances. Mick Crawford had been delighted.

'This is great!' he had said when they had met in his office in between bites of an egg sandwich. 'The public wanted you dead. But they won't like the fact that someone else wanted to do it. The British public enjoy two things: supporting an underdog and doing their own dirty work. You're in the clear!'

And it turned out that he was right. Whereas before they had been faced with angry eyes and probing questions, now the journalists looked at them in piteous sympathy and interviewed them gently before roaring fires. It was confusing, but Mark was just happy to come in from the cold.

At home, things with Jess were decidedly less warm. With all the media attention on himself, it had taken little time for news of Jess's affair to filter into the press. Apparently it had been leaked by a member of the firm. Jess had been more concerned about who had leaked it than the fact of her infidelity nor its effect on their relationship.

'It'll be Zane,' she had muttered angrily, before throwing her iPad down on the sofa in annoyance. 'I bet he did it just to turn the knife one more bloody time.' Realising she had her boyfriend in the room, she had then turned doe eyes on Mark and simpered while putting her hand on his chest, 'I'm so sorry you have to go through this because of him.'

'Listen,' Mark had said, slowly backing away. 'I think it would be best if you left.' He wasn't sure how to handle it all. He knew he should be furious. Incandescent. She had cheated on him. And with someone who looked like his grandad. But the feeling coursing through him was… What? He searched his emotional index.

Relief. Yes. It was definitely relief.

'Come on Mark,' Jess had cooed. 'Don't let one little incident risk us.' She was looking up at him now with what seemed like a mix of lust and desperation.

Oh g-d. She was going to make him dump her. This was hideous. Dumping someone even in normal circumstances was bad enough. Now he was expected to do it as a result of a national newspaper? He felt like he was on a bad reality show.

'Jess, this relationship has run its course,' he said, trying to maintain a modicum of dignity and composure. 'Admit it. You don't love me anymore.'

When she looked at him sulkily he said, 'You can keep the car and the clothes.'

'Fine,' she said in an offhand retort and flounced off to pack.

He hadn't seen her since. Or at least not in person. She had been doing the rounds on the pundit circuit, putting in her two cents and telling her 'side of the story'. Rumour was, at least according to Mick, that she had been fishing for a role on one of the bigger reality shows, but had been refused by Strictly Come Dancing as well as Celebrity Big Brother.

CHAPTER 23

'Nicky I'm here with 220 lottery winners on the twenty second anniversary reunion of the National Lottery. And I have with me four special winners in particular,' the stunning blond radio presenter called Sarah Sloane was saying into a microphone. 'Before we speak to the lucky winners, let me set the scene. It's a beautiful day here in Hyde Park near the Serpentine. I can see children playing, horse riders, cyclists and more, but I can also see a massive picnic taking place and over 200 people being counted and labelled in an attempt to spectacularly beat the record for the largest ever gathering of lottery winners.'

'The last record, if I have my figures straight, Sarah, was set in 2015 and was just 120 winners,' Nicky Campbell interjected. 'So this must be massive.'

'That's right Nicky and you should see this,' Sarah continued. 'Millionaires as far as the eye can see.'

'I bet there are some very busy pickpockets around,' Nicky sparkled down the line.

Sarah tilted her head back as she and Nicky laughed in a controlled but jovial manner as if on cue and then quickly stopped.

'Quite right, Nicky,' Sarah said, abruptly completely straight faced. 'Now let me introduce my first guest, Kai Mangle.' She put her microphone under the face of a skinny man with a long, greasy mullet and a small pot belly, his body covered in a tracksuit that was struggling in vain to find a curve to cling to. 'Kai, you became famous as the Lottery Layabout when you squandered your money on booze, drugs and partying. Your story was so sensational they turned it into a musical. How have you turned your life around?'

'Well Sarah,' Kai began slowly in his languid Manchester accent. 'I've discovered I have a talent for modern art. I'm now selling my sculptures for a bob or two.' Kai was leering appreciatively at Sarah as he spoke and winked as he finished talking.

'Now Nicky this is a family show so I won't describe Mr Mangle's depictions of the female form in detail, but suffice to say that they are *special*,' Sarah said, now hurriedly transferring the location of her microphone.

'And now onto my next guests. Mark Jones, Paul Baker and Rick Gordon. Now you might remember these three, listeners.'

'I know I do!' Nicky interrupted. 'Listeners we all remember these guys as part of the lottery club, the support group for national lottery winners. These three in particular became famous after their attempt to raise money through the Three Peaks Challenge turned deadly.'

'Yes Nicky,' Sarah said through gritted teeth, looking only slightly annoyed that Nicky had stolen her thunder. 'Mark, Paul and Rick were at the top of their final peak, Mount Snowdon, when a crazed Avalon employee who had deemed himself an 'angel of mercy' tried to kill each and every one of you. In fact, he ended up plunging to his own death in a freak fall which climbing experts have called physically impossible.'

'What was his name again, Sarah?' Nikki asked over the line.

Sarah looked panicked. She started making frantic gestures at her producer to find the name. Her producer, a tall thin man called George, started Googling with gusto while shaking his head, but to no avail. She looked to Mark, Rick and Paul, but they shrugged.

Like the pro she surely was, Sarah rose above it.

'Mark, how much did you end up raising for your charity of choice?' she said determinedly.

'Well, with all the publicity it ended up as £20,000,' Mark said proudly. 'And every member of our support group matched that so we ended up giving £160,000 to The Multiples Trust.'

'And your stories have been turned into a box office smash now, haven't they? The Lottery Club. It grossed £2 million on its opening weekend alone.'

'Yes,' Rick said smoothly, pushing his head in front of Mark's and into the line of the microphone. 'I'm played by Colin Firth. A lot of people say we're very similar.'

Sarah clearly decided to ignore this.

'And of course all that money has also gone to charity,' Paul added.

'What great things you've all achieved,' she gushed. 'So, besides that, what are you all doing now?'

'Well, I've gone back to my roots,' Paul said proudly. 'I'm now a builder on House Rescue 007, a new home makeover show on Channel 5.'

'And of course I've written my FHM Men's Book Prize winning book, 'I'm More Than A Money Man,' Rick added. 'It's about a handsome millionaire who's a jackpot hit with the ladies.'

'Brilliant,' Sarah said deadpan, 'And you Mark? Are you still beavering away as a lawyer?'

'Actually I've taken a break from the office. I'm just about to travel the world with Lawyers without Borders,' he said. Mark was so happy to be able to say this out loud. Ever since all the business with Jess's affair and their break up, things had been so difficult and work at the firm had seemed pointless. He had struggled for a while to find something else to do. But then he had seen the advert for Lawyers without Borders. The organisation offered pro bono legal help to the world's neediest people, It had seemed so perfect.

'Right, well that all sounds fascinating guys, but we're just coming up to the news so we'll have to bid you farewell,' Nicky said.

'Thanks guys,' Sarah said before taking off her headphones and shaking their hands.

Mark, Rick and Paul watched as she walked away chattering to her producer and then went to find the rest of the gang. They spotted Annie first. She smiled and waved at them. Ever since her appearance on This Morning, Annie had become a bit of a media darling and was due to appear on this year's Celebrity Big Brother. She was hoping that this would propel her already fledgling presenting career to new heights. This had, of course, meant that her education was on hold.

Derek soon joined them. Today he was wearing a t-shirt that said 'My Train of Thought is... Delayed'. He was there for the day, having flown in from China, where he now lived. After his second place at the NEC Fair, he had realised that, when it came to finding a place that took train modelling seriously, it didn't come any bigger than the land of the red dragon. So, he had packed his things and headed for the bright lights of Shanghai, where he now lived with his cat. Trainton Abbey had been purchased by an enthusiastic, but reclusive train spotter who had turned it into a national attraction. Entry cost a reasonable £5 and kids could ride the train for an added £1.

Margaret and Gerald couldn't be there that day. Having finally received their passports, they had gone on one trip to Tenerife and firmly caught the travelling bug. They were now halfway through their round the world trip and enjoying every minute. They had even signed up to Facebook so they could share their photos with the gang. They were last seen in the Antarctic with some rather large penguins.

'Where's Holly?' Mark asked.

'Over there,' Annie said, pointing at where Holly was taking photos of her children with several lottery winners. 'Practicing her skills.'

Holly had really been enjoying her photography course and apparently showed real promise in the area of capturing human emotion.

All of their attention was suddenly focused towards a large set of speakers which shrieked into life.

'Oh, sorry,' a loud, orphaned voice said over the speakers. 'That was a bit loud. If everyone with the numbers 1 to 50 can head to the steps we've set up over by the lake, we're ready to start taking the photos. We're calling up in sections, so 1 to 50 go to the steps.'

They proceeded to call group after group, filing them in step after step like a school photo. It took around forty minutes for everyone to be in place. It seemed it had been done chronologically as Mark and the guys were spread out amongst rows 1, 3, 4 and 6, with Mark being nearest to the front, Rick and Paul further back. Once everyone was in, a photographer came to the front where a large camera stood on a tripod.

'Look at you lot!' He yelled, to a happy laugh from the assembled group. 'Ok, now I think we can do this in one shot. I'm feeling lucky today. Don't know what it is, maybe the fact that I'm looking at over 200 winners.' Another laugh emerged.

'Ok. On the count of three, everyone say, Lucky!'

ABOUT THE AUTHOR

Elli Lewis grew up in North London, the second of three sisters and, consequently, in a home that was bursting at the seams with shoes.

As a teenager in the 90's, she experimented with Sun In, wore a standard uniform of combat trousers and vest top and shed tears over the breakup of Take That. She soon recovered and went on to study law before qualifying as a solicitor.

In the course of her career, Elli has worked for some of the UK's most prestigious law firms, representing a host of A-list clients. Her time in the City gave her a unique insight into the deepest depths of high society and the dizzying heights of fame. It was a world where pampered pooches roamed multi-million pound mansions and where ex-spouses had endless resources with which to wreak revenge; experiences that would later inspire her literary career.

In 2008, she went on to found a successful copywriting agency, with clients including national newspapers and media brands, including the BBC. The books came later. Suffice to say that one day she started typing and never stopped. Indeed, Elli wrote Trophy Life, The Lottery Club and The Anti-Natals in the same year and published the first of them early in 2016.

Elli can now be found back in North London in the house she shares with two boisterous boys, one exhausted husband and a colossal Siberian cat. Her favourite pastimes are drinking coffee and sleeping, ideally at the same time.

Printed in Great Britain
by Amazon